FIRST LIGHT

Other Folly Beach Mysteries by Bill Noel

Folly
The Pier
Washout
The Edge
The Marsh
Ghosts
Missing
Final Cut

FIRST LIGHT

A FOLLY BEACH MYSTERY

BILL NOEL

FIRST LIGHT
A FOLLY BEACH MYSTERY

iUniverse Star
an iUniverse LLC imprint

iUniverse books may be ordered through booksellers or by contacting:

iUniverse
1663 Liberty Drive
Bloomington, IN 47403
www.iuniverse.com
1-800-Authors (1-800-288-4677)

Cover photo by Bill Noel.
Author photo by Susan Noel.

ISBN: 978-1-4917-8514-0 (sc)
ISBN: 978-1-4917-8515-7 (e)

Library of Congress Control Number: 2014918579

Printed in the United States of America.

iUniverse rev. date: 12/11/2015

CHAPTER 1

Flickers of sunlight animated the soft cumulus clouds on the horizon. A handful of seagulls circled above the breaking waves along the untouched predawn beach while a lone pelican crashed into the sea in search of breakfast. The distant rumble of a truck's engine was the only sound I heard that summer morning as I walked along deserted East Arctic Avenue away from the center of town.

This was my favorite time of day on the small barrier island that I call home. I carried my camera in hopes of capturing sunrise photos over the ocean fifty yards to my right, and I was thinking about leaving the road and going between two houses to the beach access when a voice startled me.

"Hey you! Wait."

I instinctively pulled the camera close to my side, stopped, and turned to see who had disturbed my peaceful walk. It was still mostly dark, so I could only make out the silhouette of a man about ten feet behind me and closing in rapidly. *Great,* I thought. *Am I going to be robbed in the middle of the street? Should I run?* I was in my midsixties, out of shape, and slightly overweight, so I doubted that I could outrun anyone faster than a lame turtle. I couldn't see the man's face, but he appeared to be about five foot seven—roughly three inches shorter than me—and didn't have anything in his hands.

"Didn't startle you, did I?" he said as he stopped beside me.

If he only knew. "No," I said through clenched teeth.

"Good. Saw you and thought I'd say hi. I walk through here nearly every morning and don't usually see anyone out this early."

I smiled. "Then, hi."

He started up the street and waved for me to follow. I was at his side when he said, "What's your job?"

A strange question, I thought, but before I could answer, he said, "My name's—"

The roar of an engine behind us drowned out the introduction. I glanced back and saw a car, headlights off, barreling toward us. I grabbed my new acquaintance's arm and yanked him to the left side of the wide one-way street to give the car room to pass. As I pulled, the speeding mass of steel swerved in our direction. I lunged toward the berm, yanking the stranger. But not quickly enough. The sickening sound of steel on flesh filled the air as the car slammed into the unsuspecting pedestrian. His arm was wrenched from my hand; the wind draft from the vehicle smacked my face. The man's body flew over the hood, collided with the windshield, and then tumbled over the roof. The car's brake lights never lit. It never slowed.

I dropped to my knees and watched in disbelief as the one-and-a-half-ton weapon sped a couple more blocks and turned away from the beach. The victim lay prone five feet from me. I struggled to catch my breath, slowly pushed up from the pavement, shut my eyes, and prayed that it had been a dream. It was a prayer not answered. I walked over and hesitantly looked at the body. He appeared to be in his fifties. His legs were bent in directions that they weren't designed to go. Blood oozed from his knee and his mouth, because his heart was as dead as the rest of him. There was nothing I could do for the poor soul, so I turned and slowly moved back from the body and looked around. The sky was getting lighter, but there were no moving vehicles, no early-morning joggers. There was no one around. I punched 911 on my cell phone.

The throaty siren from one of Folly Beach's fire trucks leaving the station less than a mile away broke the silence. The shrill sound of one of the beach's patrol cars rapidly approached from the other direction. I felt light-headed and lowered myself to the sand on the side of the road, turning away from the body.

How could a beautiful morning turn so tragic so quickly? I didn't have time to think about it before the fire truck lumbered to a stop. Two firefighters who doubled as EMTs jumped from the cab. One grabbed a medical kit from behind the seat and rushed to the body on the street. I watched in silence but knew the medical kit was useless and that rushing was wasted energy. The other EMT came over and asked if I was hurt. I said no, not physically.

The patrol car that had approached from the other direction came around the block and stopped beside the fire truck, blocking the street. I heard the sirens of two more police vehicles. The porch lights from the elevated house on the beach side of the road flashed on, and a face silhouetted in the window stared at the commotion.

I didn't know the EMTs but recognized the first police officer on the scene. I had met Allen Spencer the week I had arrived on Folly some eight years earlier. He was new to the force and had appeared no older than the shoes I had been wearing. Since our first meeting, he had added roughly thirty pounds of muscle to his formerly trim six-foot-tall frame. He had attributed the buffing-up to surfing and weight lifting, two activities the two of us will never share. Spencer looked over at me, nodded recognition, held up his forefinger, and quickly moved to the first responders. I assumed he meant for me to stay where I was. He needn't have worried; my legs were shaking too much to carry me anywhere.

A second patrol car, LED lights flashing and siren blaring, skidded to a stop behind Spencer's vehicle. The officer ignored me and rushed to the body, looked down, and said something to Spencer, who then slowly walked over to me.

"Good morning, Mr. Landrum," the always-polite officer said.

I nodded. "Allen."

"What happened?" He tilted his head in the direction of the body, as if I wouldn't have known what he was talking about.

Tragically, I did know, and I explained about walking down the street in hopes of getting sunrise photographs with palmetto trees in the foreground when the gentleman started talking to me and about the car pulling out of the side street and what happened next. I realized I was rambling and shut up.

"You're lucky," Spencer said. "It looks like the driver didn't see you all." He jotted something in a spiral notebook.

I waited for him to stop writing. "No, Allen. The driver saw us, swerved, and intentionally hit him."

Spencer lowered the notebook to his side, looked at the body and back at me. "Crap."

I figured it wasn't a police acronym and agreed.

Spencer told me to hang on while he shooed the bystanders away. I said I wasn't going anywhere. He then herded them back and walked to a black Ford Crown Vic that had pulled in behind his patrol car. It was now light enough for me to see that it was Police Chief Cindy LaMond. Her window was down and

Spencer leaned on the windowsill. Then he stepped back and pointed at me.

The chief headed my way. My legs had regained most of their strength, so I pushed myself up, brushed off my shorts, and gave the chief my best feeble smile.

She shook her head. "Chris," she said in her Tennessee drawl. "You okay?

I nodded.

She looked toward the body. "What in the holy hell have you got yourself into now?"

Cindy, Chief LaMond, was nearing fifty, was sturdily built at five foot three, and had curly dark hair and a quick smile. She was married to Larry LaMond, owner of Folly's small hardware store, and was a good friend. She knew that over the last few years I had stumbled across a few murders, and with the help of a few left-of-quirky friends, had helped the police bring the murderers to justice and one to an untimely demise. It had nearly cost me my life, and Cindy had played a part in solving a couple of the crimes. I was glad to see her, sort of. She looked around and suggested that we move to the comfort of her car.

"Front or back seat?" I asked. One of my defense mechanisms was to mask fear with humor. Most of the time it helped, and much of the time only I found it humorous.

"Front," she said. "Unless you want me to arrest you for something."

Cindy had moved from East Tennessee to Folly six years before to join the Folly Beach Department of Public Safety, which included both the police and fire departments, and had been appointed chief earlier this year after the long-term chief, Brian Newman, had been elected mayor. Her appointment was controversial in some circles; she was iconoclastic, drastically different in style from Chief Newman, and, heaven forbid, a female. She was a great choice.

I slid in the passenger's seat and quickly accepted a bottle of water. The shock of coming within inches of being splayed out on the street with the victim combined with the sweltering South Carolina humidity had drained me. She waited for me to take a long draw before asking for details. I repeated the story, and she listened without interrupting. She asked me to wait while she conferred with her guys, and then she left to talk to the EMTs and police officers who had gathered around the body. Another police vehicle had arrived, and two more officers were draping yellow crime-scene tape across the street. Nine locals, and probably a vacationer or two, had inched up to the restricted area.

I closed my eyes, replayed the incident, and shuddered as I pictured the car plowing into the man who was simply walking down the street, minding his own business, and talking to me. Cindy opened the door and startled me out of my nightmare. She called dispatch and asked them to contact the Charleston County Sheriff's Office to send a crime scene unit. Our tiny island was in Charleston County and had its own police department but relied on the sheriff's office to investigate major crimes. The working relationship between the two departments wasn't always harmonious, but Cindy knew the limitations of her small department. She'd told me before that she had often taken Kenny Rogers's advice: "You've got to knows when to hold 'em, know when to fold 'em." Had I mentioned she was from East Tennessee?

She finished her call and said to me, "My guys say it looks like an accident."

I started to interrupt, but she stuck her palm in front of my face. "Whoa, let me finish."

I closed my mouth and shrugged.

"They said the driver was probably drunk, and since it was dark, he probably never saw y'all."

I tilted my head, looked at the group gathered around the body, and turned back to Cindy. "Drunk before six?"

Cindy grinned. "You wouldn't believe how many drunks we pull over this time of morning. You know how Folly is—like Vegas. No clocks, no worry about time, and access to enough alcohol to kill all the germs and reality within thirty miles."

I knew what I'd seen. "The driver zipped around that corner." I pointed to the intersection of Second Street and East Arctic Avenue. "When we walked past there, nothing was moving, no engine running. It was like someone had been waiting for him."

Cindy looked back at the intersection. "Did you see the car parked there?"

"I didn't notice, but it was quiet and I would've heard the motor running. When it started toward us, it was in the right lane. I moved to the left and pulled him with me. It had plenty of room to go around us."

I caught my breath and Cindy stared at the gathering around the corpse like she was trying to picture the chain of events.

She started to speak, but I interrupted, "Cindy, it swerved and pointed toward us like a guided missile. It never slowed. After it hit … him, it kept going. Your people weren't here. They didn't see what happened. It was no accident."

Cindy put her hand on my shoulder. "Chris, I've known you for a long time; you don't jump to conclusions. You saw what you saw, and I can't argue with that." She hesitated. "Let's wait and see what the forensics folks come up with."

There wasn't any sense arguing. I didn't know what they could tell from the scene, but I knew that I couldn't prove what I was certain of. "Any idea who he was?"

Cindy shook her head. "Afraid not. No ID, no wallet, nothing other than three crumpled-up dollar bills. I didn't get a good look at his face, but I don't think I recognized him. Did you?"

"He looked vaguely familiar," I said. "But I don't know from where, maybe just around town."

"His clothes are pretty ratty. Looks more like one of our loveable bums than a vacationer or one of our upstanding citizens."

"Hard to tell the difference sometimes."

Cindy smiled. "That it is."

"He said he walked the same route nearly every morning," I said. "I suppose he lived nearby."

We talked for another half hour, and she took notes of everything I said about the event. Then a white Charleston County Sheriff's Office crime-scene SUV pulled in behind us. Cindy said she knew where to find me if she needed anything and politely excused me before going over to the man and woman who had exited the forensics services vehicle.

I walked the three blocks home and wondered whether I had only imagined that the driver had intentionally hit the victim. No, I was certain. And then I wondered who the target was. Could it have been me and the driver had missed—by less than a foot?

CHAPTER 2

I was still shaking. It's not every day that I nearly get run down and witness a murder. I paced around my small cottage, downed two cups of coffee, and stared at the walls, all while visualizing what had happened and questioning myself about what I could have done to prevent it. I also wondered who the poor soul was who had taken his last breath in the street.

I decided that I'd be better off at the small gallery I owned than sitting around the house replaying the tragic event. Landrum Gallery was a money pit that allowed me to display and occasionally sell prints of photos I'd taken over the years. Before moving from Kentucky to the Edge of America, better known as Folly Beach, I'd participated in a few art shows and would have preferred to attend more, but my day job in the human resources department of a multinational health care company had managed to eat up most of my time and energy. I had long envisioned opening my own gallery.

I was able to live that dream on Folly, but like most dreams, reality didn't jibe. I'm far from wealthy, but through a couple of profitable real estate ventures, a pension from the company that I had given most of my life to, and an unexpected inheritance from an appreciative, eccentric Folly old-timer, I was able to operate the gallery at a loss, until recently. It had taken me a couple of years to figure out that being retired shouldn't include keeping the business open six days a week or, for that matter, having to be anywhere that often. Visitors spent most of their money on weekends, so now I opened the gallery only Friday through Sunday.

The business was located on Center Street, the figurative and literal center of retail on the six-mile-long, half-mile-wide island. There were no sidewalks on the long block from the house to Center Street, and I cringed each time I heard a vehicle approach. I began to relax once I reached the sidewalks along the city's main drag, and I walked two more blocks to my destination. The dozen or so pedestrians I saw along the way were going about their early-morning business, oblivious to what had happened.

I had poured my first cup of coffee from Mr. Coffee in the work area–office–gathering spot-for-friends–all-purpose room in back when the jangling bell on the front door announced someone's arrival. I glanced at my watch and realized that it was only a little after eight, much earlier than I usually arrived, and nearly two hours before the usual opening.

"Isn't anyone going to wait on me in this damned picture store?" bellowed the familiar voice of Bob Howard.

I smiled and peeked around the corner, and I saw Bob glancing at a large print of a sunrise behind Folly Pier. "Good morning, Mr. Howard. Interested in purchasing one of these fine prints?"

"Hell no," he said. His four-day old beard, burly six-foot frame, faded shorts, and Hawaiian-print shirt made him look more like a homeless bum than a successful Realtor. "Why would I waste my hard-earned money on a picture of something I can see down the road?"

In addition to his rumpled exterior, Bob had the charm of a

pit bull, no offense to pit bulls. He was also a friend. During my first year here, the surly Realtor had helped me after my rented house was torched with me in it. Bob had found me a place to live, helped me move in, and sold me my home. On another occasion, he had provided valuable information that helped me catch a killer.

He stared at the mug in my hand.

"Want a cup?" I asked.

"Does an octopus poop in the ocean?" He headed to the back room.

His G-rated language surprised me. "Poop?" I said.

"Cleaning up my vocab." He shrugged. "Betty said I'm a bad influence on young 'uns."

Betty was Bob's near-saintly wife, and everyone who knew them wondered how she had put up with him for several decades. I was among that group.

"Good for her," I said.

"Damned right!"

By now I'd forgotten the question and he'd forgotten Betty's advice, but I thought it had to do with him wanting coffee, so I followed him to the coffeemaker and found a nearly clean mug.

"Have five—no, make that six—pancakes; three eggs, scrambled; sausage; grits; and biscuits?" He looked around the room as if he expected to find a full-service kitchen.

"Plumb out," I said. "How about a stale Oreo and a moldy bagel?"

"Hard to turn down, but this'll have to do." He hoisted the mug in my face.

I poured a refill as Bob plopped down in one of the rickety wooden chairs by the yard-sale table. One of these days his seventy-five-year-old obese body would go right through the chair. Thankfully, today was not that day.

I sat facing him. "So to what do I owe the pleasure of your company? You're not here to buy anything, my food selection is limited, and the gallery doesn't open for two hours."

He huffed like I had slapped him. "Couldn't I have stopped to see a dear friend?"

"No," I said and stared at him.

He took another sip and then held the mug at arm's length.

I rolled my eyes and got him more.

He came close to thanking me but simply nodded. "You know, the lease on your gallery is up in two months."

I hadn't remembered. "Of course."

"The landlord called. The old codger said he wants you to sign an extension."

"Mm-hmm," I mumbled.

"Hold the drum roll." Bob tapped his palms on the table. "Your outstanding Realtor was able to use his decades of finely honed negotiating skills and got the damned greedy landlord to offer you a five-year extension with no increase in rent." He bowed his head. "You're welcome, you're welcome."

I smiled. "He couldn't find anyone else who wants it."

Bob waved his arms toward the showroom. "Hell no. Who'd want this dump?"

I laughed and knew Bob was right. "Exactly what were you able to get from him with your superior negotiating skills?"

"Let's see," Bob said. "He wanted a ten-year lease, but I told him that you were getting long in the tooth and probably would kick the bucket before then. He'd be stuck with all your photo crap."

"Good strategy," I said with a nod and an overabundance of sarcasm.

"Also told him that the way you keep stumbling on murders, you'd probably get yourself killed long before a five-year lease was up, but he said the bank needed that long so he could refinance this dump—excuse me, prime class-A rental property."

Bob's mention of murders reminded me of what happened earlier, and I interrupted his tale of real estate negotiations to share my morning with him.

"Damn, damn, damn, Chris!" Bob rolled his eyes toward the ceiling. "I need to get you a month-to-month lease—hell, maybe day-to-day. You're not going to live five years. What in the hell have you stuck your foot in now?"

It was not yet nine o'clock and I'd heard the same sentiment twice already. I told him that I wasn't involved and that I had simply been walking down the street.

The sound of hammering from next door distracted Bob before he got too far into telling me how big an idiot I was, how if I got myself involved in another murder, he wouldn't wait for a killer to do me in, that he would kill me himself.

"What's going on over there?" Bob interrupted, pointing to the wall that separated my gallery from the attached space. "Sounds like Woody Woodpecker on steroids."

"It's someone from that new church that meets on the beach," I said.

Bob looked at me and then at the wall where the racket was coming from. "I'm not good at geography, never much gave a flying flounder about where places were, but after being a highly successful Realtor for just shy of seven hundred years, I can tell you where the beach is." He frowned and nodded toward the pounding. "It damned sure ain't that direction."

"Wow, you are good. Since you've been around that long, you probably know that the weather isn't always great on Sunday mornings. They're fixing up a space for when they can't hold their services on the beach."

"Let me guess. That space next door."

"I repeat, you are good. That's going to be the foul-weather sanctuary of First Light Church."

"What's a First Light Church?"

"It started a year ago. I hear they have members ranging from street people to successful businesspersons."

"What denomination?" Bob asked as he continued to stare at the adjoining wall.

"Nondenominational."

"Cripes," Bob said to the wall. "Just what we need, another make-believe church." He looked back at me. "Another damned church preaching that the key to salvation is determined by what direction a banana peel is facing. Or God spoke to the fake leader through a Hershey bar and told him to save the world while gathering all the money he could collect along the chocolate way, or that every last word in the Bible should be taken literally regardless how radical it is. Or—never mind, you get my drift."

His drift was more a tidal wave. He was often short on tact, politeness, and civility, but he never lacked an opinion.

"Wouldn't most traditional denominations have been considered radical and maybe nondenominational when they began or broke off from another church? Every religion started somewhere."

"Don't get all theological on me," Bob said. "All these new-fangled churches want is money. They're full of con artists preying on the lost and confused souls. What do you think all those out-of-work used-car salesmen are doing now the economy's tanked?" He held out his arms but didn't wait for an answer. "That's right, they're preaching."

It's never wise to step in front of Bob's rant, so I nodded and asked, "Since you're so knowledgeable about nontraditional religions, what do you know about First Light?"

"Not a damn thing."

"Then, know anything about the building over there?"

"Why would I?" he said.

"You're a leader in the real estate community. I figured you would know about the building that's been vacant since I've been here. Don't you know everything?"

"You're being a smart-ass again, aren't you?"

I smiled.

"I'll check it out," he said.

"Good."

"Now that you managed not to get killed this morning and we got your nosiness out of the way, let's get back to your lease."

I hadn't expected to get into this with Bob, especially this morning, but he had been a good friend, and I knew he could offer helpful wisdom. "Business sucks," I said. "I've lost money nearly every month I've been here. I'm thinking about shutting down, and the end of my lease would be a good time to call it quits."

Bob turned from the dividing wall to the door leading to the showroom. He didn't say anything, and I thought he may not have heard what I'd said.

"Chris, you're not rich; I understand that. If you were, I would've conned you into buying one of those oceanfront McMansions and stuck your gallery into a building that wasn't falling down. Losing money ain't much fun; not profitable either."

"You did get something out of your Duke economics degree."

"Smart-ass!" Instead of pointing his mug, he slowly lifted himself from the chair and poured another cup. He took a sip and returned to his chair. This time he lowered himself into it more slowly. "Remember what happened the last time you wanted to close, about three years ago, if memory serves me correctly?"

I knew what he was referring to, and it was a strong argument for staying open. "Charles's reaction?"

"Your uber-nutty friend Charles went bonkers," Bob said tactfully.

Charles Fowler was my closest, and most unlikely, friend. We'd met my first week on the island, and for reasons that could only be uncovered through years of psychoanalysis, he latched on to me and I bonded with him. To say we were opposites in most everything would be an understatement. When I opened the business, he became my unpaid, self-proclaimed executive sales manager and had said that the gallery was his life. It had given him purpose, something that he had been lacking since he "retired" to Folly from Detroit at age thirty-four, some twenty-nine years before. He'd never had a steady income but performed odd jobs for local businesses. He prided himself on being a private detective, but that's a story for another time.

He may not have become clinically depressed when he learned that I had planned to close, but in laymen's terms, he was deeply saddened, angry, and frustrated to the point of making everyone around him miserable. I would have to fight the same battle again, but he wasn't the one losing big chunks of money each month. I was and had to make the call.

Since there were a couple of months left on the lease, I told Bob not to tell the landlord anything. I figured the owner wouldn't lease it out from under me if I decided to extend my stay. Bob asked whether I would consider staying if he could get me a lower rent. I said that I would consider it, but it would have to be a significant reduction. He said he would try. Finally, Bob said that if I couldn't do any better than a moldy bagel and a stale Oreo, he would have to leave this dump and get some food before he wilted and blew away. I doubted that months on a desert island without food would wilt Bob, and he'd never blow away.

"Bon appétit," I said.

His crusty exterior cracked briefly when he patted me on the arm and said, "I'm glad you weren't squashed."

CHAPTER 3

Bob hadn't been gone five minutes when the door bell announced another arrival.

"Did I see Bob waddling away?" the visitor asked as he pulled the door closed behind him.

"You did," I said.

"What'd he want?"

"Just stopped by, didn't want anything," I said.

The new arrival, at five foot eight, was a couple of inches shorter than me, regretfully twenty pounds lighter at one hundred sixty, and was wearing a long-sleeved green-and-gold University of Alaska Anchorage T-shirt and a canvas Tilley hat with a sweatband discolored by years of wear and Low-Country humidity. To complete his look, he carried a handmade wooden cane, purpose unknown. As was the case with my previous visitor, the new arrival could have been mistaken for one of Folly's homeless, but he was my best friend Charles "Don't-You-Dare-Call-Him-Charlie" Fowler.

I would have to talk to him about closing the gallery, but this wasn't the time. He would be hurt and after what happened at daybreak, I wasn't ready to go through whatever he would drag me through.

Charles walked to the back of the gallery and looked at the

near-empty coffee carafe. "Looks like Bob was here long enough to do more than just stop by."

"Fix more if you want it," I barked.

"Why so cranky?"

He started to fix another pot, and I went over to the sink to help. "Sorry," I said. "It's been a rough morning."

I told him about the hit-and-run and how I was sure that it was intentional. He asked what the police thought, and I told him that they said it was an accident; a drunk, or someone falling asleep.

"You okay?" he asked.

I lied and said yes.

"Who was it?"

The hammering next door resumed. Charles looked at the wall. "Enough to wake the dead." I cringed at his comment as we moved to the table and as far away from the irritating noise as possible.

"Don't know," I said. "He looked vaguely familiar. He didn't have any ID."

"Then how are we going to find out who it was?" Charles asked as he stood and watched the carafe fill.

"I'll call Cindy later."

The pounding stopped, and Charles whispered, "Yeah."

We enjoyed the silence for a couple of minutes. Little happened on Folly that Charles didn't know about. He had few true friends, but over the years he had woven together a network of acquaintances so extensive it would make the CIA envious.

The silence was broken once again by the front door bell. Charles assumed his executive sales manager's role and headed to the showroom. I watched with mixed feelings as he tapped his cane on the well-worn wooden floor as he scampered to greet the new arrival.

"Hi, Preacher Burl," he said.

I wasn't surprised that Charles knew the visitor. I was a bit surprised to hear the visitor say, "Hello, Brother Charles."

I went into the gallery where Charles was shaking hands with the man I assumed was Preacher Burl. He was no more than five foot five, shaped like a football—portly, in more polite terms—had a milk-chocolate-colored mustache, a balding head with a comb-over, and was pushing fifty.

The newcomer looked toward me in the doorway. "Have you two met?" Charles asked.

I'd seen him around, but we'd never spoken. "No," I said.

The preacher took two steps and held out his pudgy right hand. "Brother Chris," he said, and I wondered how he knew my name. "I'm Preacher Burl Ives Costello. I should have come in before but we've been so busy fixing it up next door, I never had enough time. Pleasure to finally meet you."

I shook his hand and needlessly told him my name. His hands were callused; he wasn't immune to manual labor. A closer look at his face told me that he had been handsome in earlier days. His blue eyes sparkled when he smiled; I suspected he could be charming.

He stepped back between Charles and me. "I didn't mean to interrupt."

"We were just talking," Charles said. "You didn't interrupt."

I thought that was the definition of *interrupt* but remained silent.

"Good," Burl said. "Question. Would you happen to have a crowbar? We have two-by-fours to pull off the wall." He smiled. "The claw end of a hammer won't get it done."

"Sorry," I said. "The closest we have to a tool is a plastic fork."

Burl laughed. "Without divine intervention, that won't suffice."

"What're you doing over there?" I thought it was better than asking, "Why are you making all that racket?" I already had a rough idea of what was going on but didn't know what else to say to the visitor.

Burl looked at Charles. "As Brother Charles can attest, we hold our services on the beach a couple of football-field lengths left of the pier. On occasion, the devil garners enough strength and lashes us with water, wind, or frigid temperatures. We will not let the son of Satan be victorious." He bobbed his head as he spoke. "Through tithing of some generous benefactors—praise the Lord—we have been able to secure the space, and we are preparing it to serve as our sanctuary to ward off the effects of evil upon our flock."

Preacher Burl made sense and appeared sincere, but I kept hearing Bob's words in my head, especially when the preacher mentioned *tithing of some generous benefactors.*

Burl looked toward the door. "I'd better get back. I don't want the benevolent volunteers to think that I have deserted them. Brother Charles, will you be joining us to do the work of the Lord? We need all the help we can get."

Charles looked at me and back at Burl. "Chris and I have a couple of business matters to discuss, and then I'll be over."

Burl nodded, smiled, and turned to me. "Brother Chris, you are more than welcome to join us. We can always use an extra set of hands to do the Lord's work."

I returned his smile and said that I had to keep the gallery open but that perhaps I would help another time. He said that would be nice and that I was always welcome to join his flock on Sunday. He repeated where they gathered, as if I wouldn't be able to see a church service on the beach. I thanked him.

"A nice fellow," Charles said as Burl closed the door on his way out.

I hadn't known Charles to go to church. "Have you been attending?" I asked.

He slowly walked to the back room, filled his mug, and sat in the chair that Bob had vacated. "You know that I've been depressed since Aunt M. left us." Charles stared at the coffee. "George W. Bush said, 'Faith gives the assurance that our lives and our history have a moral design.'"

Charles had a habit of quoting US presidents. The accuracy had long been questioned, but so far, no one had taken the time or enough interest to disprove them. Personally, I didn't care.

"I'm not certain about what George W. said," he continued, "but figured that getting closer to God may help me through these times—times that I feel lost, heartbroken, torn."

Melinda Beale, Aunt M. to Charles, had reappeared in his life last year after a thirty-year absence. She was his mother's sister and had lived in Detroit, where Charles was from. He had credited Melinda with teaching him to cuss, drink, have fun, and avoid work. She had been a superb teacher. The day she arrived she had announced that she had terminal cancer, and she only got to spend a short time with Charles and his friends before she died earlier this year. During that brief time, she shared a positive spirit, hours of laughter, and many touching moments with all who had the privilege of getting to know her. As with all good things, it had come to an end. Her death devastated Charles, and to be honest, it had left me with a void larger than I could have imagined.

He hadn't answered my question about attending church, but I remained quiet, something I was much better at than he was.

Finally, he said, "I went to the Methodist Church a couple of times. It's only a hymnal's throw from my apartment, so I figured it would be an answer to my prayers." He hesitated.

"Everyone was nice. They invited me to eat with them, patted me on the back, and did everything possible to make me feel at home." He shook his head. "It didn't take. It felt funny inside those walls. Then Lisa at Bert's told me about the new church. Figured I didn't have much to lose and gave it a try. Something about them meeting on the beach felt right."

"Why?" I asked.

Charles looked at the ceiling and down into his mug. "Know how it is when they have weddings on the beach? The wedding party gets all gussied up at the hotel and then parades through the lobby where folks are coming and going in bathing suits, flip-flops, cover-ups, and every imaginable kind and amount of clothes. The blushing bride, all pretty in her wedding gown, takes off her nice shoes and walks barefoot through the sand to the portable altar. The people sit in folding chairs and face a minister in a coat and tie pretending that there's nothing unusual about standing in the sand preaching a wedding."

I nodded.

"Then," he continued, "the wedding party stands inside imaginary walls, and other folks who have nothing to do with the wedding, who don't know who's getting hitched, move close to the blessed event. They listen to what the preacher says, all the I dos. The preacher says something about pronouncing them whatever, the bride and groom kiss, and the onlookers take pictures and applaud."

I had done exactly what Charles had described, so I nodded again.

"Those outsiders," Charles said, "feel as much a part of the wedding as the invited guests, who are all uncomfortable in their hot clothes and sandy feet. The event's inclusive. That's what First Light feels like: no walls, no dress code, no judgmental stares, and no doors to walk through to be accepted. I'm sitting there with bankers, beach bums, drunks, shop owners, and others that I have no idea what they do. I like that."

I was pleased that Charles had found somewhere where he felt at home. Somewhere where he could both grieve and rejoice.

"Is that where you and Heather plan to get married?"

Charles had proposed to Heather Lee, his equally quirky girlfriend of four years, at a spur-of-the-moment memorial service for his late aunt. Melinda's dying wish had been for Charles to tie the knot. Since the proposal, Charles had been unusually quiet about wedding plans, and I thought this was a good opportunity to pump him for information.

"Umm, I don't think so." Charles turned to look at the coffee pot. "I may have made a mistake proposing." He turned back to me.

I waited, but seeing that he had said all he planned to, and maybe more than he had planned to, I said, "Mistake?"

He then looked down at the table and back at me. "I knew Aunt M. wanted me to get married, and heaven knows Heather was onboard three hundred and fifteen percent. I sort of asked without my heart being in it."

"So you're not getting married?"

"I don't know, Chris. Honest to God, I don't know." He shook his head. "I don't want to talk about it now, okay?"

"Sure," I said reluctantly. "So you feel at home at First Light?"

"Yeah, it's a good place."

I wanted to agree, but Bob's rant still bounced around in my head. "What do you know about Preacher Burl's background and the church?"

Charles looked into my eyes and smiled. "Not a whit?"

Charles knew as much about the church as Bob did. It probably didn't mean anything, but I found it interesting.

CHAPTER 4

Something rare happened after Charles had felt the spirit move him and wandered next door to help with the remodeling of First Light's foul-weather sanctuary. Landrum Gallery was busy, busy with real customers who bought framed photographs in quantities that would actually pay the rent and other nagging expenses that had been sinking the ship. If I believed in omens, I would have taken the increased business as a sign that I should stay open. Instead, I wrote the profitable Saturday in September off to luck. It was even better luck because it distracted me from thinking about my early-morning horror.

I was exhausted when I headed home at six, not only because I had worked hard at the gallery but also because of the disaster that had greeted my day and the head-jarring hammering next door.

I pondered my newfound wealth the next morning and decided to treat myself to a hardy breakfast at my favorite restaurant, the Lost Dog Café. I had made efforts—albeit weak ones—to get in better shape and willed myself to walk more, eat better, and if worse came to worst, exercise. I was about twenty pounds on the north side of ideal, if I believed the charts that were undoubtedly created by anorexics. The only exercise I enjoyed was walking around the island with camera in hand and capturing images of the beauty and quirks of this bohemian slice of heaven. Charles often joined me on these jaunts, but less so recently. I'm an early riser and had three hours to kill before I needed to open. The Lost Dog Café was an easy ten-minute walk from the house, and this was the perfect day to get some exercise. Instead I drove, demonstrating one reason why the weight charts might be correct, because yesterday's walk had affected me more than I cared to admit.

It was cool, so I chose an inside table. The Dog was packed most Sundays, but I had arrived before the sleeping-in vacationers and found my favorite booth empty. From its vantage point by the back wall, I could see everyone entering, a habit I had acquired from inquisitive—nosy—Charles.

Amber was quick to the table with a mug of hot coffee and a smile. I had known her since my first week at the beach, and we had dated for a while. I asked about Jason, and her pride swelled as she told me that her son was taking two college-bound classes. I had known her since he was ten, so now it was hard to believe he was a junior in high school and had celebrated his seventeenth birthday. Amber and I were no longer a couple, but we had remained close. I would do anything for her, and I suspected she would do the same for me.

"Yogurt today?" she said and grinned. She had worked diligently to get me to eat well, but she would have had a better chance of getting a vegan to eat fried cat than to get me to order yogurt.

Not today, not tomorrow, not ever, I thought, but I simply said, "No thanks." I compromised and ordered one egg instead of two, two strips of bacon instead of four, and with great flourish, I declined the hash browns. I felt the weight falling off as I spoke.

"I hear you were with the poor man who was killed." Her smile turned to a look of concern and sadness. "Are you okay?"

I wasn't surprised that she knew. The Dog was ground zero for rumors on Folly. Basically, if you couldn't hear it in the Dog, it didn't exist—sort of the tree falling in the forest, but on a less philosophical level.

"Yes, it was terrible. Hear who he was?"

"Don't think they know," she said. "Couple of cops were in earlier and they hadn't heard. I'll call if I do."

I thanked her, and she moved to a table in the center of the room to spread her charm to a couple who had been seated while we were talking.

The restaurant was near full when Chief LaMond came in and looked around. She saw me and waved before she stopped at the counter to talk to Matt, the owner of Cool Breeze, the island's popular bicycle rental business. He laughed at something she said, and then she came over to my table. She looked at the bench seat across from me and said, "Vacant?"

"Is now. Have a seat."

She slid into the booth. "You okay?"

I told her I was, and for a fleeing second I thought I should put a sign around my neck that read *I'm okay!*

"Good," she said. "I'm glad I caught you. What're you buying me for breakfast?"

Before I answered, Amber appeared and took Cindy's order and then headed to the kitchen.

I smiled. "I didn't think citizens were supposed to buy meals for police chiefs."

"Not supposed to bribe local officials," she said. "I'd be a mighty piss-poor chief if I could be bribed for a measly breakfast. I have standards. Lunch is another matter, and if you try to buy me supper, I'll have to haul you off to the hoosegow."

"I'll remember that the next time I want to bribe you. Why are you glad you caught me?"

Cindy turned toward the room and waved to get Amber's attention. Amber nodded and said she'd be right over, and Cindy turned back to me. "Couple of reasons. First, since you were there—and lucky to be alive, I might add—I thought you should know who the victim was and what's happening. Second, since you're one of the nosiest critters I know, I figured I'd better tell you before you start calling and pestering me."

"No wonder you're Folly's top law enforcement official," I said. "Lovely, brilliant, perceptive, and can be bought for lunch."

"Yep." She blushed. "Now, you going to keep sucking up, or do you want to hear what I know?"

"Info, please," I said.

She pulled a notebook out of her pocket and flipped through a few pages before setting it on the table. "They found the car: a 2009 Nissan Altima, black. It'd been reported stolen by a landscaper in Charleston. The genius left the car running at a gas station while he went in for 'only a sec' to buy cigarettes." She paused and grinned. "Proof that smoking kills."

I rolled my eyes.

Cindy shrugged and continued, "Anyway, the Charleston police found the car a quarter mile from where it was taken, parked along the Battery in one of the free parking spaces. Whoever docked it came too close to the wall and knocked the side mirror off and scraped the paint. That's what got the cops' attention. They found fifteen empty beer cans on the floor and in the backseat. Some person or persons unknown had quite a party."

"No idea who was driving?"

"You are so correct. The cops think that someone saw the car running at the gas station, decided to take a booze-infused joyride here, and while drunk out of his or her gourd, didn't see you, hit your walking buddy, and panicked."

"Were there prints on the steering wheel or door handles?" I asked.

"And your sidekick Charles thinks he's a detective." Cindy shook her head. "All clean. He probably wore gloves."

"Drunk, joyriding, with gloves in September? Does that make sense?"

"Do drunks ever make sense?" Cindy said.

"Doesn't matter. I know what I saw, and the car swerved toward us. He was hit on purpose."

"I don't know." Cindy squinted and pulled on her earlobe. "I've shared your thoughts with the cops over there, but I suspect the official report will chalk it up to an inebriated driver."

I shook my head and then took another sip of coffee.

"We know who the victim is," Cindy said as Amber quickly returned with Cindy's food, a perk of being chief.

I waited for her to take a bite of bagel and then motioned for her to continue.

"Guy's name is Jeremy Junius Chiles, age forty-two, no permanent address."

"Junius?" I said.

"Would I make that up?"

"How'd you find out?"

"Fingerprints."

"He had a record?"

"Want to join the force? We could use a perceptive guy like you, although you're way too old." She smiled and snapped her fingers. "You could be our mascot."

"Thanks. Record?"

"Yep. Six years ago in Savannah, he spent a deuce in prison after he borrowed a few hundred dollars from a store without telling the clerk when he would be bringing the money back. The clerk happened to be distracted by a gun in Jeremy's hand. After that, he had a couple of disorderly conduct arrests down there, but he only spent a few nights in jail each time. He apparently got tired of Savannah's tax-supported accommodations and arrived here awhile back. I hear he made a career of bumming money on the island and hitchhiking to Charleston to give gullible tourists an opportunity to part with some of their vacation cash. One of my guys said that Jeremy spent some nights in River Park. He hung around some of our fine bars until closing. Seemed to be harmless; no reason for anyone to want him dead."

"Someone did," I said.

"That's what you say. Another one of my guys said that he had stopped Jeremy Junius twice on the side of the road. He was drunk but not causing any harm to himself or others, so my guy let him go." She looked back at her notes. "That's it. No one knows when he got here. Everyone will know when he left."

"What now?" I asked. "I'm certain that—"

Cindy's phone vibrated on the table. She held up her hand for me to wait, and answered.

The look on her face told me that it wasn't her husband calling to say how sweet she was. She tapped End Call and said that she had to go. Said that a body had been found in a beach house on West Ashley Avenue.

"Go ahead," I said. "I'll get your check, and would you—"

She put her hand in my face. "Yes, I'll let you know about it when I get a chance."

I smiled as she left. I'd trained her well.

CHAPTER 5

I drove home, left the car, and walked the short distance to the gallery. It wasn't time to open, but since I was already out and moving, I figured I might as well be there as sitting at home. Charles usually beat me to work and chided me for arriving close to opening time. In his alternate universe, on time meant thirty minutes early, but I wanted to think that I was a resident of reality and didn't follow Charles Standard Time.

I was surprised to see my friend near the gallery painting the door trim on the foul-weather church. He wore a long-sleeved College of Saint Elizabeth Screaming Eagles T-shirt with cargo shorts that had a large blob of white paint on the front.

He looked up. "You okay?"

I wanted to remind him that I wasn't the person on a slab in Charleston but nodded and pointed to the shirt. "Church school?"

Charles probably had the largest collection of college and university T-shirts outside of Dick's Sporting Goods. Only his apartment-stuffing wall-to-wall collection of books exceeded the quantity of his shirts. He had never said where he got the long sleeves or why he constantly wore them. A word to the wise: don't bother asking. I'd tried countless times, more or less, to no avail.

He looked down at the front of the blue-and-white T-shirt. "I'm in the spirit," he said. "Want a brush?"

"I'd love to," I said, "but have to open. It appears that my sales manager is indisposed."

"*Executive* sales manager. I'll be here if the crowd gets too much for you."

Someone inside hollered, "Charles!"

He balanced the brush on the paint can, opened the door, looked in, and said that he'd be there in a minute. He turned to me and said, "Come in and say howdy to your neighbors."

"Later," I said. I had been reared Baptist and attended Sunday school and worship services regularly until I was in my twenties. I considered myself spiritual but not big on organized religion. To my recollection, I had only been to one church service since leaving the Baptists' roll, and that had been a year or so before, and days before my ex-wife had been murdered. She had come to Folly to escape her second husband's killer; sadly, the move failed to save her after he sabotaged her brakes, causing her to meet a tragic end on the bridge connecting Charleston with Mt. Pleasant. The wreck nearly killed me as well, but my habit of wearing a seat belt saved me from the same fate that took her life.

"Why all the work now?" I asked while Charles resumed slapping paint on the door. He had spread almost as much paint on his clothes as he had on the wood. I knew who not to ask if I ever needed anything painted.

"Passing a collection plate on the beach doesn't attract as much money as it apparently does in bigger churches," Charles said. "Preacher Burl said that until a month ago the offering wouldn't cover the cost of renting sunshine and sand."

"Near nothing?"

"I'm no accountant, but that sounds about right."

I waved my hand toward the door. "So what happened?"

"Social Security would be like hitting the lottery for most of Preacher Burl's flock. Occasionally someone from the business community, a vacationer, or someone who has a few extra dollars to donate to the cause will attend. Those folks are as rare as a snowstorm in August."

I looked at the door and back at Charles. "Was the answer in there?"

"I was almost there," he said. "Six months ago a fellow named Timothy something started attending. The first few times, he wore those shiny thousand-buck shoes like rich folks in Charleston wear to the office. None of us knew what to think about him. He finally wised up and started wearing flip-flops. Anyway, a couple of months ago, he went to Preacher Burl and asked what he could do money-wise. The Sunday before a big ol' thunderstorm had come rolling through the middle of the service. Preacher Burl figured that was God telling him what Timothy could do."

"So, Timothy funded the remodel?" I asked.

"Every dollar, but only if flock folks did the work. That's the long version of why I'm painting."

"What's Timothy do for a living?"

"Stockbroker. He's with one of those old firms in Charleston with some dead guy's name followed by *and Associates*. Timothy's one of the associates."

"It's nice that he came along," I said, more to make conversation than make a point.

"You bet it is," said Charles, who had already forgotten someone inside had requested his presence. "Oh yeah, Mad Mel and Caldwell said they'd try to stop by before the service. I'll have them stick their heads in the gallery to say hey."

Mad Mel, aka Mel Evans, was a friend we had met a few

years back. He operated a marsh-tour business that catered primarily to college students who wanted to get on a boat, go to a secluded part of the marsh, drink like adults, and act like children. Lessons on flora, fauna, and marsh geology were optional and seldom requested. Mel was a textbook example of someone successfully catering to a niche market. Caldwell was Mel's significant other. He made a living as a music promoter for Low Country bars and small concert venues.

"Are they members?" I asked.

"Members is a bit strong, and according to Preacher Burl, unnecessary to be part of his flock. According to the good preacher, all who attend are part of First Light. But yeah, Mad Mel and Caldwell attend. See what you're missing? Now get out of here so I can get finished in time to get to the eleven o'clock service."

I looked at the clear sky and back at Charles. "On the beach?"

Charles nodded and dipped his saturated brush back in the bucket. I watched him as he slopped more paint on the door frame. "Didn't someone want you to come inside?" I asked.

"Whoops," he said. "Knew I forgot something."

CHAPTER 6

I was to meet Karen for an early supper at the Black Bean Company. Karen, Detective Karen Lawson to her colleagues in the Charleston County Sheriff's Office, and I had been dating for almost three years. Over the last week, she had been more than knee-deep in a homicide investigation, so this would be the first time I'd seen her in several days.

The Black Bean Company was known for its all-natural, healthy foods; but to me, someone whose food order usually began with the word *fried*, I was drawn to its warm, welcoming interior. And the restaurant was four miles from my house and near where Karen was investigating a murder.

I arrived ten minutes early, ordered a Diet Pepsi, and grabbed one of the three cushiony leather sofas at the back of the building. It was midafternoon, so the comfortable seating section was empty. Two groups of college-age guys were at the tables along the wall watching a sports talk show on one of the flat-screen televisions.

Karen arrived fifteen minutes late and apologized for her tardiness and her appearance. Her shoulder-length chestnut-brown hair looked like it had been in a wind tunnel. She wore a navy-blue pantsuit, her traditional work attire, but it was more wrinkled that usual and had what looked like gravel dust on the knees. She had said that the case she was working on was a tough one, and her appearance reinforced it. Regardless, to me, she was lovely.

She caught her breath and said that she had had to run down a suspect and ended up in a tangle with him on a sidewalk. The suspect didn't know that the trim detective had run high school track, and although she was nearing fifty, she could still outpace most anyone. I asked if she was okay, and she gave a feeble smile and said I should see the other guy. I smiled appropriately. She wanted to run to the restroom and to reestablish the look of a human being, so I asked what she wanted, and she said anything as long as there was a lot of it. I envied her metabolism.

Karen attacked a Beach Burrito like she had attacked the suspect, and mango salsa seeped out the side of the wrap. Chasing murder suspects was good for the appetite. She finally paused and apologized again, this time for gobbling her food; she said that all she had eaten today was a piece of toast. I munched on my gyro and repeated that apologies weren't necessary.

She finished her wrap, took a sip of Pepsi, and looked at the college students in the front of the restaurant. "I had Joe put to sleep," she whispered.

Joe was a twelve-year-old cat named after Joe Friday from the old television show *Dragnet*. He had been sick for months, and she had known that his life outside cat heaven was coming to an end. That still didn't make it easier.

"I'm sorry," I said, putting my hand on hers across the table. "Why didn't you call? I would've gone with you."

"It was something I wanted to do by myself. We'd been together since he was five weeks old. He's better off, but I already miss him."

It was touching that the lady sitting with me could be chasing a murder suspect across a parking lot one minute and grieving over a feline that had been her companion for a dozen years the next.

"Anything I can do?" I asked.

"You're doing it." She put her other hand on top of mine.

We sat silently and watched others in the restaurant. She tried to make small talk, but it was forced. The death of her cat must have been hard, but it was clear something else was bothering her. I asked what it was.

She hesitated but finally said, "It's Dad."

Her father, Brian Newman, had been Folly Beach's police chief—more accurately, director of public safety—for more than eighteen years before winning a special mayoral election. The former mayor had resigned to the displeasure of almost no one. Brian had reluctantly run for office, and from the time he announced his candidacy, Karen had been against it. He was nearly seventy but had spent his adult life in law enforcement—thirty years in the military and then several years as Folly's chief. He had suffered two heart attacks since I'd known him, and Karen was afraid that moving out of his comfort zone would cause additional stress.

"Is he okay?" I had known about her fear for his health but hadn't heard anything about new issues.

"Says he is," she said. "But I see fatigue in his eyes. He's putting up a good front, but I'm positive that local politics is taking a toll."

I didn't want to downplay her concern, but I also felt that she was being overly protective. Brian was well entrenched in the community, had a clear picture of the pitfalls and plusses of the local government, and was well respected by most citizens. Rather than sharing that, I nodded.

She shook her head like she was shaking off her misgivings. "Know what I'd like to do?"

I didn't and said so.

"Walk on the beach."

"Do you have to go back to work?"

"Not really," she said. "The guys have everything under control, and I have a meeting early in the morning."

"Leave your car and I'll drive you over, and we can walk on the beach to your heart's content. I'll bring you back whenever."

She said that it was the best idea she'd heard all day. I didn't figure that meant much considering the day she'd had. She grabbed a pair of shorts, a polo shirt, and tennis shoes that she kept in her trunk for such emergencies, and we headed to Folly. We parked at the house, she changed clothes, and we walked two blocks to the sand, surf, and sea breeze where small groups of vacationers were enjoying one of the last sunny Sundays of the summer.

I wanted to tell her about the hit-and-run and ask if she thought I'd overreacted by thinking it had been intentional. Considering her mood and what she had been through, though, I couldn't bring myself to mention it. Maybe later.

The crowds thinned as we moved away from the pier, and the laughter of small children frolicking in the surf quieted until the only sounds we heard came from a few seagulls overhead and the waves spanking the shore. It was low tide and the beach was wide, so we walked at least a mile. I could almost see the tension leaving Karen's shoulders, and her talk turned to the weather, the beauty of the ocean, and the cruise ship that we watched as it entered the Charleston harbor. She was leaving her grief over Joe and the day's work behind; the ocean was working its magic. I thought that First Light Church's meeting on the beach would be much more appealing to many than services held in a building.

Karen could have walked to the end of the island that

overlooked the Morris Island Lighthouse on Lighthouse Inlet, but my aging legs told me that it was time to turn back. On the return walk, I lightly broached the hit-and-run.

She stopped and reached for my hand. "Are you okay?"

I told her that I was fine, and she listened before responding that she understood why I had thought it wasn't an accident but that I should leave it to the experts to determine what had really happened.

She nudged me in the ribs. "Here's a radical idea. Why don't you leave police work to the police? It goes against your grain, and especially Charles's, but give it a try."

It wasn't what I wanted to hear, but I didn't argue. With fingers crossed, I said I'd try.

A cool breeze blew in our faces as we reached the pier, and she agreed that coffee sounded good. We stopped in Roasted, the coffee shop in the Tides Hotel, got two cups of Starbucks, and sat on the deck overlooking the pool and the outdoor bar. The sun was descending behind the hotel, and Karen had finally relaxed.

Soon the little coffee we had left was getting cold, and we were too. Karen said that she needed to get home to get some sleep before her morning meeting, so I reluctantly returned her to her car in the restaurant's parking lot. She thanked me for helping her out of her funk, gave me kiss that lingered longer than most parking-lot kisses, and headed to her house on the outskirts of Charleston.

The bright oval of the setting sun was barely visible behind the windswept trees adjacent to the marsh as I crossed the bridge to Folly, and the red reflected off the slowly rippling water in the Folly River and off the tops of the sailboats anchored in the stream. The end to another wonderful day on Folly.

Or so I thought. The phone rang while I was seated in my

well-worn lounge chair sipping a glass of chardonnay, stuffing my mouth with Cheetos, and reflecting upon everything that had happened the last two days. I was out of spring water and tofu.

"Did I wake you?" asked Chief Cindy LaMond's familiar voice.

"Why would you think that?"

"Let's see, it's almost ten, and I know you old folks peter out around nine. Plus, everyone knows that you go bonkers when someone bothers you this late."

"Enough, Cindy. I'm awake. What's up?"

"Whew, I'm glad. I've had enough people going bonkers on me tonight. Enough chitty-chat talk. Want to know what happened on West Ashley?"

I didn't want to be considered bonkers, so I calmly said, "Uh-huh."

"Here goes," she said. I heard papers rustling. "Timothy Mendelson, age fifty-six, Caucasian, was found totally dead by his housekeeper in his great room. I might add, his great room is really great, with a mile-high ceiling and windows larger than my car that overlook the Atlantic. The late Mr. Mendelson was stabbed three times, once in the back, twice in the chest."

Something tickled the back of my memory bank, but I couldn't put a finger on it. "What happened?"

"Don't know," Cindy said. "The doors were locked. No sign of a struggle, no defensive wounds. I'd say Mendelson knew the killer. It'll be up to the medical examiner to tell for sure, but I suspect the stab in the back came first. No one's going to let someone with a big-ass knife insert it in his chest without trying to deflect it. The vic still had a god-awful-expensive gold Rolex on his deceased wrist and five hundred dollars and several credit cards in the wallet in his pocket. Robbery unlikely."

"Married?"

"Why, Chris, you flirt, you know I am."

"You know what I meant, Chief LaMond."

She giggled. "He was single. No evidence of a female residing on site. There were pots and pans in the kitchen, but I've been told that some men—although not the one I'm married to—actually know how to use those things."

"I don't think I knew him. Has he been here long? What'd he do?"

"I'm not certain how long he's lived here, but one of my officers said it's been at least five years. He had given Mendelson a speeding ticket around then and remembered it because the guy raised a stink. He was a stockbroker. We're trying to identify his next of kin. I'll let you know what we find out."

I thanked Cindy for not waking me up and for sharing the update. She said that it would never have entered her mind not to have shared it with me—she lived to feed my curiosity. I told her that she was wise beyond her years; she called me a smart-ass and hung up. Citizen-police relations at their best.

It then struck me why he sounded familiar. Timothy is a fairly common name, at least it was in my day when people weren't named after the seasons, modern technological companies, and combinations of letters that only can be pronounced by Swedes. *Timothy something* was the benefactor of the First Light Church—*Timothy something* who happened to be a stockbroker.

I called Charles and hung up after five rings. He didn't have an answering machine, so I knew he wasn't home. His apartment was so small that when he was there, he was never more than three rings away. He also didn't have a cell phone. His refusal to leap into the twenty-first century had frustrated me on several occasions and at least once had nearly cost him his life. I would have to wait until tomorrow to talk to him about Mendelson.

I then lived down to Cindy's expectations and fell asleep in my chair.

CHAPTER 7

The next day started for me like most others on the sleepy island—half awake, sensory underload, then spiked with coffee. It was unusually cool for September and thunderstorms had rolled through overnight. The rain had slackened, but it was still coming down enough to discourage me from going outside. It would be a good day to do nothing.

I picked up the phone to call Charles, but it rang before I could dial.

"Dude dialing," said the high-pitched voice of Jim "Dude" Sloan, owner of the surf shop and another unlikely friend. He was in his early sixties but had never left the golden age of hippies.

"Chris listening," I said, and smiled.

"You be at *su casa*?"

"Yes."

"Be sloshin' over," he said, and then the line went dead.

Seconds later there was a knock on the door. Dude may have been stuck in the 1960s, but he had surpassed Charles in technology. He had a cell phone. The rain dinged loudly on the metal roof, so it must have intensified in the last few minutes.

I opened the door to the pitiful sight of the five-foot-seven, scrawny, aging hippie. His long, curly white-gray hair was plastered down the sides and front of his face, his colorful tie-dyed shirt looked like it had been just pulled from the ocean, and water dripped from his green shorts.

Besides his current soaked state, Dude looked like he always did. What was different was a red rhinestone-studded leash in his hand that was connected to a small bundle of wet fur standing at his feet.

"Got drying rag?" Dude asked.

Dude had never met a sentence that he couldn't screw up. His spoken language, somewhere between surf talk and gibberish, convinced most listeners that he was either a blithering idiot, a visitor from another planet, or a genius who didn't waste time with proper English. Actually, I had only heard one person attribute Dude's unique command of the language to his being a genius, and the odds were that it had been said in jest. I had learned years ago not to underestimate my friend; he was bright, had a sense of humor, and was loyal to his friends, something in short supply in the world.

I told him and whatever creature was at the lower end of the leash to wait on the screen porch while I got a towel. I returned with one, and instead of drying his dripping locks with it, Dude bent down and wrapped it around what was now beginning to look like a dog and carried the bundle into the living room.

I nudged Dude toward the kitchen table. "You're soaked. Let me get another towel."

He shook his head, and water flew in all directions. "No big whoop." He shook his head again. "Me be surfer. Water be friend."

Dude rubbed the dog with the towel. Other than the dog's hair being light brown and the dog's being approximately five feet shorter than Dude, I was struck by how much they looked alike. I had never heard Dude speak about a pet, so I thought it was appropriate to ask about the sad-looking bundle of wet fur. "Who's your friend?"

"Be Pluto," Dude said as he continued to rub the soaked canine.

"Like Disney's Pluto?" I asked.

"Nope. Be named for dwarf planet, FKA Pluto."

In addition to being known as the strange hippie surf-shop owner stuck in a time warp, Dude was Folly's expert on astronomy. Charles had often said that Dude's curiosity about the science was the result of his coming from another planet; I thought it was simply an interesting hobby. I remembered a lengthy conversation—lengthy for Dude—that we had had a couple of years ago when he was peeved because something called the International Astronomical Union had kicked Pluto off the official list of planets. Dude apparently wasn't over the slight.

I asked Dude if he wanted coffee. He asked if I had tea. I said no. He declined the coffee but asked if I had 2 percent milk for Pluto. I said no. He said water would do, and I filled an ice-cream bowl and set it on the floor beside the nearly dry pooch. Pluto licked my hand in appreciation.

I ruffled the dog's head and looked at Dude. I wanted to ask more about Pluto—where he had come from, what breed he was, and why Dude was out walking him in the pouring rain—but I figured there was a more important reason Dude had showed up at my door on such a miserable day.

"What's up?" I asked.

"First," Dude said after he settled into one of my underused kitchen chairs, "formal intro Pluto." He reached down and put his arms around the fifteen-pound version of himself and lovingly lifted him and kissed his forehead. "Pluto be Australian terrier."

I looked at Dude and then at the dog that I would have sworn grinned at me. "Pleased to meet you, Pluto. I believe you're the first Australian terrier that I've met."

Dude smiled, and Pluto continued to grin. "Vetster say he be Australian terrier derivative." Dude looked down at the dog. "Me just say Pluto."

Since Dude apparently wanted to surf this wave, I asked, "I didn't know you had a dog."

"Didn't until last full moon," he said.

As with many things my friend says, I wasn't certain what that meant. "Oh," I articulately responded.

"Traded surfboard for Pluto. Board old, Pluto new."

"Oh," I repeated.

"Me be stoked." Dude hugged Pluto and carefully returned him to the floor.

"I'm glad."

"Intro be done. Chrisster, you be detective, private-like. Me need detectin'." He looked back down at Pluto, who had returned to the water bowl, and back up at me.

Unlike Charles, I had never said or thought I was or aspired to be a private detective. Along with Charles and a few others, I had merely stumbled upon several murders, way more than any one person who wasn't taking a paycheck from law enforcement should ever have to. Through luck—mostly good, occasionally tragic—and with the help of friends, I had assisted the police in catching some evil people. I didn't know why Dude had thought, even in his scrambled brain, that I was a detective, but I was about to find out.

"Dude, I'm not a detective."

"Horseshoe close," Dude said.

Pluto had finished hydrating himself and was at Dude's feet, looking up and whimpering. I considered whimpering but refrained since I had opened the door. Besides, I was curious.

"Why do you need a detective?" I reached over and patted Pluto. Dude had given into the whimpering, and Pluto was now happily seated on my friend's lap.

"Me be sun god worshiper; Helios mostly, Surya when spirit strikes." Dude who pointed to the ceiling like I wouldn't know where the sun hung out during the day. "Sunday pray, sing from book, steeple churches not my thing. First Light religion of different color. Preacher Burl be like preacher nonpreacher. Don't preach about sun god, but he cool with Helios. Spends most time talking about Jesus and his buds. That be boss, meet outside and me whisper to my gods."

"You attend their services?" I asked, hoping to speed up his story.

"As Christians say, religiously. Stand in sand, gander at surf, raise eyelashes to sun. Boss."

From Dude, that was quite a sermon. For the last year, First Light hadn't been on my radar, and in the matter of three days, it had become the topic of discussion with Charles, Bob, and now Dude. My mind drifted. Could this be an omen that I should return to church? After all, I was rapidly getting into my most senior years and hadn't been a regular churchgoer for more than four decades.

In a soothing way, Folly Beach had become my heaven. The afternoon summer sun could bake skin to a few degrees shy of blackened; traffic during vacation season could give an aspirin a headache. The small beach community was home to a few nefarious characters who wouldn't be able to find the Pearly Gates with a map, much less meet the entry requirements. No, Folly Beach wasn't heaven, but it was my heaven. Folly cared little about the multilayered pasts—good, bad, whatever—of its residents. The future was a concept seldom dwelled upon. And eccentricity was worn on one's sleeve, not like a chip to be knocked off but like a general's epaulette. But was there more? Was First Light an omen?

"Yo, Chrisster," Dude interrupted my reverie. "Dudester to Chrisster. You be earthbound?"

"Sorry, Dude, what?"

"Rumor be you see smash between man and machine. Nearly squashed yourself."

"Unfortunately, true." I shook my head. I shared the gory details with Dude and Pluto. I think Dude understood everything I said, something that seldom happens the other way around. Pluto seemed confused or else was wondering why I didn't have 2 percent milk.

"Me might help," Dude said.

"Explain?"

Dude had a mysterious way of evaporating words out of everyone's sentences.

"One of Preacher Burl's flocksters be named JJ. Hear hitee have funny J name."

"Jeremy Junius Chiles," I said.

"If me be he, my handle'd be JJ."

"Good point, Dude," I said. "What do you know about JJ?"

"He not always there Sundays. He unconstrained by job." Dude looked at me like he expected me to say something; Pluto stopped smiling and licked Dude's arm.

"Know anything else about him?"

"Low to ground and drug-shrunk thin." Dude returned Pluto to the floor. "Got bugged-out eyes, noggin barely holds them." Dude hesitated, closed his eyes tight, and then continued, "Wore corduroy shorts; could be cut-off corduroy britches."

I'd never known Dude to be so observant, but then again, I hadn't known he was a dog lover. The description fit the man who joined me on the street. "Anything else?"

"Always be asking questions. Not only church stuff but things about peeps."

"Like what?"

"Where from? Why here? What job? Favorite color, or food, or toothbrush?"

"Really?" I said, and then remembered how strange it had been when Jeremy Junius had asked me what I did.

"All but toothbrush." Dude smiled. "Said to see if you be listening."

I grinned, and so did Pluto. "Did he seem to have anyone he spent time with in the congregation?"

"Flock, not congregation."

"Sorry," I said. "Flock?"

"Nope. Maybe Preacher Burl, maybe not."

"Anything else?" I asked.

"That be it. Check him out?"

I wasn't about to commit to anything, but it seemed certain that Dude's JJ was Jeremy Junius.

"Why didn't you go to the police to find out?"

"Fuzz and Dude not always surfin' same wave," Dude said.

Dude had become a staple on Folly. He was the unlikely intermediary between the police, what the rest of the world would consider the normal citizens, and the surfers and other bohemian residents, some with homes, some without. He wasn't perfect, and I doubted there were any outstanding warrants on him, but there were gaps in his past; gaps that no one seemed able to fill.

"One other bit," Dude said. "Got hunch JJ had checkered past—no facts, Jack, just vibes."

Dude had good instincts, so I took him seriously and told him that his description of JJ fit Jeremy Junius.

Dude looked at me and then down at Pluto. He shook his head and said, "See, Pluto? Told you he be ace detective."

CHAPTER 8

I wasn't a fan of exercise, but the morning was so pleasant that I had walked a half-dozen blocks to City Park on the edge of the Folly River. I was surprised to see Charles watching a small sailboat meandering upstream. I sat on the bench beside him and told him about Dude's visit. Charles's sun-wrinkled face seemed to have more wrinkles since Melinda's death. He wasn't as quick to smile, and I occasionally caught him daydreaming. When I asked about it, he'd shake his head and look away.

One thing that seemed to pull him out of his dark mood was hearing the latest rumors, so I shared what Dude had told me about JJ. Charles said that he was surprised that he hadn't seen the person Dude had described at First Light. He admitted that when he had attended, he had been lost in thoughts about Melinda and hadn't paid much attention to others.

Charles modest interest in my story became enthusiasm and intense questioning when I mentioned Pluto. I was able to answer some of his questions, like what the pooch's name was and what breed it was, but when he got to what Dude fed it and what vet he was using, I threw up my hands and said that he'd have to talk to Dude. Charles must have figured that he'd gotten as much information about Pluto as he could and agreed that he would head to the surf shop later to meet the new addition to Dude's family. He returned to our earlier conversation about JJ's attending First Light and suggested that we see if Preacher Burl was at the foul-weather sanctuary.

We entered First Light's storefront and were greeted by the gravelly voice of a gentleman perched atop an eight-foot ladder with a paintbrush in hand.

"Our prayers are answered," said the painter, who appeared to be in his seventies. "The Lord has sent us more workers."

A man and a woman were also in the room. Mr. Gravelly Voice stepped off the ladder and approached us. He was tall, probably six foot two or so, and had a long white beard that looked like it had slipped down off his bald head. He transferred the paintbrush to his other hand and reached out to shake Charles's hand. Charles introduced himself and pointed over his shoulder and told him my name.

"I'm Six," the painter said, and then coughed.

"Like the number?" Charles asked.

Six stared at Charles but didn't seem to be focused. "Know any other kind?"

Charles stammered, "Umm, no."

I knew when to remain silent, although I did wonder if Six was his first or last name.

Mr. Six, or probably Brother Six, took in at Charles's blue long-sleeved T-shirt. "What's that?"

I assumed that he was referring to the strange looking creature on the front. I was used to Charles's eclectic shirt collection and had stopped commenting on them.

"Petey the Griffin," Charles said like it was obvious. "Mythical creature with the head of an eagle and body of a lion; mascot of Canisius College in Buffalo, New York. It's—"

Six waved his brush in the air. "Who gives a sh—"

"Whoa, Brother Six," interrupted the woman who had been

painting in the nearby corner. She had moved close as Charles gave his fascinating lesson on mythical creatures. "You are in the house of the Lord." Her voice was barely above a whisper.

Six bowed his head, coughed, and mumbled an apology.

"I've seen you at church," the woman said softly as she stuck out her hand to Charles. She was in her forties and probably had been beautiful until she had been zapped by life. Her long brown hair was either poorly cut or displaying a new style. I suspected the former, probably self-butchered. But unlike Six, she had hair. She shook Charles's hand and turned to me and did the same. "Name's Lottie," she said to both of us. "I hope Brother Six was right when he said you were here to help."

The smell of paint hung in the air, and my eyes watered. Charles smiled and said that we were actually here to see Preacher Burl.

The third worker finally joined our group and said, "He's off ministering to a young couple that lost their baby—God rest the young 'un's soul."

He was roughly Lottie's age. He looked emaciated and had a chiseled face and dark-brown hair and stood a good half foot shorter than Six.

Charles told me that the third person was Sharp and that they had met when painting a few days earlier. As with Six, there was no hint if this was his first or last name.

"So if you're not here to do the Lord's work, what do you want with Preacher Burl?" asked Six, the least friendly of the trio.

Charles wasn't deterred by Six's surliness. "Perhaps you can help us." He waved his cane toward all three so they knew that whatever he was about to ask included all of them. "Maybe you know the man who was tragically run down by an automobile the other morning. His name was, umm." He turned to me.

"Jeremy Junius Chiles," I said.

"That's right," Charles said. "We think he may be JJ, one of our flock."

"Oh my God," Lottie whispered.

"Didn't know anybody was kilt," Sharp said. "What happened?"

Charles summarized the hit-and-run.

Six shifted his weight from foot to foot and kept looking toward his ladder and paint bucket. "Don't recall anyone by that name."

Lottie turned to Charles. "That don't mean much coming from Six. Most of the time he don't remember who I am, and we've been going to First Light since Preacher Burl started it."

"Humph," Six said, punctuating this with a cough.

"Smoker's cough," Lottie said as she pointed at Six. She turned to me. "Was he real thin-like?"

I said yes.

"I might remember him," she said. "If it's who I think, he's a nice guy. Talked a lot to Preacher Burl."

"Now I know who you mean," Sharp said. "You saying he got hit on the street made me remember him. He was always walking around. After you get off this street, there ain't a lot of sidewalks, and the guy was always walking in the street." He hesitated and then nodded. "Not just in the street, but in the middle of it. God rest his soul."

"It's dangerous out there," Six said. "Surprised more people aren't run down." He took his paintbrush over to the can, pounded the butt on the top of the can, and then rejoined the group.

"Anyone know anything about him?" Charles asked.

Six grabbed a metal folding chair from the corner, turned it around, and straddled the back. I didn't know if he wanted to start a prayer meeting or rest. "JJ reminded me of a student in my class at the community college," he said. "Always asking questions."

"Thought you didn't remember him," Lottie said.

"Didn't, then Sharp said he was always walking the streets. It clicked. He spent most of his time with Preacher Burl. Don't rightly know what they talked about. Called it *apple polishing* back in school."

"Your college have a mascot?" Charles asked.

Only a question Charles would ask, I thought.

"Don't remember no mascot," Six said.

I knew that I had to redirect the conversation or Charles would go as far as asking if Six would undergo hypnosis to remember the mascot. "Have you been members long?" I asked the group.

Lottie said that she and Six had been part of the flock since nearly the beginning and politely pointed out that First Light didn't have members and that anyone who decided to attend was considered one of the flock. Membership was for the walled churches. Sharp said that he had started attending six months before. All three had settled comfortably into the conversation and didn't appear in a hurry to get back to work.

"First Light saved me," Six said. He ran his hand through his beard, coughed, and then said, "Grew up piss poor—sorry, Lottie—near Birmingham. First of anyone I knew to go to college. Didn't finish, but spent two years there. Got a job selling televisions when there were actually television sales-and-repair shops." He laughed, the first time I'd heard this from him. "I remember when there were tubes in TVs. They kept burning out, and we could actually replace them and fix the TV without needing a degree in electrical engineering."

"The good old days," added Charles.

"Sure were," Six said. "Then the small shops were squeezed

out of business by large appliance and furniture stores that sold TVs. And then they all were gobbled up by Walmart." He paused and pointed toward the ocean. "Sort of like small fishes out there being eaten by larger fishes, and larger fishes being eaten by larger ones." He coughed.

"Don't guess we know anything more about JJ," said Lottie, who had apparently gone down memory lane as much as she wanted to with Six.

"You know all I know," Sharp added.

I walked toward the door.

"Then I went to selling insurance," Six said, oblivious to the rest of us. "Was back when insurance men went house-to-house selling policies and then back to the houses each month to collect the premiums." He shook his head. "Got myself fired. I had to go in homes where it didn't take a genius to see that the folks didn't have the money to make their payment. I let a lot of them slide. Got canned but didn't care; couldn't take those folks' food money."

"Sorry to hear it," Charles said.

That was all it took for Six to continue. "Got a bartending job." He coughed and then sighed. "Big mistake. Bartending put me close to booze. Slid right into hell. Ended up on the street and, when I was lucky, homeless shelters."

I glanced at Lottie and Sharp as they watched Six. Their expressions said that they'd heard his story before, probably more than once.

"Then, praise the Lord, I found my way to Folly and Preacher Burl."

"Amen," Sharp said.

"Gotta get back to work," Lottie said. "Lot of God's work to do in this ol' space."

I looked around. Two of the walls had been painted bright

white. From where it had been chipped, I noticed that the concrete floor had had several coats of paint over the years, from dark brown to brick red to battleship gray. The last coat had been light blue. There were four mismatched pews shoved against the back wall that looked like castoffs from a church remodel; two had warped backrests and had seen the underside of a flood.

Lottie was right, there was still a lot of God's work to be done.

I told them that I had the photo gallery next door and to holler if they needed anything. Sharp said that I looked familiar and that he must have seen me there. I said that I had to get to work, and Charles said he would stick around and help.

I left the work in progress knowing little more about JJ than I had when I entered but a lot more about Brother Six. Lottie and Sharp undoubtedly had equally tragic stories, and I was glad that they appeared to have found a way out of their downward spirals. For that, I thought Preacher Burl should be praised, regardless of what Bob had said.

At least I thought that was right.

CHAPTER 9

Saturday night was unusually quiet. Nothing caught my interest on television, and no one knocked on the door. I poured a plastic wineglass of chardonnay and sat on the screen porch to watch the parade of vehicles in front of the house.

The events of the last week tweaked thoughts about my life before and after moving to Folly. My pre-Folly years had revolved around work in a highly structured environment that had been bureaucratic to the *n*th degree. Risk taking was an alien concept, and nothing about me stood out with my traditional attire, socially acceptable vehicle, and house in a middle-American subdivision. My Folly friends correctly described my former life as boring, boring, boring.

Then I ended up here, and things began to change almost from the first time I crossed the bridge. Not only did I stumble on a murder, but I stumbled upon a cadre of friends. More accurately, they stumbled upon me. During my first two years, I got closer to more people than I had been close to in my first sixty. I couldn't explain it but counted it among the greatest blessings that had been bestowed upon me.

First-time visitors to Folly Beach generally had one of two reactions to the island: they loved it or hated it. From my experience, it appeared that those who fell on the negative side arrived imagining Folly to be like many coastal resort communities, dotted with luxury high-rise condo buildings featuring pools with floating bars and Jacuzzis and pristine white beaches with firm-bodied college students delivering umbrella-topped drinks to their umbrella-shaded beach chairs. They couldn't fathom a beach without a major outlet mall within a couple of miles featuring stores with familiar names selling second-quality goods to those found in their malls back home. And they weren't comfortable unless they could pay a premium for status-logoed tennis and golf equipment and apparel to use at the courses and courts feet from their condos.

Inexplicably, I fell into the second category. At first I thought that I had entered a time warp and gone back to the 1950s. Most of the houses had the precentral-air feel about them. They were sturdy, but no one would accuse them of being upscale. The *Charleston Visitors' Guide* had described the island as "a charming bohemian enclave perched on the self-anointed edge of America." I wholeheartedly agreed with the brief, albeit a bit too poetic, description but told newcomers that it had more of an aging-hippie, beer-for-breakfast-shared-with-your-Doberman feel. It wasn't filled with wealth but was crammed with locals who cared about one another and who knew about one another but who did not judge lest they be judged.

The beauty might not have been quite on the same level as nearby Kiawah Island, the per capita income would not match that of Daniel Island, and it would be hard to find the entertainment opportunities of Myrtle Beach, but Folly met my needs. West of Center Street were forested areas, east had the rocky, turbulent waterfront of the Washout, and the far east had an isolated section awash in nature and beauty with an awesome view of the iconic Morris Island Lighthouse. If I were exercise inclined, I could walk miles on the lightly populated beach with my toes in the Atlantic Ocean, watch pleasure boaters traversing the Folly River in their small sail- and powerboats, or watch dolphins frolic in the peaceful streams throughout the marsh that bordered much of the inland side of Folly.

The love-hate attitude of many first-time visitors could also be found in the recesses of locals' minds. They loved the arrival of vacationers, who brought money to the economy. Outside dollars supported businesses and, indirectly, many of the residents. But with the outside money came increased traffic, both vehicular and human. Finding a place to park could be as difficult as finding a Roman coin in your change from Target. Waiting for a table in a local restaurant could take longer than the lifespan of a housefly. And during vacation season, the usually simple task of returning to the island from nearby Charleston could overheat your radiator and your temper.

Folly Beach was perfect for First Light; so in hindsight, I wasn't surprised that not only did it get its start here but that several people I knew attended. My prayer was that it was as positive as my friends said it was.

Between my second and third glasses of wine, I began to think again about how many times First Light had been thrust upon me in the last few days. It seemed more than coincidence, and if I had learned one thing the last few years, it was that there was no such thing as coincidence. Why not attend tomorrow's service? I could see what the fuss was about. And if nothing else, it would shock Charles and irritate Bob. That would make it worthwhile. I laughed. A large palmetto bug climbing up the screen in front of me apparently didn't see the humor and continued at a leisurely pace.

My thoughts then drifted to Timothy Mendelson's murder. He had been a stockbroker, so I wondered whether Bob had ever crossed paths with him or whether he knew anything about the successful businessman. It was still before ten, so I figured my Realtor friend would be awake. I called, and Betty answered. Unlike boorish Bob, she seemed genuinely pleased to hear from me. I shared a couple of pleasantries and filled her in on the activities of some of my friends when I heard Bob in the background. "He didn't call to talk to you. Hang up or give me the phone."

Who could not love Bob?

"What in the hell do you want pestering my wife in the middle of the night?" Bob boomed.

"And a pleasant Saturday evening to you as well, my friend," I said with a grin.

"Yeah, yeah, yeah," he said with a little less bluster. "What do you want?"

"You hang around with Charleston's rich and famous, and you're the most knowledgeable Realtor in the business, so I figured you'd know something I was curious about."

"Crap! That much frickin' fake flattery means you want something, something big. Spit it out."

"Do you know Timothy Mendelson?" I asked.

"You mean something other than his mug was plastered all over the Channel 5 News all week? Something other than he's dead?"

"Yep," I said.

There was a pause, and I heard Bob whisper, "Okay, sweetie, I'll be up shortly. I love you."

"Ew," I said with a chuckle.

"Shut up," he said. "So what about Mendelson?"

"Anything," I responded.

"Don't know much. I heard him speak at a Board of Realtors' meeting a couple of years ago. Wasn't much of a speaker; all he wanted to talk about was the stock market, how it's up and down, bears, bulls ... could have been talking about penguins as far as I cared. I fell asleep somewhere after he started telling how the term bear came from London bearskin jobbers, blah, blah, blah. Hell, all I wanted to know was when people'd start buying houses again. Is that what you called in the middle of the night to find out?"

I told him that if that was all he knew, it'd have to do.

"Why do you want to know?"

"No reason. I heard some folks talking about him and was curious about his death."

"Oh no, holy damnoly. Don't tell me." He sighed. "You're sticking your wrinkled old neck somewhere it don't belong. Again."

I told him that it was nothing like that and that I was simply curious.

"The same curiosity that killed the damned cat," he replied.

I once again tried to reassure him that my interest was no more than curiosity and that I had no intention of getting involved. He said that he didn't believe a word of it, but since he couldn't stop me from barging into the middle of a mess and probably getting myself killed, he would make a few calls and see if he could find out anything about Mendelson that might help.

"Try not to get yourself killed before I can get back with you," he said and was gone.

CHAPTER 10

Sunday morning, when the laid-back island was even more serene, had always been my favorite time of the week. The roar of work trucks heading off-island or arriving at work sites disturbed the early morning quiet most weekdays, and vacationers and day-trippers cluttered the streets on Saturdays. But before the more devout residents left their homes to attend services at the local Catholic, Baptist, and Methodist churches, traffic was nearly nonexistent on Sundays.

I stepped out of my cottage and looked at the cloudless sky, felt the early morning warmth and humid air that permeated September, and listened to the sounds of silence. This was going to be the perfect summer morning; a perfect day to attend my second church service in four decades.

The beach entry closest to the service was two blocks from the house, but I had seldom ventured in that direction on a Sunday morning. It was fifteen minutes before the service was to begin, but I knew that Charles would be there. It was easy to spot the gathering. The Folly Pier transected the portion of the beach to the right of the pier, where visitors to the Tides and the large Charleston Oceanfront Villas dominated the surf and sand in season, and the portion to the left, where the crowds were lighter. That was where a five-foot-high homemade wooden cross was embedded in the sand beside a portable lectern that could have spent its better days in a high school gymnasium as the focal point of bored students forced to listen to their principal. In front of the makeshift pulpit were twenty-five folding chairs, and behind them six rusting card-table chairs and three surfboards arranged in a semicircle.

Preacher Burl was on the ocean side of the lectern and surrounded by approximately twenty others. Each held a Dixie cup; some were drinking and three were standing at a large plastic dispenser pouring what looked like lemonade. I had thought I would be early, but I hadn't gotten word about preservice refreshments. Charles tilted the dispenser so an elderly couple could fill their cups with the dwindling liquid.

The elderly gentleman nodded thanks to Charles, and my friend spotted me as I self-consciously moved toward the group. He wore his summer Tilley and one of his more muted shirts. It was off-white with a tiny University of Arkansas logo on the breast pocket.

"Welcome, Brother Chris," he said with a nod.

I wasn't sure if he was serious, so I nodded back and apologized for missing whatever First Light called the preservice event. Charles said that he accepted my apology and politely told me he was glad that I was there—no criticism for my being late, no snide remark about anything. God had to be grinning, if not baffled.

Preacher Burl had moved behind the pulpit and called for us to take our seats. Charles said that there were more chairs than people and that I could join him in the second row.

Preacher Burl held out his arms and said, "Shall we begin?" He wore a flowing white gown that looked like a poorly sewn bedsheet; when he held out his arms, it reminded me of a kite readying itself to be taken by the wind. I shook the vision from my head.

"We can't control most of the distractions around us," the preacher said as he waved toward the kids yelling over the side of the pier behind the makeshift church, and then he pointed toward a City of Folly Beach ATV as it chugged past us on one of its patrols. "But we can control one thing." He pulled his phone out from under his sheet—correction, robe. "Please silence thy portable communication devices."

I assumed that was preacher speak for cell phones and flicked mine to mute.

While others were completing this task, I turned to see who else was here. I was pleased to see Mel Evans in the row behind me. His significant other, Caldwell, wasn't with him. Mel nodded and smiled. Two elderly couples were to my left. Both men wore knee-length white socks that almost reached their navy-blue shorts, and their spouses wore flowery-patterned long dresses. There were three middle-aged couples in attire more suited for church in town than on the beach: the men wore white dress shirts, dark dress slacks, and black shoes, and the women wore fashionable dresses. They looked as out of place as an abacus in an Apple store. On the surfboards now sat two young men and a woman. There were still empty seats close to the pulpit, but I recognized the three helpers from the foul-weather sanctuary standing behind the surfers.

While the preacher was waiting for everyone to silence thy portable communication devices, one of the white-socked gentlemen handed out packets of approximately twenty sheets of paper stapled together. They appeared to have been photocopied from a church hymnal. Burl then asked the gathered group to turn to the third page and join him in singing "Morning Light Is Breaking."

After two verses from the plagiarized songbook, I decided that that the only way the singing could have been worse was if Charles's main squeeze Heather had been there. One of my morning prayers was answered when Preacher Burl raised his hand for us to stop "singing" after three verses.

"Brothers and sisters," Burl began, "this is a sad day indeed. Most of you already know, but our beloved Brother Timothy Mendelson's life was recently taken from this flawed earth."

From the gasps behind me, it was clear that some had not heard the news.

"Brother Timothy," Burl continued, "had not been part of our flock long, but in the few short months he had made an everlasting impression."

Burl went on to describe how Mendelson had offered to help the struggling church by generously giving his time, his prayers, and his tithes. The preacher didn't dwell on the financial contributions but made it clear that Mendelson had made church-altering contributions and had promised more as needed.

I wondered if Burl was going to mention the passing of JJ, and then I wondered if he knew about it. I planned to ask Charles after the service. I also irritated myself by wondering if Mendelson had left anything in his will to First Light.

Burl finished his lengthy, heartfelt eulogy and said, "Brother William, would you honor us with a heavenly rendering of Brother Timothy?"

I hadn't seen William Hansel arrive. He had been seated directly behind me, and when Preacher Burl made his request, William walked to the front of the assembled group. In an operatic bass voice, he sang "Rock of Ages."

William had been my neighbor when I first moved to Folly. He was in his early sixties and was about my height but not as heavy as me. He was a professor of hospitality and tourism at the College of Charleston and one of the few African Americans living on Folly Beach. William was friendly in a stuffy professorial way but was a friend, and he had one of the most beautiful singing voices that I had ever heard. Not only did he have the full attention of First Light's flock, but several beach walkers and three kids riding their bikes stopped to enjoy his touching rendition of the hymn.

> When I soar to worlds unknown,
> See Thee on Thy judgment throne,
> Rock of Ages, cleft for me,
> Let me hide myself in Thee.

Besides William, most of us in the congregation couldn't carry a tune in a sand pail, but we did speak our amen in one voice.

Preacher Burl choked back tears after William's awe-inspiring rendition, wiped his nose with a white handkerchief, and opened a leather legal-pad holder.

"When I was in the seminary, I studied the various traditional messages and how to conduct services under unusual circumstances, but nothing taught me how to begin after hearing an angel of the Lord deliver a musical message like we just experienced. Thank the Lord for giving us someone with such a heavenly voice. Thank you, Brother William."

I knew William was blushing, but it was masked by his cocoa-colored skin. He was introverted and hated attention. He mumbled thanks. I patted him on the leg when he returned to the chair behind me.

"God is everywhere, so pray anywhere." Preacher Burl had regained his composure. He studied his notes. "I know you've heard me say it before, but brothers and sisters, it's one of the founding tenets of First Light's ministry: God is everywhere." He stopped and waved all around him. "The Bible tells us that Jesus walked among everyone. He didn't discriminate against the poor, the hungry, the sinners. His ministry was among the trees, under the stars." He smiled. "And along beaches. We are outside because we don't want to be constrained by walls and the limits they impose upon us. I repeat, God is everywhere, so pray anywhere." He looked skyward, then toward the sea, and back at his flock. "I know you've heard this story, but it bears repeating. Is it from the Bible? No, but it was divinely inspired. There once was an elderly gentleman walking along the seashore. Could, in fact, have been on this wonderful beach." Burl pointed to the seawater lapping the shore. "He saw a young lad, oh, perhaps ten years of age, reaching down in the sand and carefully picking up starfish and then throwing them back into the sea." Burl made a tossing motion like he was skipping a rock on a pond. "The elder gent stopped by the youngster and shook his head. 'Son,' he said, 'you can't possibly save them all. You can't make a difference.' The youngster looked at the critical elder and said, 'I know, but I made a huge difference for that one.'" Burl paused for the message in the often-told story to sink in. "We can make as much a difference as that young lad made. We cannot save the world. We cannot stop war. Eliminating pestilence is outside your and my control. We cannot solve world hunger. But what we can do is touch those around us, those who are suffering, those whose lives can be made greater simply by showing we care."

I hadn't known what to expect, but I was surprised by Preacher Burl's message and how the eclectic mix seating in front of him appeared to be taken in by his words and mesmerized. He spent the next fifteen minutes translating the complex and often hard to understand gospel with everyday examples and explaining how it could directly help each of us. A handful of passersby stopped to listen.

It was before noon, but the direct sunlight had brought out beads of sweat on most of our faces, and Burl appeared sensitive to how uncomfortable his followers were becoming.

"Let me tell you about Luke 5:4–6," he said. "Jesus said to Simon, 'Throw them fishing nets into the sea.' Simon said, 'It won't do any good—already tried, caught nothing,' but anyway, he did what the Master had said to do. Guess what? They caught fishes aplenty."

Charles leaned over to me and said, "Don't think that's exactly how the Good Book said it."

I agreed but was struck by how effective Preacher Burl's version was.

He asked us to turn to page seven in our made-for-First-Light hymnal and started singing "Onward Christian Soldiers."

I remembered the hymn from when I attended Vacation Bible School at my Baptist church in Kentucky. It seemed that we sang the song each day, but my fading memory could have been wrong. I honored God's request to "make a joyful noise unto the Lord" by remaining silent; with my terrible singing voice, it was the best contribution I could make. As soon as the song ended and Preacher Burl thanked us for coming, I nudged Charles and said, "I thought a nontraditional church service on the beach would feature someone playing a guitar and singing contemporary religious songs."

Charles nodded in the direction of Preacher Burl, who was shaking hands with an elderly couple. "He says that most of his flock are older citizens, you and me, sort of, and those folks over there. He says we can identify with the old church songs more than the newer stuff. He wants us to be comfortable."

A small group of the flock now gathered around Preacher Burl as he pulled the cross out of the sand. Six and Sharp, who had remained standing through the entire service, quickly went to the front of the makeshift church to fold the chairs and stack them beside the pulpit. Lottie, the other helper I had met at the storefront sanctuary, came over and thanked me for coming. Her DIY haircut was neater than it had been the day before, and she wore a long burgundy dress. I could barely hear her over the roar of the surf when she said that she would welcome me when I ventured to the storefront to help her finish painting. More accurately, she said, "Such a handsome fellow like you is welcomed anytime." My blush was more obvious than William's had been.

Both Six and Sharp were painting at a pace that would make a snail seem like an Olympic sprinter, she said. "Six is so slow that the danged paint dries on the brush before he reaches the wall with it."

I smiled and said that I had to open the gallery but would try to get over when I had time. She left to help Sharp and Six with the chairs, saying that if she didn't push them they'd still be there next Sunday.

Charles had been talking to William, and they came over to me when Lottie walked away. I knew it would embarrass him, but I still told William that it had been an honor to have the opportunity to hear him sing. He stumbled through a thank-you. His car was parked on the street in front of the hotel a block from the service, and Charles said we would walk him to it. On the way, Charles told William why he was attending Preacher Burl's church, a story that I'd already heard.

"Shall I tell you why I attend?" William asked as we approached his eight-year-old Buick.

I was surprised he asked but pleased. I was curious but never would have broached the topic with the professor.

"I would be interested," Charles said.

"I grew up in black churches, attended with my parents, sang in the choir." He watched a car pass us. "My wife and I attended an AME church in Charleston until she passed. After her death … golly, it's been some fifteen years now." He slowly shook his head. "I continued attending. But, I must confess, disillusionment diluted my faith. Perhaps it was from my feeling of loss for my wife, perhaps my increasingly jaded perspective of the world. I am not certain the cause, but I noticed that even though my church preached inclusion and equality of all, I felt deep-seated emotional segregation. I began attending one of the Holy City's large, predominantly white congregations. I will not disclose the name for fear of biasing you against it. The parishioners were outwardly friendly and said that I was welcome in their midst, but my vibes, as my students say, told me otherwise."

"Sorry," I said.

"As am I," the professor said. "I reluctantly acknowledge that after that experience, I drifted away from the light. And then I read about First Light from a flyer posted on the eclectically adorned entry to Bert's Market. I couldn't quite put my finger on the reason, but I was intrigued by the concept." He smiled. "Perhaps it was because the services were held outside and I could scurry away if they were not to my liking."

I didn't hear what William said next; I was having trouble picturing the apposite, staid professor scurrying.

Charles patted William on the back. "First Light is blessed to have you among its flock." He turned and looked at me. "I was glad to see Chris here joining us this morning, but God must not have been around when his vocal cords were built. His singing sucks."

William laughed and thanked Charles and said that he was sure that I had other gifts I could bless the church with. "Each of us offers something to the Lord."

That reminded me. "William, do you remember someone named JJ attending? Dude said he thought JJ had been there some."

William looked over at the hotel and back to me. "I cannot say that I recall anyone with that moniker." He looked at the sidewalk. "I have on occasion shirked my Christian duty and failed to attend. Your Mr. JJ could have been there and I not. Why the inquiry?"

"Just wondering," I said.

William snapped his fingers. "Ah, could this JJ have been the unfortunate soul who was struck down by a vehicle? I heard about it at Bert's. I believe you were with him when the accident occurred."

"I was there and, most likely, he was one and the same." I didn't correct him about it not being an accident.

"Unfortunate, quite unfortunate." William shook his head. He opened his car door and turned back to me. "Stop by anytime for a glass of tea. I'll let you help me eradicate weeds from the garden."

Some of my fondest early memories on Folly were of visiting William's house and sitting under a shade tree overlooking his small garden sipping ice tea. Gardening was his passion and his escape from complaining students.

Charles turned to the Tides and suggested a trip to their outside bar for an adult beverage. I quickly agreed.

I felt energized after the church service. The weather was perfect; what a great day.

CHAPTER 11

Two hours later, Charles and I were still at the outdoor bar at Blu, the hotel's upscale restaurant, where he had convinced me, with minimal arm twisting, that God wanted me to enjoy the beautiful day instead of opening the gallery. The bar was packed with an eclectic mix of merrymakers. Hotel guests in bathing suits walked to and from the nearby pool or the beach, locals from other churches enjoyed lunch after their services, and several day-trippers from colleges in Charleston leaned against the railing and griped about classes, finding somewhere to park, and the multitude of other things college students gripe about. Two elderly couples from First Light had been beside us for the first hour, and we talked about the morning's sermon. One of the couples thought that they remembered JJ from a few Sundays back. They said he had spent quite a bit of time talking with Preacher Burl. The couples had then left to get to their afternoon nap. I thought that sounded like a good idea but wasn't about to tell Charles.

My friend had nursed his second beer for the last hour and made three trips to the bar for water refills. We watched as two men in their early twenties paddle surfed about thirty yards from the pier. Dude had given me a surfing lesson several years before, and I swore that I would never get on a surfboard again, so I couldn't imagine how someone could stand on one and paddle around in the ocean, regardless of how large the board was.

"Paddle surfing's called *hoe he'e nalu* in Hawaiian," Charles said.

"Everyone knows that," I said with a straight face.

He looked at me from under the brim of his Tilley. "Right. It reminds me of Jesus walking on water. Been reading about it." He looked back at the paddle surfers. "You may know Hawaiian, but I bet you didn't know that the Sea of Galilee is really a lake. That's what Jesus walked on. His disciples saw him and said, 'You truly are the son of God.'"

Charles had never expressed a special interest in religion, but after the heart-wrenching death of his aunt, he had been searching for answers by reading nearly every book in his book-cave apartment, so I shouldn't have been surprised by his knowledge of the Bible.

I surmised that he didn't want a response, so I took the last sip and watched the paddle surfers do their thing.

"Think I'll head home for a nap," Charles said.

Yes! I thought. "Okay," I said.

Charles thanked me for attending church with him, a strange sentiment, I thought. I then remembered that I had turned my phone's ringer off and was surprised to see that I had missed six calls and two voice mail messages. I couldn't remember my last voice mail message, so I put my hand up for Charles to wait while I listened. I hit Play, and my day went straight to hell.

"Chris, Brian," came the garbled voice from the speaker. It sounded like Mayor Newman was in a hurricane, but he was probably speaking hands-free from his car. "Karen's been shot. Taken to Roper. I'm on my way." I heard tires screeching and then a horn blast. "Shit! Get out of my way." A horn blasted again. "What I'd give to have my cop car back." There was a pause, and then he said, "Hurry."

The message had been recorded an hour ago. I stared at the phone. My knees felt weak.

"What?" Charles asked. He reached over and grabbed my elbow.

"Hold it," I said and tapped Play for the second voice mail message. It was also from Brian and recorded ten minutes before.

"Chris," Brian said, "where are you? Crap. I'm at the hospital. She's in surgery. They won't tell me anything other than she's in critical condition. Gotta go."

The fun-filled laughter of the people around me was muffled by the ringing in my ears and the panic-stricken voice of the usually calm Brian Newman. I grabbed the edge of the bar and slid onto a stool. Charles moved closer but didn't sit.

"What?" he repeated.

I stammered through the rest of Brian's brief messages that I needed to get to the hospital. Charles put his hand on my shoulder. I shook my head.

Charles kept his arm on me as I stood and slowly walked toward the hotel. "*We* need to get to the hospital," he said.

Traffic was light, and luckily, police patrolling Folly Road were also light, so I made the ten-mile trip in under twenty minutes. Parking near the emergency entrance was at a premium, so I squeezed in a space reserved for motorcycles. Let them tow the car; I didn't care. There were a half-dozen Charleston County Sheriff's Office patrol cars double-parked in front of the door; two still had their blue LED lights on. Brian Newman's black Jeep Grand Cherokee was in the No Parking space by the door.

Charles stayed in the car with the promise that he would move it to the first open parking spot. I stepped through the emergency room door and Brian grabbed me. He wore gray sweatpants and a red T-shirt; I'd never seen him this haggard. He probably had been on his treadmill when he got the call.

He pulled me to a corner of the packed room. "Thank God you're here," he said. "I was afraid you wouldn't get my messages. I was about to get Chief LaMond to run you down."

I told him I'd been in church and asked how Karen was.

"I don't remember what I said in the message." His eyes were bloodshot, and he rubbed his hand through his short, more-salt-than-pepper hair. "She's in surgery. The EMTs that brought her in stayed around in case the detectives had questions. One of them said that she'd lost a lot of blood, was breathing but barely, when they got here. Said it was touch and go." He shook his head and looked toward the door leading to the bowels of the hospital. "He said that he'd be surprised if she made it. Sorry."

I didn't know what to say. The only time I'd seen Brian in less than total control was in this same building five years before after his near-fatal heart attack. He wasn't big on things touchy-feely, so I resisted putting my hand on his shoulder.

Five uniformed sheriff's deputies and four off-duty officers were huddled on the other side of the room. I didn't recognize them besides Burton and Callahan, two detectives I had dealt with. Charles rushed into the crowded waiting room mumbling about having to almost push a geezer out of the way to grab a parking space. He asked Brian about Karen and received the same pessimistic prognostication.

A nurse came out the door from the exam rooms and waved for a young couple with two small children who had been sitting behind us to follow him. After they left, I suggested that we take their seats. Brian looked at the doors like he was afraid to get comfortable, but he reluctantly followed Charles's lead and took one of the vacant chairs.

"What happened?" Charles asked.

Brian looked at Charles and then toward the officers on the other side of the room. "Don't know details," he said. "One of the guys over there was the first responder. He told me that it appeared that Karen had stopped for lunch at the Shake Shack. It's that hamburger joint a couple of blocks from her house."

I had been there with her, so I nodded.

"She walked in on a robbery. She wasn't on duty, just damned unlucky," Brian whispered, and he bowed his head.

Charles and I silently waited for him to continue.

"Apparently the kid working behind the counter made a quick move and the robber shot at him. Thankfully, he missed. Karen pulled her handgun from her purse and identified herself as a cop. According to a witness, the guy turned and fired twice—he never hesitated. There were people standing behind the perp, so she didn't return fire. He hit her in the chest and leg. The leg wound's not life-threatening; the chest shot barely missed her heart, but she'd lost a lot of blood before the EMTs arrived." He looked at the door that led to the operating rooms. "That's all I know."

The two detectives I knew worked their way over. Michael Callahan was the first to speak. He was probably in his early thirties, and he wore a dark-green blazer and black slacks. He said he was sorry and that if there was anything he could do, I should ask. I had met him a few months earlier when he was the lead detective on a murder case that I had gotten way too close to and that had nearly cost me my life. I told him that his prayers and catching the guy would be appreciated. He said that they would get him and that he'd already been praying. I thanked him, and he stepped back so the other detective could speak to us.

Detective Brad Burton was as different from Callahan as a

Kia is from a Crock-Pot. His suit coat looked like it had been run over by a city bus before it got caught in a lawnmower. He was days away from retirement and was as rumpled as his clothing. I'd first met him when he was investigating a murder that I had literally stumbled on during my first week on Folly. It was hate at first sight. He thought I was the killer, that I was smart-alecky (that part was true), and that I had no business butting into police business (also true). Since then our relationship had mellowed slightly, but we were far from being buddies. He expressed his concern and said that he would do everything possible to bring the shooter to justice. I appreciated this but had doubts that he had enough left in his less-than-illustrious career to catch a cold, much less Karen's assailant.

Three more uniformed deputies joined the group on the other side of the room and occasionally glanced in our direction and gave sympathetic nods. I was touched by their camaraderie with their fellow officer.

An hour passed, and then another. Brian sat motionless. He twice shared stories from Karen's childhood of how they had travelled around the country to different postings while he was in the military. He said that he regretted not spending more time with her when she was growing up and that he'd been a terrible father. I told him that was far from true and that he had had a positive influence on her. She loved him dearly and had never said anything bad to me about him.

Finally, a young doctor made his way out of the door leading to the surgery suites, the door that often separated life from death, and walked to the group of deputies. He said something, and one of them pointed to Brian. The doctor, his surgery mask down around his neck to show his grim expression, slowly came in our direction. Brian stood, and the doctor took his elbow and escorted him to a side of the room out of earshot.

Brian stood military erect; the doctor stood about a foot from him and said something. His expression remained grim. My stomach was in knots, and I caught myself holding my breath.

Brian nodded twice and closed his eyes. The doctor said something else and put his hand back on Brian's elbow.

I blinked back a tear, closed my eyes, and thought of my meeting with Karen the other night. Was that the last time that I would see her—alive?

CHAPTER 12

The doctor left, and Brian stood staring at the floor. Charles put his hand on my arm. I was torn between rushing to Brian to find out what the doctor had said and curling myself into a ball and blocking out the world. I didn't have to decide; Brian raised his head and came over to Charles and me. To Charles's credit, he fought his instinct and remained silent.

Brian lowered himself into a chair. "She's alive," he whispered. "But it's not looking good. They've stopped the bleeding, but there's a lot of internal damage. 'Hanging on by a thread'; that's how he described it." He put his head down. "Hanging on by a thread."

"When'll they know something?" Charles asked.

Brian looked at Charles and then at the group of deputies and detectives that were still standing on the other side of the room, looking toward us. "Only time and the will of God will tell."

The sheriff, who had arrived when Brian was with the doctor, broke away from his group and walked over. Brian stood, shook the sheriff's hand, and shared what the doctor had said. The sheriff expressed his deepest sympathy, said he and his office and all local police agencies were doing everything possible to catch the shooter, and went back to his deputies to update them. Then three of the deputies left the waiting area. The others remained to show unity with Karen.

The next few hours were surreal. Ambulances arrived carrying victims of other disasters large and small. Two heart-attack victims arrived within minutes of each other: the first an obese man in his fifties and the other a jogger who appeared to be in his thirties who had collapsed while training for a marathon. A woman escorted a man with a blood-soaked towel wrapped around his hand through the lobby as if nothing was wrong.

Four officers and an assistant chief from the City of Charleston Police Department drifted in to learn Karen's condition and to show support. News crews from two of the city's television stations arrived. They were politely, but firmly, escorted out and told they could film outside.

Cindy LaMond flew through the door like a midafternoon thunderstorm and made a beeline for Charles, Brian, and me. She apologized for not arriving sooner; said that she and Larry had been at the outlet mall in North Charleston when she got the call. She hugged Brian and me and ruffled Charles's unruly hair. Brian had said hardly anything the last two hours, and I told Cindy what little I knew. She said to let her know if there was anything she could do and then went to join the group of officers, which now included three of her Folly Beach colleagues.

Two more ambulances arrived, the first delivering an elderly woman who had collapsed in front of her home and the second delivering a teenager who had been the victim of a hit-and-run just off the College of Charleston campus.

Charles watched the gurney carrying the teenager while he listened to the police officer who had accompanied the EMTs tell another officer what had happened.

Then Charles leaned over and whispered, "Think there could be any connection between Jeremy Junius's hit-and-run and Mendelson's stabbing?"

He was trying to get my mind off Karen, but I wasn't ready. I shook my head and turned away.

Hours passed and the chaos lessened, or I was getting used to the constant movement and noise of an urban emergency room. Cindy stayed for a half hour and then apologized because she had to go to work. Officers came and went. Brian returned to his silence, and Charles twisted in his chair; silence and stillness were foreign concepts to him.

Brian went outside for some fresh air, and Charles asked again, "Do you think Jeremy Junius's death and Mendelson's could be connected?"

I didn't know if he was starting to believe me about Jeremy or if he was nervous and talking to hear himself talk. I preferred the former.

"I wouldn't think so," I said. "Mendelson was wealthy and lived in a big house on the beach, and the other guy, well, he had no house at all. One was *intentionally* hit by a car, the other stabbed. It doesn't seem like they had anything in common."

Charles held up his hand. "Other than being murdered and attending First Light."

Brian returned to his seat at the same time a young nurse came in and looked around the room. She spotted Brian and came over, so I moved close to hear what she had to say.

"Mr. Newman." She gave him a muted smile. "Your daughter's condition is unchanged. She hasn't regained consciousness, and to be honest, I doubt she will for several hours. You can give me a number where you can be reached, and we'll call as soon as there's any change."

Brian looked at the ceiling and then at the group of officers gathered across the room. "Thank you, but I'll stay." He looked at the nurse. "Can you tell if there's any improvement?"

"Mr. Newman, I can't make that call, but she's still hanging on, and that's a good sign. Sorry I can't be more help."

Brian and I returned to our seats and gave Charles the nurse's message. Charles agreed that it was a good sign and said he was confident that she would pull through. I wished I had his confidence. My mind flashed back to when I sat in this same waiting room with Karen after Brian's heart attack. It was the first time that I had spent time with her when she wasn't investigating a murder that I had information about. Those were bittersweet moments that I will never forget.

Charles's stomach growled so loud that I heard it over the noises of the busy emergency room. When was the last time we ate? Too long ago. Since the nurse said that it would probably be hours before there was any change, I thought it would be good for us to leave the hospital to get a break from the depressing waiting room, some fresh air, and food. I asked Brian if he wanted to go to Al's. He shook his head and said he wasn't ready to leave but asked me to bring him a burger and said that he'd call if he learned anything.

Al's Bar and Gourmet Grill was three blocks away. Bob Howard had turned me on to the restaurant, and I had met him there on a few occasions. The first time I wondered if I had the wrong address since Al's was in a nearly prehistoric concrete-block building that it shared with a Laundromat and that had probably seen its last coat of paint during the Kennedy administration. The lower half of its large plate-glass window had been painted black to provide privacy for its diners, and I had never seen the exterior neon sign illuminated, and I suspected that anyone who was a preteen hadn't either.

Fats Domino's version of "Ain't That A Shame" blared from

the jukebox as Charles and I entered the near-black interior. The only light came from the shaded sunshine through the top half of the front window and a Budweiser and Bud Light neon sign behind the bar. One table was occupied with customers I didn't recognize, and the owner, the only other person in the restaurant, slowly hobbled around the bar to greet us.

Al wrapped his bone-thin arms around me and squeezed and did the same to Charles. "And to what does this old man owe the pleasure of a visit?"

The bar's owner was in his late seventies but looked older. His skin was somewhere between dark brown and gray and had more wrinkles than a slept-in linen shirt. His coffee-stained smile was radiant, and his enthusiasm for life far exceeded his arthritic body's ability to express it.

I said that I'd tell him why we were here once Charles got some food in his stomach because I was tired of hearing it growl. Al pointed at the booth in back of the restaurant that he had dubbed Bubba Bob's Booth since it was where Bob insisted on sitting. I gave our order before we sat so Al wouldn't have to walk to the table more than he had to.

Al stopped at the jukebox and punched in some numbers, and Fats Domino was replaced by Randy Travis singing "Forever and Ever, Amen." Al had seeded his jukebox with some of Bob's favorite classic-country songs, to the chagrin of his predominantly African American clientele. For reasons that fell beyond mystic, Bob and Al were close and had been for years. Al knew that I was a fan of traditional country and selected what he knew that I'd like.

Al soon returned with my cheeseburger and fries. During my first visit here, Bob had said that Al's cheeseburgers were the best in the world. I doubted that Bob had sampled all the cheeseburgers in the world—although his waistline suggested that he could have—but I did agree that they were the best I'd eaten in years and had ordered one each visit. Charles was more adventurous and had ordered a fish sandwich, probably to be different. The comforting, familiar aroma of my burger beat the proprietor to the table.

"What's up?" Al asked as he pulled a rickety wooden chair from a nearby table and joined us.

He had met Karen several times, and each time he told her that she was the loveliest white woman he'd ever seen and was by far the prettiest cop of any race, creed, or color. I delicately told him what had happened.

"Oh my Lord," he whispered. "Allow me to say a prayer."

We bowed our heads, and Al gave a heartfelt prayer for the lovely young lady. He was no stranger to violence and other terrible things that this world had no shortage of. He had heroically saved seven fellow soldiers in the Korean conflict, and after returning home, he and his wife had adopted nine children. One was now an emergency room doctor in the hospital where we had spent the last several hours.

He asked if they'd caught the shooter; I said not yet. He asked if I wanted him to call his daughter to see if she knew anything new about Karen's condition; I said that Brian was there and would let us know if they told him anything. He asked if there was anything he could do. I said to keep praying.

Eddie Arnold's smooth, sophisticated country voice filled the restaurant with "Make the World Go Away." I completely agreed.

Then my phone rang. I looked at the screen and saw it was Brian. My heart stopped. My finger trembled as I touched Answer.

"Chris," Brian said. "First, there's no change. I wanted to let you know they caught the shooter. He was two blocks from the Shake Shack and didn't resist." He sighed. "Know what he had on him?"

Of course I didn't, but I figured Brian didn't expect an answer, so I said, "What?"

"The damned bastard had exactly thirty-seven dollars and fifteen cents. That's what he got from the food joint." He exhaled. "That's what he shot her for. Shit!"

I agreed.

"Wanted you to know," he said.

I thanked him and moved to hang up.

"Oh," he said, "one other thing. One of the Folly officers came in a few minutes ago and said that if I saw you to let you know that Jeremy Junius Chiles went by JJ. He's the one who went to First Light." My phone went dead.

"What? What?" Charles said before I had time to set the phone on the table.

I relayed Brian's message.

"Thank the Lord," Al said. "What's that about a church?"

Charles, who by now had filled his quota of silence, said, "Chris has had a bad week. He was almost killed the other morning. Guy with him wasn't as lucky."

Al put his hand to his mouth. "My Lord, what happened?"

"Hit-and-run," Charles said. "Chris and this other fellow called JJ were walking down the street and a car came out of nowhere, hit JJ, and nearly got Chris."

"That's terrible," Al said. "Didn't the driver see you? Was it dark, or what?"

"Chris thinks it was *or what*," Charles said before I could answer. "He thinks the driver intentionally ran him down. Good old George Herbert Walker Bush said, 'I have opinions of my own—strong opinions—but I don't always agree with them.' At first I thought Chris was, you know, hallucinating, but now that I know poor JJ went to the same church as Timothy Mendelson, he might be right."

"I am," I barked.

"Got it," Charles said, and then he turned back to Al. "The police think it was a drunken joyrider who stole a car and didn't see them in the street. It was hard to see that early, so they've got a good point. But the church thing's a scary coincidence."

"Mendelson," Al said as he rubbed his cheek and closed his eyes. "Isn't that the stock guy who was killed?"

I said that it was and briefly explained what I knew about First Light.

Gene Watson sang "Farewell Party," Al pondered what I had said, and Charles took the last bite of fish sandwich.

Al rubbed his arthritic right knee. "Chris, you stumble into more trouble than a blind man on roller skates. Please tell me you're not skating down that path again."

I told him that I wasn't involved. I meant it; I really did. Then I said that we'd better get back with food for Brian.

Al fixed a cheeseburger and fries to go and refused to let me pay. "There's nothing I can do for Karen, but I can keep her daddy from starvin'. I'll be praying for her, and I'll tell my daughter she'd better keep a close eye on my favorite, lovely detective."

We thanked Al for the food, his friendship, and his prayers. He hugged us and said that we'd better let him know if there was any change in Karen's condition.

New faces dotted the gathering of cops back at the hospital, but there were still a half-dozen concerned officers silently standing watch. I didn't recognize any of them but nodded to them on our way back to Brian. He looked like he had aged a decade in the hour we were gone.

He picked around the edge of his burger and said that

Charles and I should go home and get some rest. I tried to resist, but when a former MP, retired police chief, mayor of my city, and father of my significant other insists, I wilt. He promised to call the second there was news.

I dropped Charles at his apartment and drove home. Instead of going inside, I sat in my car, pounded my fist on the steering wheel, and wondered what was going to happen next. I'd never been more scared and frustrated.

Despite all efforts, I couldn't do anything to save my dream of owning a photo gallery. I had failed to save my ex-wife from a tragic untimely death. I couldn't stop a three-thousand-pound killing machine from slamming into a hapless pedestrian. And, as much as I loved Karen, there was nothing, absolutely nothing that I could do to save her.

CHAPTER 13

The shrill ringtone startled me awake. The bedside clock showed five thirty. When I saw that the call was from Brian Newman, my heart stopped, just as it had yesterday. My hand trembled, and fear kept my finger off the button, but I finally garnered the courage to answer.

"Did I wake you?" Brian asked. His voice was strong, but I sensed he was faking it. I assured him that I was waking, and he continued, "She's regained consciousness. They haven't let me in; she's still critical. The nurse said I might be able to see her after the doctor checks on her."

I finally took a breath. "That's great. When will the doc be in?"

"Not certain, but the nurse said probably around seven. She said unlike most white coats, he's usually on time. I didn't want to wake you but wanted to give you time to get here."

I was at the hospital by six thirty; Charles would have been pleased. Brian greeted me when I entered the seventh-floor ICU waiting room. Three other people were there: two sheriff's deputies and, to my surprise, Preacher Burl, who was sitting next to Brian. Brian looked terrible. His ordinarily well-groomed hair was mussed, his normally erect posture slumped, and his face matched the rest of him. But his eyes reflected hope.

He shared that there was no change, and then Preacher Burl stood, shifted his Bible from his right hand to his left, and held out his right hand. I shook it and said that it was good to see him and asked what he was doing here.

"Brother Charles called last night and told me about the fate that has been bestowed on Sister Karen. He suggested that whoever was at the hospital awaiting news might need spiritual counsel." He smiled broadly; with his lips turned up on one side, his mustache reminded me of a centipede crawling uphill. I smiled back, but not for the reason he probably thought. "Brother Charles said that extra prayers could do no harm."

The three of us sat, and Burl placed his Bible on an empty chair.

"When did you get here, preacher?" I asked.

"Sixish." He straightened his cream-colored camp shirt over his ample belly.

"That was kind of you," I said.

"It was as it should have been," he said.

Whatever that means, I thought.

"When I was in the seminary, my classmates teased me about my wanting to visit the hospital at all hours of the day and night to offer prayer. You know," he looked Brian and then at me, "Jesus didn't wear a watch."

This was the second time that I'd heard him mention being in the seminary, a point he didn't want forgotten, it seemed. And since watches weren't invented until the fifteenth century, I didn't think Jesus's not wearing one was as profound as Burl had made it sound.

My second surprise came when Detective Brad Burton walked in and looked around. He was less rumpled than he had been yesterday, but he still wouldn't be on any best-dressed list. He nodded in our direction and walked over to one of his colleagues on the other side of the room. They huddled momentarily, and then he came over to us. Brian stood and greeted him. I remained seated and received a cursory smile and nod from the detective.

"Mind if I join you?" he asked, more to Brian than me.

Brian waved toward one of the chairs opposite ours, and Burton sat and asked if we knew anything new. Brian told him that Karen had regained consciousness and that we might be able to see her this morning. Burl remained silent, and I doubted that the detective knew who he was, so I introduced them, adding that Burton had been Karen's partner for several years and, while biting my tongue—no simple matter when speaking, I might add—that Burton had been instrumental in solving some cases on Folly. Brian knew that by *instrumental* I meant that Burton had stayed out of the way and had not hindered the investigations. I figured a little sucking up to the detective couldn't hurt, and it probably wasn't the first little white lie that had been shared with the good reverend.

"Would you be the detective investigating the tragic death of Timothy Mendelson?" Burl asked.

Burton tilted his head and looked at Burl as if he'd just seen him. "One of them. Why?"

"Brother Timothy, God rest his soul, was a wonderful part of my ministry. My flock and I will miss him. Have you by chance caught the evil incarnate who took him from us?"

"Not yet," Burton said. "Did you know Mendelson well?"

"Not well, but perhaps better than some," Burl said. "He came to us a few months ago. We met on the beach under God's great expanse when Brother Timothy stopped his walk along the shoreline to see what a group of citizens were doing listening to a chubby vertically challenged man preaching the gospel." To his credit, Burl chuckled at his self-deprecating comment.

"Brother Timothy stayed on the periphery, but after the service, he talked to me. I could tell from his first words that he was in need of a spiritual anchor." Burl looked at Brian and then at me before turning his gaze back to Burton. "Brother Timothy attended regularly from the next Sunday. He was a wonderful man. Many people of his stature would ignore the teachings of Jesus and turn their snobbish noses up at those in my flock, of whom most have not been blessed with earthly wealth and status. Brother Timothy was different. He cared, and about all with whom he had contact. Money is not important to me, and I never asked him for any, but from his first visit, he gave generously."

"Did he have enemies?" Burton asked, shifting into detective mode.

Preacher Burl held his Bible with both hands. He shut his eyes, and his head vibrated like a tuning fork. "Satan, Lucifer, Beelzebub, Belial, and by any other name, the devil was his enemy, as he is yours and mine."

Detective Burton looked down at the Bible and then up at Burl. "I was thinking more in terms of a person who might have shoved a knife in his back."

Burl shook his head. "Then I'm afraid I am unable to be of assistance. Brother Mendelson was loved by everyone in my flock. Of course, I can't speak about people I don't know. The stock market has experienced drastic fluctuations in recent years. The devil could have convinced someone that Brother Mendelson was responsible for his or her loss of considerable wealth. Never underestimate the coercive power of the devil."

"I'm certain that the police are looking at all angles," I interjected. My concern at this moment was Karen, so the direction this conversation had taken was irritating. "The doctor should be here anytime." Maybe that would slow Burton's interrogation.

"Sister Karen should be the focus of our prayers," Burl said. "But let me tell you one more thing, Detective. I and my ministry have never been about money. Our services on the beach, in addition to bringing us closer to our Lord and Savior, do not require silver and gold to survive. I have never been a monetarily wealthy man. Money is not important to me. I believe that Brother Mendelson, whose entire professional life involved money, recognized that and for that reason offered us the chance to have a sanctuary where we could meet during inclement weather. I didn't ask for anything; he offered. He asked nothing in return and was a godsend to First Light. Enemies, he may have had some, but I can assure you that they were not part of my ministry."

One of my rules of thumb was that if someone said it's not the money, it was probably the money. If I heard it twice, it was definitely the money. And on the third mention, I hid my wallet. Preacher Burl had mentioned that money was not important twice in the last ten minutes. I was waiting for him to say it the third time when the doctor who had talked to us the day before entered the room and came over.

His expression was grim.

The doctor steered Brian away from our group. I stood and followed. The serious doc said that he would like to speak to Brian alone.

"He's my daughter's fiancé," Brian said, cocking his head in my direction.

Fiancé. Did Brian know something that I didn't know?

Brian gave the doctor his police-chief stare; intimidation at its best. "He can hear whatever it is, and in the future, he has my authorization to receive updates whether I'm here or not."

The doc glanced at me, nodded, and turned back to Brian. "Mr. Newman, as we communicated earlier, Ms. Lawson's condition had improved. She had regained consciousness but wasn't alert. Time usually takes care of that, but unfortunately, she's relapsed."

I felt my chest tighten. Brian stared at the doctor and remained silent.

"The next twenty-four hours are critical," the doctor said.

"Her odds?" asked Brian.

The doctor shook his head. "I'm not in the business of guessing," he said brusquely. "If I was, I wouldn't under these circumstances. She's getting the best care possible."

Brian looked at the floor and then back at the doctor. "Then, what—"

The doctor put his hand on Brian's shoulder and nodded. "I'm sorry to be so abrupt. I know you want answers, but I don't have them. You've been here since she arrived; you're exhausted. You can't do your daughter any good by endangering your health. Why don't you go home and get some rest? Doctor's orders." He patted Brian on the back. "I have your number." He patted his pocket. "The nurses have it. We will call the second there's a change. I promise."

"He's right, Brian," I said. "You know Karen'd be worried silly." I almost said *worried to death*. "Worried more about you than she'd be about herself. Get some rest for her."

He protested but finally gave in after the doctor repeated his promise to have someone call. Brian then went to the small group of cops who were still in the room and thanked them for being there and slowly headed to the exit.

"How is she?" Detective Burton asked as soon as I returned from walking Brian to his Jeep.

I updated the detective and Preacher Burl. Burton said that

he was so sorry, and Burl offered a prayer. Then silence. The only sounds we heard in the next ten minutes were muted discussions from the officers across the room.

"I didn't know that you and Karen were engaged. Congratulations," Detective Burton said to break the silence.

I smiled. "Thank you. I didn't know it either. The mayor probably thought saying that would give me more clout with the doctors."

Burton nodded. "Smart."

"Have you heard anything about the homeless man's death?" I asked.

"As far as I know, they haven't found the joyrider who hit him," Burton said.

"Why does everyone think it was a joyrider?" I asked. "I told the police that the car targeted the man."

"Now, Chris," Burton said. "You don't know that. Ever since you moved here you've nosed into our business. Are you doing it again?"

Detective Burton had shared some information with me a year or so ago that prompted the resignation of Folly's mayor and opened the office for Brian to be elected. Until then, he had been a burr under my saddle. He was lazy, as slovenly in his investigations as he was in his dress. He was days from retiring, a moment most of his colleagues welcomed. He was not directly involved in looking into the hit-and-run, but I was frustrated by his casual attitude toward the untimely death—frustrated, but not surprised.

Little could be achieved by asking him anything else, so I turned to Preacher Burl. "Dude told me that JJ attended First Light. What did you know about him?"

Burl looked down at his Bible and then up at me. "JJ." He bit his lower lip. "Names are unimportant in my ministry. I look at the heart and dreams of my flock. We are all the same in God's eyes."

"You didn't know him?" I said.

"I don't recall him, but it doesn't mean that he did not attend. Many people wander in and out of the services; I can't keep up with all of them even if I do learn the names they are going by." He glanced at the detective and looked back at me. "When I was in the seminary, I learned that we all have something to hide. Some of us change our names to hide our past from others, even ourselves."

I gave a brief thought to strangling Burl if he mentioned the seminary again but figured that strangling a minister in front of a police detective might be looked upon unkindly. Besides, even someone as incompetent as Detective Burton could figure out who did it.

My second thought was that it was strange that the preacher didn't know JJ. His flock was small, and even if people wandered in and out and if names were unimportant to him, he had to have at least heard names mentioned. I wondered what Preacher Burl had to hide.

I didn't give it more thought, as Charles and Dude then rushed over to our small group. Dude in one of his ubiquitous tie-dyed florescent T-shirts and Charles in a long-sleeved red University of New Mexico T-shirt contrasted with the uniforms of the officers who still stood by.

"How is she?" Charles asked.

I shared the doctor's ominous news.

"Me be sorry," Dude said. He turned to Preacher Burl. "Me be hijacked by Chuckster. Groveled for ride in Dudemobile."

I wasn't sure why Burl deserved the explanation. The Dudemobile was a rusting 1970 Chevrolet El Camino that had once been green. I smiled as I thought about the first time

I'd been in it. Dude was taking me for my first—and only—surfing lesson. He had told me that some of his customers said that the large rust spot on the passenger door was the spittin' image of Moses parting the Red Sea. Given that these people were members of Surfers for Jesus, he figured they would know what Moses looked like. It probably wouldn't have done any good to ask Preacher Burl to verify this since he wouldn't have remembered Moses's name.

Detective Burton took the banter as his cue to leave, mumbled something like, "Stupid talk," and went to talk to a buddy standing with the other officers. I wondered which one could possibly be his buddy.

"Dude didn't tell me his air-conditioning was on the fritz," Charles said. "If he had, I would have bummed a ride on a beer truck or hitchhiked."

"Wheels rolled," Dude said. "Be happy."

Charles flicked his wrist at Dude to whisk away the comment and asked when was the last time Burl or I had eaten. We said we couldn't remember.

"Then it's time to head to Al's." He waved toward the door.

I protested, and then he went to the assembled police and said something. One of them wrote something, and then Charles returned. "They'll call the second someone comes out with any word. Besides, Al's is only ten minutes away even with your senior-citizen shuffle."

Bob was entering the hospital as Charles, Burl, Dude, and I were walking out. He said that he was on his way to see Karen, although in his frayed bright-orange T-shirt, yellow shorts with the legs rolled up and a dirt stain on the front, and tennis shoes that looked like they had walked to Charleston from Cancun, he looked more like he was heading to hoe weeds in the garden instead. It was Bob at his sartorial best.

I shared the news about her condition, and he asked where we were going. When I said Al's, he turned on a quarter (Bob could never have turned on a dime) and joined us. He then noticed Burl.

"Who the hell are you?" he said in his most friendly voice.

Then all hell—or, more accurately, all heaven—broke loose.

CHAPTER 14

"Holy crapola," Bob said after I told him who Burl was. "You're that fake holy man."

We weren't off the hospital property yet and already Bob was attacking the unsuspecting preacher. Burl reached out to shake Bob's hand. Bob must have realized that someday the preacher might need a Realtor, so he reluctantly, and briefly, shook Burl's meaty paw. He didn't bother lying to Burl by saying something like, "Nice to meet you."

"So, Shyster Burl," Bob grunted, "you over here getting dying patients to sign their estates over to your fake church?"

I knew that Bob's bark was usually worse than his bite, but Burl wouldn't have known it. "Preacher Burl came to comfort us," I interrupted before another holy war broke out. "He's here for Brian, Karen, and me, and I appreciate him taking the time."

I hoped that Bob would take the hint to behave.

Instead of taking offense or running for high heaven, Burl smiled. "Brother Bob, I certainly understand your position. I must—"

"Stop," Bob said. "I'm not your brother." He then pointed at Burl. "Continue."

I had no doubt that the preacher had been confronted by skeptics and was able to deflect most criticism, although most of those who had doubts about his ministry probably were not as direct, or, yes, as obnoxious as Bob.

Burl nodded. "As I was saying, I must sadly admit that there are many con artists and hypocrites who profess to be spreading the gospel when all they are spreading is a bad reputation for nontraditional ministries."

"Amen," Bob said without a hint of reverence.

We continued our slow walk toward Al's. I wished that Bob had driven.

"Amen, true," Burl said. "But let me assure you Bro—Mr. Howard, I am not among that despicable group."

Bob smiled. "We shall see."

We finally made it to Al's having managed to draw no more than verbal weapons. I held the heavy door open so Bob could barge in first, followed by Dude, Charles, Burl, and then me.

Al stepped out from behind the bar. "Heavens," he said. "This is the most white folks I've seen in here since the SWAT team stormed the place to arrest Clarence 'Big Clump' Sullivan back in ought-six."

Al pointed to Bob's table.

"You're damn right that's where we're going," Bob said.

I introduced Burl and Dude to Al.

"What be Big Clump's story?" Dude asked as he shook Al's hand, and before trivia-starved Charles could ask.

"Robbed a liquor store and stole an ambulance to get away." Al chuckled. "He drove it three blocks then drank a bottle of cheap wine and laid down on the gurney in back and took himself a nap."

"How'd he get here?" Charles asked.

"The cops who found him in the ambulance were laughing so hard they forgot to cuff him. Clarence was pretty swift when he had the need to be. Cops chasing him brought out his best running time. He stormed in here out of breath. Someone called the police and said that he had a gun and may be holding us hostage, so the police called out SWAT."

"Dumbo," Dude said.

Al grinned. "They took him to jail, not to a Mensa meeting."

Dude, Burl, Charles, and I left Al at the door and joined Bob, who had already squeezed his stomach into *his* booth. The restaurant wasn't as empty as it had been the day before. Diners at seven tables were in various stages of their meals, and I noticed a couple of them watching us out of the corners of their eyes. And why not? After all, we were the largest gathering of Caucasians since the SWAT team's visit in ought-six.

The suspicion and borderline hostility weren't lost on Al. He gave a larger than necessary laugh, slapped his knee, and gave me as big a hug his arthritis-riddled body allowed. If we were okay with Al, we were okay with his diners.

"Cut the queer-hugging crap, old man!" Bob yelled over James Brown's "I Feel Good." "We want food!"

He wouldn't say it to Al's face, but Bob considered Al a true American hero, not only for his heroics in Korea but because Al and his wife had sacrificed everything to give their nine adopted kids a stable upbringing.

Al ignored Bob and leaned close to me and asked about Karen. I gave him the same version of the news that I had shared with Bob. He said he'd been praying for her, and I thanked him. Then he said, "Get over there and shut Fatso up. Tell him that he may be the heaviest person here, but he's not my only customer. I'll be there in a minute."

"I'll be honored to share your quote with him," I said with a smile.

We sat at the table. Burl wisely chose the farthest seat from Bob he could get. Al went to the jukebox, which now played

Aretha Franklin's "Respect," reached behind it and fiddled with something, and punched some numbers in the front. "Respect" ended and the familiar voice of George Jones serenaded the group with "The Right Left Hand."

Groans came from the nearest table. One customer rolled his eyes and clasped his hands over his ears. Bob smiled from ear to ear. He proceeded to tell Dude and Burl that Al's cheeseburgers were the best in the universe. Dude hadn't spent much time around Bob and had never been in Al's, but he was an expert on astronomy, so he told Bob that these may be the best cheeseburgers on earth, but, he said, "They may not be goodest on other planets."

Bob said that he didn't care what the little hippie said. Burl continued to be immune to Bob's rudeness and thanked him for the suggestion. Bob stared at him and grunted.

Al interrupted their love fest and took our orders. With Bob's body taking up every inch of space on one side of the booth and Burl's stomach pushing the other side, I envied sardines their spacious accommodations in packing cans.

Bob leaned forward and glared at Burl. "So what makes you and your make-believe religion so different from the other fakers and con artists you so righteously talked about?"

If Burl ever did want to buy property, I was fairly certain who he wouldn't call.

"Sadly, money is the paramount concern in many of those ministries. They beg for donations to support television and radio programs where they can ask for more money from the expanding audiences—excuse me, their media ministries. Many are Cafeteria Christians who—"

Dude waved his hand in Burl's face. "Whoa, Café Christs? Me be confounded."

Burl turned to Dude. "Christians who—"

"Zealots," Bob interrupted. "Damned zealots who pick and choose whatever parts of the Bible that meet their needs. Ignore the parts they don't like."

Dude scratched his chin and said, "Buffet Bible."

My best contribution to the discussion was to remain silent.

Bob exhaled, and his stomach pushed the table into Burl, who gave it a little shove back. "You're still a made-up religion. You take donations, don't you? You want people to attend your fun-in-the-sun services, don't you?"

Burl leaned back and absorbed Bob's darts without reacting. He took a sip of water and asked, "How does that differ from mainstream religions? Don't they all seek donations and evangelize?"

Bob stared at him, hesitated, and then said, "Just freakin' does, Burly Burl."

The pot calling the kettle black immediately sprang to mind, but the moniker beat "Shyster Burl."

Dude pointed to the ceiling. "Me follower of Ra. He be Egyptian solar deity."

Burl nodded. "Brother Dude told me about his belief in the sun god following the first service he attended. He thought that I'd be angry or would try to convert him. But what did I tell you, Dude?"

Dude shrugged. "Be okeydokey."

"That's right," Burl said. "Dude said that the only reason he had stopped was because it was outside and he had a clear view of the sun. I said that my God, and probably his, worked in mysterious ways. Belief is better than no belief; faith better than no faith."

"Ra doesn't beg for money," Bob said.

"Neither does First Light," Burl responded in a prickly tone.

"Then let me ask you," Bob continued, "where did the money

to rent the space next to Chris's gallery come from? Who paid for the paint, the drywall, and the other stuff you're using to fix it up? And, oh yeah, who's paying you to carry on your so-called ministry?"

"Excellent and legitimate questions, Brother—sorry, Mr. Howard. Our congregation was blessed by the most generous benefactor, Brother Timothy Mendelson. And lest you wonder, Brother Timothy approached me about making his contributions. I did not ask him for anything."

"Right," Bob said.

Burl waited for Bob to say something else. When he only huffed, the preacher continued, "All expenses related to our walled sanctuary were paid by Brother Timothy. And to the question I suspect is foremost on your mind, I do not receive a salary. Granted, I will occasionally take a few dollars that are freely donated to cover my meager expenses, and on occasion someone in our flock will offer me a meal." Burl smiled and patted his stomach. "You can see I am not prone to skip eating."

Bob came close to smiling. He was an expert on not skipping meals.

"In deference to your alleged holy status," Bob said, "I will limit my comment to *bunk*!"

Burl did smile. "My arms are always open to you *Brother* Bob. My heart will welcome you." He chuckled. "And my ears will not take offense at your proclamations."

Bob grunted. "Our proclamations will not cross."

Charles, who had amazingly remained silent, turned to Burl. "George W. Bush said, 'You can fool some of the people all the time, and those are the ones you need to concentrate on.'"

Al then arrived with our food and his well-honed smile. The tension could have been cut with a table knife. From the jukebox, Johnny Paycheck told his boss to "Take This Job and

Shove It." And I closed my eyes and thought about Karen battling for her life a few blocks away.

Charles gave his best shot at brokering a cease-fire when he told Al that Dude had a new dog. Al had spent many years working the bar, where tensions escalated to physical fights on a fairly regular basis, so a sideways glance in my direction told me that he knew what Charles was up to. Even though Al had just met Dude, he asked about Pluto, fawned over Dude's every brief word, and asked Burl and Bob if they had pets. We casually walked on safe ground through the first half of our burgers.

Our pleasant discussion didn't last.

I had heard all I wanted to about religion from Preacher Burl and Bob, a person who I had never associated with being a biblical scholar, so I took a sip of chardonnay and turned to Burl. "Preacher Burl, have you given more thought to JJ?" I still had trouble believing that he hadn't heard the name of a member of his flock.

"Umm, no," he said with a smile. "Back when I was in the seminary they taught us to remember names by associating the person's name with something familiar. Sadly, I couldn't remember what something familiar was, so it didn't do any good."

I resisted the urge to grab a butter knife when he said *seminary* and mentioned that I thought he might have remembered something since I had asked him earlier.

Dude turned to Burl. "You remember JJ," he mumbled through a mouthful of ground beef.

All eyes turned to Dude.

"JJ," Dude repeated as he held both hands out in front of him like the gesture would help the preacher remember. "Two full moons ago. You be jabbering with him after service." Dude stopped as though that should do it.

Burl had started fidgeting with his fork and his napkin when the discussion turned to JJ. "I don't remember."

"Sure you do." Dude was not to be deterred. "Ankle breaker rolled in. You be at edge of water with JJ."

Charles, my Dude-speak translator, whispered to me, "Ankle breakers are small waves."

"And?" Burl said.

"JJ be aggro. Kicked sand on your preacher pants."

Charles leaned over again. "*Aggro* means—"

"I got it," I said.

Burl pointed at Dude. "It's coming back. The individual you call JJ was asking me questions about the Bible."

I had a hard time thinking what he could have been asking that caused him to kick sand on Burl's preacher pants.

"Dude, why did you think JJ and Burl were arguing?" I asked.

"JJ kicked sand, said words not okay in church, Preacher Burl shoved him."

That was enough for me. I asked Burl for his opinion about it.

"He was probably trying to con money out of whoever JJ is," Bob interjected.

"Be squeezing gold from prune," Dude said. "JJ growed lots of hair on chinny-chin-chin, and lots of broke."

Burl smiled at Dude, something that's easy to do, and continued to do an admirable job of ignoring Bob's insults. "That man, JJ, had many questions. As I recall, he was asking me about a verse in Leviticus that I had referenced during the sermon." He paused and turned to Dude, and then to Charles, and then to me, but not to Bob or Al, who was returning to the table after getting someone else a beer. Burl then continued, "Leviticus is a difficult book, chock full of rules and regulations for Christians. The book is often tedious, and I was glad that someone was interested in exploring it further. Brother JJ had many questions, but some of what I interpreted for him brought ire to his heart. He became irritated."

I tried to picture the scene but couldn't quite imagine JJ becoming so irritated by what Burl could have said about Bible verses that he would have kicked sand. I couldn't think of anything to ask for clarification, though. It simply didn't feel right.

Bob had remained quiet during the discussion; not a record time for him to be silent but close. It couldn't last. "Now Burly Burl," he said, "while we're on Bible talk, let me bounce something off you."

Burl appeared to want to be anywhere but here, but he maintained his courteous tone as he said, "Of course, Mr. Howard."

"It seems to my doctrinally-challenged mind that many religions hold to the belief that if someone is not a member of their group, upon death, he or she will go to hell."

"That's a fairly accurate statement," Burl said. "Simplistic, but—"

Bob waved his right hand in Burl's face. "So, how the hell is hell big enough to hold those gazillion people?"

I suspected that Bob was playing with the minister, but Burl could only have seen Bob as rude and boorish, so I sat back as he pondered a response. Al didn't give him a chance.

"New rule in Al's," the smiling bar owner said. "Bob can talk about country music, real estate, his saintly wife, and how good my food is. No more about religion."

Bob smiled up at Al. "Damned dictator."

I smiled too, but not at Al. After having known Bob for several years, I suspected that much of his bluster now was an attempt to distract me from worrying about Karen. Below, way below, the Realtor's gruff exterior was a caring, sensitive person. But I wouldn't tell anyone his secret, and if I tried, no one would believe me.

Burl seemed to have taken all Bob's love and my questioning about JJ that he could stomach, as he said that he had to visit a sick follower. Bob said that he had all Al's rules that he could stomach and that he didn't have to be anywhere but that he'd had enough of us. They got up at the same time and almost twisted the table off its base. Then they left, not quite arm in arm, but at the same time.

"Don't think Burl converted Bob," Charles said.

You couldn't slip anything by Charles.

It wasn't until Bob was gone that I remembered that I'd asked him to see what he could learn about Timothy Mendelson. Had he found out anything? What, other than First Light Church, could Mendelson and JJ have had in common? And why did I feel that their deaths were connected?

CHAPTER 15

Dude had to return to the surf shop to save the buying public from Stephon and Rocky, his two employees and poster children for poor customer service. Charles asked if I wanted him to return to the hospital with me, but I said no, there was nothing he could do there. He and Dude headed back to Folly, and I walked to the building that I had come to loathe.

At the hospital, the deputy keeping watch over the waiting room came over to say that I hadn't missed anything. I spent the next two hours looking at the door to the ICU. In addition to the police officer, two families had arrived to await word on their loved ones who were recovering from surgery. Fortunately, the ICU waiting room was quieter than the one for the hectic ER. I drifted off, but I was awakened by the same doctor I had spoken to earlier. His expression gave nothing away.

"There's no change, sir," he said. "To be honest, I doubt there will be any today. She's stable and that's a good sign. Why don't you go home? I assure you we'll call you and her father when there is anything to report. That's all I can offer." He gave a weak smile and left me sitting.

I rubbed my forehead. The deputy came over and asked what the doc had said. I repeated the message, and he echoed the suggestion that I go home. I didn't want to leave but didn't know how I could help by staying.

I called Brian on my way home and shared what I had learned. He sounded exhausted and simply thanked me and hung up. I spent the rest of the evening staring at the television. I had no idea what I was watching, and I didn't care. My mind wandered between thoughts of what was going on in the ICU and the many wonderful moments I had spent with Karen. She was smart, funny, and beautiful. I wondered what she saw in me. I was several years older, and although I had been told that I was nice-looking, I would never be a contestant in a Mr. Anything pageant, and to quote Bob, I was "always stepping in problems like they were piles of dog shit."

Soon after remembering Bob's kind words, I must have fallen asleep in the living room chair. Someone pounding on the door jolted me awake. I jumped up and tripped over the ottoman but caught my balance. I shook my head awake and looked at the clock; it was six. I had been in the chair all night. I stumbled to the door and slowly opened it.

Mel Evans stared at me from the porch. His six-foot-one frame stood erect, befitting the former marine that he was. To complete the ex-marine look, he wore a leather bomber jacket with the sleeves cut off at the shoulders and camo field pants sheared off at the knees. He looked me up and down. "Caught you sleeping the day away," he said.

"It's only six," I said with absolutely no enthusiasm.

"My point exactly. You civilians waste so much time. We once-and-always marines get more done by now than you lazy asses do in an entire day."

"I've seen the ads. What's going on?"

He pushed past me and sniffed loudly as he raised his nose in the air. "Sleep in those clothes?"

I looked down at my wrinkled slacks. "Yeah, but—"

"Never mind," he said. "How's Karen?"

"No change. How'd you hear?"

"Damned draft-dodging hippie told me." Mel looked around the room and toward the kitchen.

Mel and the draft-dodging hippie, better known as Dude, had been friends since Dude had saved him from drowning after he had been caught in a rip current. That was nearly two decades before, and they had traded insults ever since. Their picture could be found in Wikipedia under "Opposites." Mel was much taller than Dude, much balder, more profane, and much more gay. Dude was laid-back; Mel was, well, a former marine.

"Speaking of food," Mel said, although neither of us had been, "got any grub?"

I wasn't ready for the question but knew the answer either had to be nothing or near nothing. "Bread, maybe?" I caught myself and shook my head. "Hold on. What are you doing here?"

He charged into the kitchen. "Food first." He opened the refrigerator. "Any eggs, cheese, red peppers?"

I shook my head. "No, no, and no way."

"Got bread, sugar, butter, cinnamon?"

I rolled my eyes. "Bread, butter, sugar, yes. Cinnamon, dream on."

"Go check," he said as he grabbed the butter from the refrigerator door. "I'll fix cinnamon toast. Gotta eat breakfast, the most important damn meal of the day. What're you waiting for?"

I probably averted a terribly unpleasant moment when I found a can of cinnamon. It must have come with the house because I would've sworn that I never bought it. Nothing was wiggling around in the can so I figured it was okay.

Fifteen minutes later I had managed to change into less-wrinkled clothes and wet and brush what hair I had left to get it headed in the same direction. Mel had morphed into a short-order cook and had two plates on the table. The aroma of broiled sugar and butter whet my appetite. I had exhausted my culinary talents when I fixed coffee, and I prayed that Mel didn't want milk in his.

"Speaking of my commie pinko hippie bud." He swallowed the third and last bite of his first slice of cinnamon toast. "He said you'd been asking about one of his church amigos."

I hadn't been speaking about Dude anymore than I had about food, but I chose to go along with whatever direction Mel was headed and said, "JJ?"

"Affirmative," Mel said. "JJ would be the Jeremy Junius you saw taken out."

"How do you know?"

Mel looked around the kitchen as if he was afraid someone was taking notes. "You may want to write this down. It's my secret technique for extracting information." I didn't make any effort to find paper and pen, so he continued, "I asked him what JJ stood for."

"Wow," I said. "Did you learn that in the marines?"

"Smart-ass. It wasn't quite that simple. I threatened to hang him by his feet from the nearest palmetto until he told me his real name. He confessed it was Jeremy Junius, and I told him it was a damned prissy name." Mel stuffed half of his second slice of toast in his mouth and mumbled, "Kidding about the hanging part, but I did call Junius prissy. Anyway, that's what he said it was, so he's the guy you saw offed."

I savored the last of my first slice of toast, surprised that my kitchen could be the site of such a breakfast feast, and pondered whether I should tell him that the police had already confirmed that the late Jeremy Junius was, in fact, JJ. *Oh, why not.*

"The police told me yesterday." I waited for an explosion.

Mel stared at me like a drill instructor getting ready to erupt on a green recruit. "Why in the hell did you waste my time telling you?"

I wasn't a green recruit; I was seven years older than Mel and wiser—okay, maybe not wiser, but definitely older.

"Could I have stopped you?" I smiled.

"Hell no." He returned my smile.

"I let you because you may've said something that I didn't know."

"Yeah," he said. "The damned pinko hippie told me that you imagined that JJ was run down on purpose. If history tells me anything, you've already commenced recon."

I shook my head. "If that means that you think I'm trying to find who killed him, not really. I know what I saw and shared it with the police."

"Then what about Timothy?" Mel said.

"What about him?"

Mel gave me another one of his intimidating glares. "I've known you for what, two years?"

I nodded.

"In that time you've blundered into a couple hundred murders, and did the cops' job. And now you've found JJ's accident to be a cold-blooded killing without even considering that Timothy was murdered. Why the hell wouldn't I think that you'd tripped into this one?"

"Mel, I've shared my information with the police. I never met JJ or Timothy. It's not my business."

"Yeah, right," he said in the same tone I suspect he used with a group of college kids who wanted him to take them on a marsh tour saying they were interested in learning about the ecosystem. "Now that you've given your obligatory bullshit disclaimer, want to know some secrets about JJ?"

My house was not on Mel's way to anywhere, so he couldn't have stopped by simply to tell me that Jeremy Junius was JJ. "Wouldn't want you to have made the trip for nothing." I brought him more coffee.

Mel took a sip. "He was a QLT."

"Huh?" I said.

"Queer little turd. Queer like peculiar, not queer like me. He was always asking questions."

"Like what?" I asked.

"Nosy, personal stuff. The first thing he asked everyone he met was what they did and then where they were from."

I remembered the seconds before his tragic death; he had asked me what I did.

"What's unusual about that?"

"Context," Mel said.

I shrugged confusion.

"Like if someone at church said, 'Good sermon, wasn't it?' JJ'd say, 'Where are you from?' If someone said, 'Did you see that dolphin?' queer JJ'd say, 'No, where do you work?'"

"Got it."

"He asked me personal questions like how much my boat cost and how much money I had. Didn't ask them once, but over and over. Like he had OCD, ADD, ODD, or some other psychobabble syndrome. If you ask this old marine, I think it was just QLT disease."

I didn't bother to ask him about his years studying to be a marine psychiatrist, but I did find JJ's compulsions interesting. "Know anyone who'd want to kill him?"

Mel rolled his eyes. "And you're not going to get involved. I repeat, yeah, right!"

"Just curious. You brought it up."

"Let me tell you something I learned when serving your country. When you ask a jarhead a personal question and don't get an answer, you'd damn well better not ask again. Boundaries, my friend. Good-fences-make-good-neighbors kind of crap. QLT didn't know a fig about fences. You can take it from me, that'd piss folks off."

I agreed.

"Maybe one pissee figured JJ'd make good roadkill. Just a thought." He shook his head. "No, I don't know who."

"I'll share that with the chief," I said.

"You might want to share something else if she don't already know it." He took the final bite of breakfast.

I waited.

"Your JJ had a shady past. The boy spent time in the pokey."

I knew that but wondered what Mel knew. "Why?"

Mel laughed, a rare show of emotion for him. "The boy told me that he had a habit of writing checks for more moola than he had in his piddlin' bank account."

I thought I knew where the story was going, but I guessed I was a little off.

"He covered the bad checks by making withdrawals from his savings account, one that looked a lot like a 7-Eleven store. He didn't have a PIN so he used a gun instead of a debit card." Mel smiled. "JJ told me that the person he'd written the bad checks to didn't care where he got the money, but the 7-Eleven manager didn't take too kindly to it and called the police. The cops didn't appreciate JJ's method of covering the float and threw him in the brig."

I asked if he knew anything else about JJ.

"Hell, isn't that enough? I only talked to him after church and a couple of times at Rita's. If I'd known you wanted his whole bio, I would've applied pilliwinks."

It was bad enough that I had to learn Dude-speak, but now Mel had his own language. "Pilliwinks?"

"Thumbscrews, of course. Everyone knows that."

"How could I have forgotten?" I hoped he appreciated the sarcasm.

"Anyway, that's all I know about your QLT." He stood and headed toward the empty cabinet. "Anything else to eat in this galley?"

"Let's see, for breakfast, the dessert menu is a pack of Oreos or bag of stale Cheetos."

"As tempting as those are, I'll pass. Want to hear what I know about Timothy Mendelson?"

"Okay," I said. "What do you know about Mendelson?"

"Damn little. I only saw him at church. He tried to look common like the rest of us. Couldn't carry it off in his tailored, pressed sport shirts and thousand-dollar Mezlan alligator shoes."

I'd been called a borderline illiterate when I didn't know what pilliwinks were; no way was I going to ask about Mezlan shoes. "He was a successful stockbroker," I said in defense of his dress.

"Sure, I knew he got rich selling stocks. That stock stuff's only pieces of paper, or was in the good old days. Now it's all computer bits and bytes and crap. Worthless, if you ask me. You can't eat it, shoot it, drive it, or live in it."

"Did you ever—"

He held up his hand. "Okay, Predictable Chris, before you

ask, no, I never saw JJ talking to Timothy." He lowered his hand and stared at me.

"Any idea who'd want him dead?" I asked.

"Hell, he was as stockbroker. In this economy, the key word in that profession would be *broker*. Most of his clients probably wanted him dead."

"Were any members of First Light clients?"

He shook his head. "From what I know about the flock, the closest most of them ever came to stock was at the state fair. Moo!"

Mel stood again and opened the empty coffee carafe, huffed, and looked out the kitchen window. "Let me tell you something else. I've heard that some upstanding citizens are badmouthing First Light, calling Preacher Burl a quack, calling his flock—calling us—a bunch of sinners looking for a way out, getting their damned stuck-up noses out of shape."

Bob came to mind, although I wouldn't have been surprised if others fell into the group too. I said that if there were people like that, it was their problem and not First Light's.

Mel returned to the chair. "Caldwell and I have attended other 'gay friendly'"—he punctuated this with air quotes—"churches. The preachers said the right words, but their vibes said otherwise. First Light is truly nonjudgmental. Preacher Burl's the real thing. That's why his flock has all kinds in it: rich, but dead, stockbroker; bums; hippie, commie, sun-worshipping Dude; everyday folk; and a double-bonus feature, Caldwell and me, a gay interracial couple." Mel smiled. "Hell, if I had any money, I'd give it to Preacher Burl."

It was interesting that Mel's reasons for liking First Light were similar to William's after he'd attended both black and white churches. I thanked Mel for sharing his feelings. He shrugged off my comment and talked more about Karen's condition and offered to do anything I asked that would help.

Finally he said that he didn't have anywhere to go but had had as much of me as he could stand and headed to his Camaro. Mel had exceeded his quota of warm and fuzzy.

CHAPTER 16

I thought JJ's and Mendelson's deaths were somehow tied together, but their attending First Light seemed to be no more than a coincidence. What else could have connected them? JJ was homeless, a vagrant who few people knew much about, and Mendelson a successful stockbroker; two paths that would seldom cross.

According to Mel, if JJ's past was an indication, he could have regressed to a life of crime. Could he have targeted Mendelson, maybe worked a scam to reduce Mendelson's net worth? If someone had wanted JJ dead, why did he or she go to the trouble to steal a car and run him down? Was it important that it looked like an accident? Mel and Dude had said that JJ was always asking questions. Could he have stuck his nose fatally close to somewhere it didn't belong?

Mendelson had given a substantial amount of money to rent and renovate the storefront for First Light under the condition that as much of the work as possible be done by church volunteers. I had met Six, Sharp, and Lottie plying their skills there. No one had mentioned JJ, but had he been involved in the renovation? He could have had contact with Mendelson there. If Mendelson's murder had something to do with his being a stockbroker, what would that have to do with JJ?

There were two more possibilities that I had tried to ignore. The first was that I was the intended target and JJ had simply been collateral damage. I couldn't think of anyone who had it in for me. No way was I the target—no way. But had I just convinced myself of that?

Then there was the chance that I was wrong about JJ's death. Could it have been what everyone else had said, a tragic accident? Since I had arrived on Folly, I had been exposed to more unnatural deaths than I could have ever imagined. Charles had told me once that we had been in the middle of more murders than Jessica Fletcher had in Cabot Cove in the *Murder She Wrote* series. He had read all the books, so I couldn't dispute his claim. Could I now be seeing murder in every death on Folly? My gut said no, but could I trust it?

It was nearly ten o'clock and I hadn't heard from the hospital. Was that a good sign? I'd drive myself crazy staying here worrying.

I went next door to Bert's for coffee on the way to the hospital. Omar, one of the owners, was behind the counter and talked me into a slice of pound cake to go. I told him that it would be the perfect food to follow up my breakfast of cinnamon toast. He laughed and agreed. The cake was gone before I reached the hospital's parking lot.

Two sheriff's deputies were seated in the far corner of the waiting room. Their heads bobbed; they were more asleep than awake. I didn't have to disturb them to learn what was going on. Preacher Burl was in the same seat where he was yesterday.

"Good morning, Brother Chris," he said and shook my hand. "No one has come out with information." He nodded toward the door to the ICU.

He said he'd been here since seven since he knew that Sister Karen needed all the prayers that she could get. I thanked him.

"God hears prayers from anywhere, of course," Burl said. "But when I was in the seminary, I was taught that praying in proximity to the person in need could be more effective."

"For the family?" I said.

"Yes. To couch it secularly, praying is like yawning. When one does it, those around also pray. The more the better."

He learned that in the seminary?

"You've mentioned attending a seminary," I said. "Where?"

Burl smiled. "You are inquisitive like everyone says. I attended Golden Gate Baptist Theological Seminary in California."

I didn't know where to go with that, so I changed the subject. "Do you know anything JJ and Mendelson had in common other than attending your church?"

He looked at me as if he were trying to read the question's intent in my face. "I believe I told you before that I didn't really know Brother JJ. He just attended a few services and showed interest in one of my biblical references." He paused and smiled. "Brother Timothy is another story. He was there nearly every week. He was the answer to our prayers. He wanted to give money, a large quantity of money, to us and also wanted to donate to whatever charities that I identified."

He slowly shook his head. "Other than wanting to share in God's good graces, Brother JJ and Brother Timothy had nothing in common. I'm certain of that."

He may have been certain, but I wasn't. "Since Timothy donated heavily to the storefront and requested that other parishioners do much of the work, could they have crossed paths there?"

Burl gave me a sideways glance and lowered his head. "I don't recall seeing Brother JJ at the project. I'm not there each time others are working, so it's possible that he may have graced the doorway. Brother Timothy was there quite often. Some thought he was checking up to see if the volunteers were carrying their weight, but I had the impression that he was proud of what was happening and wanted to share in the joy."

His answer wasn't definitive, so I thought I should check with Charles or the others I'd met there. I was ready to ask Burl about the last time he'd seen Timothy, but all calmness was sucked out of the room when Bob charged in. He glanced at the deputies and headed to Burl and me.

Bob ignored Burl and grabbed the seat on my other side. "Update?" he said, pointing in the direction of the ICU. I told him that I didn't know more than I had known yesterday. He uttered a profanity.

Bob still didn't acknowledge Burl, who seemed to take this as a not-so-subtle hint when he told me that he had to get back to Folly. I thanked him again for being there and said that I was sure his prayers were helping Karen's recovery.

"What were you and the huckster talking about?" Bob asked as soon as Burl was out the door. "Still have your wallet?"

"What's your beef with Preacher Burl?" Bob had been described as insolent, crude, loud, and rude many times, and he tended to lean in the negative direction, but I had never heard him be so consistently so to anyone as he had been to Burl.

He waved his hand at the door that Burl had just exited. "A story for another time," he said.

I took his *another time* to pointedly mean never, so I told him what Burl and I had been talking about.

"Hell, I'll tell you what JJ and the stockbroker had in common. That charlatan." He pointed at the chair where Burl had been.

"They both attended First Light," I said. "But what—"

Bob put his hand on my shoulder. "Listen. I'd say he killed both of them. The only thing that would have stopped him was that to be a successful con artist, he needs a larger flock to attract more unsuspecting, naïve followers." He looked at the ceiling. "Whoa, here's a thought. I bet the shyster conned the rich guy to leave his estate to the First Light. How's that for a reason to kill the goose that crapped out the golden egg?"

The doctor who had previously talked to us stepped into the room and looked around. He came over and asked if Karen's father was in the building. I explained that Brian wasn't here and reminded him that he could share updates with me.

He hesitated but finally said, "There are some optimistic signs. Ms. Lawson is awake. She's talking some but not making sense. That's progress."

Bob moved close behind me to listen.

I was both elated and frightened. "Is that normal?"

"Not usually," the doctor said, "but I've seen it. It's still a good sign that she is conscious and able to speak. I'm afraid it will be hours before we know more."

"May I see her?" I asked.

The doctor looked at Bob and then back at me. "Not now. I only came out to report her improved condition. I, or someone else, will call Mr. Newman when he can see his daughter." He pivoted and left the room.

I told Bob that I needed to call Brian. He nodded and sat down again. I took the elevator down and walked outside. Brian was in a meeting at City Hall but listened as I told him what the doctor said. I heard excitement and relief in his voice as he said that he would be over as soon as he finished his budget talks. I repeated that it would be hours before there was any change, so he said I should go home but that he was still coming.

I returned to the seat next to Bob. He patted me on the leg.

"See," he said, "me being here did more for Karen than all those prayers from that damned man."

Either way, I breathed a sigh of relief and silently prayed that it wasn't premature.

CHAPTER 17

After I left the hospital, instead of going home, I decided that the gallery needed cleaning. To be honest, cleaning could be done anytime, but if I went home, I knew I'd only worry. My hand shook so much I had trouble unlocking the gallery door.

This reinforced that I was exhausted. The last year had been devastating. I had been reunited with my ex-wife only to lose her to a cold-blooded killer; I had nearly lost my life simply because I had tried to help a young friend; and I had my mortality thrown in my face as I watched the slow death of a friend I had come to love. Now in the last few days, I had been nearly killed and witnessed a murder-by-vehicle, and Karen was in intensive care fighting for her life.

I went directly to the back room, fixed coffee, and plopped down at the table. I stared into the glimmering dark-brown coffee and wondered—whether Karen had suffered permanent brain damage, what my future was with the charming, strong, loving, yet much younger police detective. Was she ready to commit to something more than our casual, meet-when-we-can relationship? For that matter, was I ready? And was it only my overactive imagination that saw JJ's death as murder? The coffee didn't offer answers.

Pounding on the wall from the storefront church shook me out of my thoughts, or, more accurately, my feeling sorry for myself. The storefront had been vacant since I opened the gallery, so I hadn't known how much sound traveled between the spaces. My overhead lights flickered, and it sounded like a herd of elephants might crash into my space. I smiled knowing that thought was a figment of my imagination, but I decided to check out what was going on anyway. It would distract me from things I couldn't do anything about.

Lottie, Sharp, and Dude surrounded two long benches lying on their sides along the wall separating the space from the gallery. Pluto was supervising the trio from his perch on a chair in the corner.

Dude spotted me when I entered. "Yo, Chrisster, sand a spell."

Lottie and Sharp looked my way. Both were in short-sleeved T-shirts, Lottie's oversized and Sharp's skintight. Lottie wore jeans, and I suspected her overall frumpy attire was intended to mask her attractive figure and deter unwanted attention. Sharp also had on running shorts and tennis shoes that probably had been white a decade or so ago, and he held an electric sander. Dude, of course, wore one of his glow-in-the-dark tie-dyed shirts adorned with a large peace symbol. Pluto was the best dressed of the group with his red rhinestone-covered collar.

Sharp gave me a distracted glance and went back to sanding the side of the bench, which looked like it had either been a church pew or one of the long benches from a 1940s bus-station waiting room. The lights blinked each time Sharp squeezed the sander's trigger, and the tool's motor made it impossible to hear, while a cloud of fresh sawdust filled the air, making it difficult to breath. Sharp didn't appear to care. Lottie gave him a dirty look and walked over to me. Dude followed.

She leaned close and shouted. "Hey, good-looking, we need a break. Let's go outside." Dude, Pluto, and I followed her out.

The late-afternoon sun was focused on our side of Center Street, and it must have been in the upper eighties. I started to ask if they wanted to go in the gallery where it was at least fifteen degrees cooler when Sharp stuck his head out the door.

"Come in where it's cooler," he said. "Sorry about the noise; I wanted to get the sanding done so we could start staining."

Lottie didn't need a second invitation. She was on Sharp's heels as he returned inside, and the rest of us followed. One of the pews was now ready for the first coat of stain. The other one looked like it had spent a few years outdoors. It's multiple coats of paint had bubbled, and splintered bare wood stuck out on the seat. Neither pew would match the other four pews that had been in the room during my first visit, but they would accommodate everyone during inclement weather.

"How be Cop K?" Dude asked as soon as we got inside.

I gave him a brief update and he said, "Cool."

"Where'd the benches come from?" I asked, more to steer conversation away from the depressing topic than out of curiosity.

Lottie smiled. "Brother Timothy found them at an architectural salvage store in North Charleston." She lovingly caressed the side of the bench that Sharp had finished sanding. "Preacher Burl borrowed a pickup from a guy who runs a furniture store, and Six and him got them." She nodded toward Sharp. "Going to be great once we get them fixed up."

She pointed toward the back of the space, which would be the front of the church once everything was in place. "What do you think about that?"

She was referring to a seven-foot-high tin cross with neon tubes lining the edges of the fixture leaning on its side against the wall. Before I could answer, she said, "Brother Timothy found it. He said it would be the perfect *crux ordinaria* for our humble place of worship."

"Whatever that means." Sharp rolled his eyes.

Lottie glared at him. "Brother Timothy said it's Latin for the Christian cross. Brother Timothy was such a brilliant man and kind to give us this space."

Clearly there was no love lost between the two volunteers.

"It be boss," Dude said.

I didn't think he'd taken that out of a Latin-to-surf dictionary.

"It will definitely make a statement," I said.

"Need an electrician to fix us a plug back there before we can hang it," Lottie said. "There's a 220-volt wire there, but an electrician has to do something I don't understand to make the cross work. It'll be magnificent once it's lit."

She had opened the door to talk about Mendelson, so I stepped in. "Do you know much about Mend—umm, Brother Timothy?"

Sharp grabbed an old towel from the floor and wiped his hands, flicking sawdust on the floor. "Nope," he said. "Only saw him at church and in here a few times. Seemed snooty. Money'll do that to you."

"I thought he was, uh, interesting," Lottie said. "He had that big house right on the ocean. Must've cost a mint. He had all the money in the world and could've gone to any church. I figured that he would've liked one of those rich churches in Charleston." She hesitated, looking around the storefront, and then waved toward the cross. "Yet he chose First Light. He was there nearly every Sunday, and look at all he's given us. Praise the Lord and praise Brother Timothy, none of this would have been possible without the dear man."

Lottie talked so fondly about him that I wondered if they

had been more than fellow flock members, or if she wanted them to be.

Dude snapped his fingers. "Where be Six?" he asked like he had just noticed the other volunteer's absence.

Lottie wrinkled her nose at him. She probably worried that Dude had heard something she had so lovingly said about Timothy. "Six ain't here. Gone away a few days. Don't know where he went."

"Oh," Dude said, like that explained everything. He pointed to each of us. "Anything new about JJster?"

Lottie looked at the rest of us, and when no one answered, she said, "Not much about him, but he sure wanted to know a lot about us."

"Meaning?" I said.

"I'm not in the habit of speaking poorly about the departed, but JJ was the nosiest person I've ever known." She waved her hands around the room. "He was here several times, twice when it was only the two of us. Questions, questions, questions!"

"Like?" Dude said.

"Like, he wanted to know if I'd been married," Lottie said. "Then once he asked if I'd ever stole anything. Can you believe that?"

Dude nodded. "He be nosy."

Lottie pointed to the far corner of the room. "One day, right over there, he hemmed and hawed and asked if I'd been a prostitute. That turd—excuse me, Lord—really asked that. I was shocked, I repeat, shocked."

"What'd you say?" Dude asked.

He was the only person here who could have gotten away with asking.

She stared at the surfer. "Nothing. I walked away."

Sharp had remained silent until now. "Brother JJ was way

too curious," he said. "It was like he didn't have a … what do you call it that keeps you from driving too fast?"

"Cops," Dude said.

Sharp shook his head. "No, something in the car."

"A governor," I suggested.

"Yeah, that's it," Sharp said. "JJ didn't have a governor on his mouth. He'd ask anything."

"That's why I like Preacher Burl," Lottie added. "He accepts everyone. He doesn't care about someone's past. All he's interested in is the here-and-now and the future. Names, police records, past addictions, past sins are not his thing. He treats us all like important parts of his flock." She shook her head. "I do worry about him sometimes. Not all people can be saved, and I wouldn't be surprised if someone tries to bring harm to him. A viper will still bite you even if you try to treat it kindly. That's basically what a viper is."

Considering the two deaths in the First Light family, I wondered if Lottie's words could come to haunt the church.

"Lottie, Sharp, you knew JJ and Mendelson," I said. "Give some thought to anything else that may have tied them together, anything that may have led to their deaths."

Lottie raised her hand over her head. "Wait," she said. "Are you figuring that JJ's death wasn't an accident?"

I nodded.

The population of the storefront increased by one when Charles flung open the door and walked in like we were expecting him. He wore a white long-sleeved T-shirt with a black-and-gold creature on it that looked like an angry wasp stalking its prey.

Charles made a beeline to Pluto, gave him a hug and a kiss, and then clapped and pointed at me. "Holy moly," he said. "The walls will come tumbling down. Heathen Chris is in the house!"

Lottie chuckled. “If having heathens in this house is that bad, the walls would have tumbled long ago.”

“Probably why First Light meets outside where there ain’t no walls,” Sharp added.

That was the first glimmer of humor I’d heard from the acerbic pew sander.

“What’s that?” Lottie said, pointing at Charles’s shirt.

Lottie hadn’t been around Charles enough to learn not to ask unless she wanted to hear far more than she wanted to know.

“Glad you asked,” said Charles, who winked at me and then turned to Lottie. “It’s Corky, the Emporia State University hornet.” He turned back to me. “That would be in Emporia, Kansas.”

Lottie didn’t appear awestruck.

Charles turned serious and asked about Karen. I shared the same information that I had told Dude. He said he was relieved. I knew he wouldn’t dwell on it but that he was truly concerned.

Lottie asked who Karen was, and Charles proceeded to give her a slightly abbreviated history of my relationship with the detective, her father the former police chief and now mayor, and a bio on Joe, Karen’s recently departed cat. Lottie seemed to lose interest somewhere between what street Karen lived on and where the cat’s name came from. Sharp hadn’t made it past Karen’s occupation and had returned to prepping the pew for a coat of stain. Dude listened attentively even though he already knew the stories.

“Lottie be momma,” Dude said after Charles had either finished Karen’s bio or stopped to take a breath.

I looked at the surfer and wondered what that had to do with Karen. “Oh,” I said. Dude wasn’t the only one with few words.

Lottie frowned at Dude and turned to me. “Every time Dude hears someone mention children he tells about me.”

I didn't know what to say to that, not one word.

Lottie lowered her head. "See," she said barely above a whisper, "I got hitched in high school, had two young 'uns by nineteen, divorced by twenty-three." She shook her lowered head.

This was the kind of story that Charles lived for. "What happened to your children?" he asked.

"The three of us struggled a long time," she said as she raised her face to Charles. "Not much opportunity for a high school dropout trying to raise two babies. Next door neighbor watched the kids when I got a part-time job at the local five-and-dime. Then a big ol' Wally World opened a mile away and shut down my store and my job. Tried to get a job there but couldn't work the shifts they wanted and still raise kids."

"All stuff five or dime?" Dude interrupted, a trivia-collecting Charles in training.

Lottie grinned. "Nah, owner thought it sounded better than Thirty Bucks and Under."

"Then what happened?" I asked to get back on the right path.

"All I had was two kids and, according to some men, good looks. I became the age-old stereotype, I turned to stripping."

Sharp stopped staining the pews and walked over to us. "Lottie, you don't have to tell that to total strangers."

"It's nothing I'm ashamed of, Sharp. I wasn't a hooker, and I had to support the kids."

"Little 'uns be where?" Dude asked.

"Don't know." Lottie glanced at the neon cross leaning against the wall. "Both boys're grown; both took off as soon as they finished high school. At least they finished high school. They went out west. Used to send me Christmas cards, but I moved over here and somehow they didn't get my new address.

They can't find me; I can't find them." She looked back at the floor and then at Dude. "Think Sharp's right; enough about me, except that Preacher Burl saved my life. That man's a godsend."

"Did you tell JJ your story?" I asked.

Her eyes widened. "Lord, no! He'd never've stopped asking questions. That man is—was, a question-asking fool." She smiled for the first time since I came into the storefront. "I told him my past was too painful to talk about, and even shed a tear. He stopped asking. Hallelujah!"

"What about you, Sharp?" Charles asked.

"What about me?"

"Did you tell JJ your story? I figured you spent a lot of time in here, talking and working, working and talking."

"I shared what brought me to First Light," he said hesitantly.

"What it be?" Dude asked.

Sharp gave Dude a look that could have meant either "none of your business" or "huh?" He turned to Lottie. "I told him some to keep him from continually pestering my friend here."

"Past be what?" Dude repeated.

Sharp smiled. "Past be crappy."

Dude returned the smile since they were speaking the same language. "Crappy how?"

"Actually," Sharp said, "it wasn't so bad. I'd stumbled into some trouble over the years but not nearly as bad as folks I hung with." He shook his head. "I had a friend who was headed down the wrong track. Truth be told, he got quite a ways down the wrong track before he met a chaplain in the homeless shelter where we were staying. The preacher man grabbed ahold of my buddy and got him into church. Suppose he saved my friend from stuff you don't want to talk about."

"Sounds like Preacher Burl," Charles said.

I wondered if Sharp was talking about himself.

Sharp blinked and lowered his head. "Got another buddy big into drugs. Started going to church; ended up dead anyway. Damned shame."

Finally Lottie said, "Preacher Burl's better than that. He could've saved your buddy."

"Maybe," Sharp said.

"Did JJ have enemies?" Charles asked.

"Darn, Brother Charles," Lottie said in mock—or I thought it was mock—exasperation. "You're sounding like JJ and your buddy here." She tilted her head in my direction.

"Don't think so," Sharp said before Charles could respond. "JJ was a pesky little bugger, but I doubt it would've bothered anyone too much." He pointed to Lottie. "Except her." He laughed.

Lottie also laughed. "Pesky, he sure was. But once you shut down his questions, he wasn't such a bad fellow. I'll miss him."

"Church save me from nothing," Dude said. He had been following the discussion, but apparently he'd gotten hung up on the how Sharp's friends and Lottie were saved. "Just went to worship under sun."

Not surprisingly, no one had a response. Or if we did, we waited too long, as Preacher Burl bounded through the front door just then. He reminded me of a bowling ball plummeting down the alley.

"Praise be the Lord," he said. "My prayers continue to be answered. Even with the tragic loss of Brother Timothy, you wonderful volunteers continue to do God's work. I thank you."

"It's a pleasure," Lottie said.

"I'll second that," Sharp added.

Dude and Charles both said they didn't have anything else to do, and I remained silent. I wondered if Burl realized that neither Charles, Dude, Pluto, nor I had done anything constructive.

I wanted to like Burl, I really did. His smile was infectious, and he seemed to have a positive effect on so many people. I was touched and appreciative of his being at the hospital for Karen and those gathered there to pray for her recovery. But as hard as I tried, Bob's outpouring of skepticism still bounced around in the back of my mind. I kept picturing the car that hit JJ and then thinking of Timothy's murder. The only connections I could see between the two were First Light and Preacher Burl.

CHAPTER 18

Charles stayed in the storefront while I returned to the gallery to juggle three overdue invoices to see what to pay next. At one point I fantasized about how much more fun I would have had painting next door. That highly unlikely thought reminded me once again how much I needed to shut the gallery and totally retire.

The door bell dinged before I could become more depressed. Charles's cane tapped its way on the wooden floor to the back room.

"Are you starved?" he asked.

I hadn't given it much thought, but I realized that it was almost midafternoon and that I hadn't had much to eat.

"Starved, no; hungry, yes," I said, doing my best Dude impression.

"Then get your wide butt out of the chair and let's get to the Dog before it closes."

I was surprised that it was already two thirty, a half hour before the restaurant closed. I grabbed my Tilley and slid the invoices back in their folder; out of sight, out of mind—temporarily.

The restaurant's covered patio was nearly empty, so we chose a table against the railing and were promptly attended to by Richard, one of the few male servers. Charles barely glanced at the menu before ordering a hot dog and telling Richard to heap as much goop on it as possible. The helpful waiter clarified that *goop* only meant cheese, onions, kraut, and relish. Charles added mustard and mango salsa. I tried not to traumatize Richard and ordered the Thai wrap with nothing extra, goop or otherwise.

"I like Preacher Burl," Charles said out of the blue.

"Why?"

Charles picked flecks of dried paint off his fingers. "He's real, and look what he's doing for his ... umm, flock. Look at how he's helped Lottie, Sharp, Six, and Dude. Well, Dude won't admit it, but he gets more from the services than being outside under his sun god. And there's—"

"He does help," I interrupted before Charles gained steam and started telling me how each person benefitted. "But there've been a lot of preachers in my lifetime who conned people rather than helping them find the way."

Charles opened his mouth to say something, but I held up my hand to stop him. "I'm not saying Burl's one of them—he may be as sincere as Jesus—but I keep thinking about what Bob said about new churches and their preachers."

Charles rolled his eyes. "Let me get this straight. You're using Bob Howard as your expert on religion?"

I laughed. "Even Bob can occasionally be right."

Cindy LaMond pulled her unmarked Crown Vic into an empty space directly in front of us and tapped her horn before Charles could say that Bob was never right. The chief came in and pointed to the chair beside Charles, and I waved for her to join us.

"How's Karen?" she asked before sitting.

I gave her the stock answer that I'd shared with everyone this morning.

"She's strong," Cindy said as she put her hand on my arm. "She'll make it; she'll be fine."

I wish I had that much confidence and wondered if Cindy believed what she was saying.

"Thanks," I said. "Any update on Mendelson's murder?" I asked because I didn't want to tear up in front of Charles and the chief of police, and because I really wanted to know.

"Yep." She nodded. "He's still dead."

"No wonder you're the chief," I said and smiled.

Cindy returned my smile. "Yep."

"Anything else? Beyond the obvious."

"Nothing specific," she said. "Seems that the brilliant detectives are speculating that the murder had something to do with a deranged client who'd turned a pot load of dough over to the stockbroker to invest and make dough plus. Mendelson's stockbroker wisdom managed to turn the investor's dollars into cents."

"Is he deranged or just angry because Mendelson lost money?" Charles asked.

Good question, I thought.

"She," Cindy said. "The client, Renee Baker, sent Mendelson a dozen threatening e-mails. Said that if he didn't find a way to get the money back, she would off Mendelson's head. Think the detectives figured *off Mendelson's head* chucked her into the deranged category. The other e-mails told Mendelson what other body parts he would lose if the money wasn't returned."

"Alibi?" I asked.

Cindy smiled. "One of these days, Chris, I'm going to let my fingers do the walking on the Internet and buy you a shiny detective's badge you can stick on the front of your boring golf shirt."

"Get me one too," Charles said.

Cindy ignored him, another sign she was chief. "Her alibi's solid. Seems she was at a Dale Carnegie training session with a dozen other becoming-self-actualized attendees. Funny, though, Detective Callahan thinks her alibi's too airtight."

"Meaning?" I asked.

"Renee signed up for the seminar late. The person who scheduled it said that she seemed more interested in what days they met than any other details."

"What's strange about that?" Charles asked. "She had to know when it met."

"Almost a good point," Cindy said, "except she missed the session the week before, and guess what?"

Neither of us ventured a guess.

"Cowards," Cindy said. "Anyway, Renee also missed the session after the killing."

"So the only meeting she attended was when Timothy was murdered," I said.

Cindy nodded and pointed at my shirt. "I see that detective badge now, stuck right over that overpriced horsey logo."

"She got someone to bump Timothy off while Renee was learning how to win friends and influence people?" Charles asked.

"You got it."

"That doesn't make sense," I said. "There weren't any defensive wounds on Mendelson's body. He must have known the killer."

"I don't totally disagree," Cindy said, all humor out of her voice. "But it's Burton and Callahan's case. Burton's work isn't worth an ounce of pluff mud, but Detective Callahan has a good head on his shoulders. He'll figure it out."

I wasn't convinced. "Don't you find it strange that both JJ and Mendelson attended First Light?"

"Not really," she said. "I've given it some thought. Counting First Light, there're only four churches here. Two deaths, one murder and the other accidental, the—"

"Two murders," I interrupted.

"So you say," Cindy said. "Back to my point, two deaths doesn't seem that strange since the church options are limited. It's tragic, but not outside the realm of reason."

"It's also the newest church; it has the smallest number of members," I said. "And it's led by a man we don't know anything about. I'm not saying the deaths have anything to do with the church, but I think Bob may have a good point about Burl's motives for starting First Light. He thinks it's a con, a way for Burl to rip off his flock."

"Whoa," Cindy said. "You're citing Bob as your expert on churches?"

Charles sat back in his chair so quickly that it almost tipped over. He folded his arms across his chest. "See."

I looked up at the ceiling, but not in prayer. "I'm not saying Bob's an expert on anything. He has concerns, probably legitimate, about what's behind First Light. The deaths may not be connected, but I know as well as I'm sitting here that JJ was murdered."

Cindy and Charles quickly agreed that Bob wasn't an expert on anything except possibly real estate.

"Cindy," I said, "how about a favor? Would you run a background check on Burl Costello?"

Cindy rolled her eyes. "Because Bob thinks he's a fraud?"

"No," I said. "Because I'm curious. We don't know much about him, and since the detectives don't think there's a connection between the deaths and First Light, someone needs to look at him."

She looked down at the table and then at me. "Middle name?"

"Ives," Charles said.

"Like Burl Ives the dead singing actor?"

I nodded.

"You're going to get me fired one of these days." Cindy gave a slight nod.

"While you're at it," Charles said, "how about running JJ and Mendelson?"

Cindy looked at Charles, then at me, and shook her head. "If I'd paid more attention in school, I'd have remembered some big ol' long word to describe you two."

"Incorrigible," I suggested.

"Brilliant," Charles said.

"Jackass stubborn troublemakers," Cindy concluded.

"That's more than one word," Charles said. "I'd stick to brilliant."

Cindy almost smiled and then stood and headed out to her car.

Charles watched her drive away. "Think that went well, don't you think?"

I said time would tell and broached the subject that I'd dreaded for days, giving Charles an abbreviated breakdown on how much money I was losing at the gallery. My stomach knotted and my tea turned sour in my mouth as I told him that the lease was about up and that I wasn't planning on renewing.

He didn't interrupt and didn't react. He bowed his head and then stared at the street. Then his jaw quivered and a tear formed in his eye, but he still didn't say a word. The silence was deafening.

"Charles, I—"

"Do what you must," he said.

"You know—"

Charles pushed his chair back, and it tipped over and

bounced on the floor. He turned and walked off the patio. He didn't look back.

I had to tell him; it had to be done. So why did I feel like crap?

CHAPTER 19

With everything that happened the day before, I had forgotten that I wanted to clean the gallery. Today, I thought mindless physical labor could get my mind off Karen and the two—yes, two, regardless of what anyone thought—murders. I grabbed coffee at Bert's and shared a few words about the weather with Julia, one of the owners, and an elderly lady who was buying an apple. The sidewalks were nearly deserted as I walked to the gallery, which strengthened my resolve not to open every day.

I gazed at the framed photos on the walls and the print racks in the corner and wondered what I would do with the inventory. I could cram it in the extra room at home, but it would be a shame for it to just sit. I had displayed my work at the semiregular art shows at River Park, so I could continue selling there.

Looking at the photos made me think of Charles's devotion to the gallery, and then my mind drifted to his second thoughts about marrying Heather and my worry at the time he proposed that he had done it solely because of his promise to Aunt Melinda. And then, for some reason, probably because I had nearly lost Karen, I wondered about my relationship with her and how conflicted I was about taking it to the next level. I shook my head. Cleaning the gallery may not have been such a good idea after all.

A scream from next door startled me. I rushed over and found the door unlocked, the lights on at the far end of the room, and someone in the back corner. There was no mistaking where a second scream came from: Lottie, on her knees, bent over someone prone and unmoving. I hit the light switch by the front door and the harsh overhead fluorescent lights blinked on. Lottie's head jerked up at the lights and then at me. I couldn't see who was in front of her, but the eight-foot ladder was on its side next to Lottie. Four tiles had been pulled from the ceiling, and the grid that had held them had been ripped loose.

I moved closer and saw Six's twisted body leaning between the ladder and the wall. Parts of a ceiling tile were on his chest. I felt for a pulse. Nothing.

I put my arm around Lottie's paint-spattered T-shirt and inched her away from the lifeless figure of her friend. Her body shook, and I was afraid she was in shock.

"Six, Six, my God, Six!" she chanted.

I turned her away from her friend and led—nearly carried—her to a nearby pew. I tried to get her to sit, but she slid off. I lifted her back on the pew, held her with my arm around her trembling shoulder, and fished my phone out of my pocket. I tapped in 911.

Minutes later, Folly's GMC fire-and-rescue pickup truck pulled up in front of the storefront; its brakes screeched to a halt. Two firefighter EMTs rushed through the door and knelt over the body. If they'd asked, I would have told them that there wasn't any reason to hurry. They conferred, and the younger EMT came over to see if Lottie needed help. She was still sobbing uncontrollably, and I suggested that the medic give her something to calm her. I had talked with him a couple of times over the years, and he was polite, but his expression communicated that he would decide what was best.

He asked what happened, and I shared that I had arrived from next door after hearing Lottie scream. He turned to Lottie, but before she could tell him anything, two Folly Beach police officers arrived. One was Allen Spencer and the other was an African American woman I'd seen around but had never met. Officer Spencer cautiously walked over to Six, and the woman came over to Lottie, the EMT, and me. She introduced herself as Officer Bishop and asked who we were. Lottie gave her first name, and the officer didn't push for more. The EMT said he wanted to get Lottie to the hospital, and Officer Bishop gently put her hand on Lottie's trembling arm and asked if she could answer a few questions first.

Lottie held her head in her hands but managed a slight nod. The medic stepped back, and Officer Bishop squatted in front of Lottie so they were face to face, and in a reassuring voice, she asked what had happened.

Choking back a sob, Lottie said, "Preacher Burl told us we could come in when we had time. Some of us had keys to the front door." She cleared her throat. "I thought I could sand the pews without being bothered, so I came in and saw the shadow of the ladder on the floor. I thought someone knocked it over, so I went over to make sure it hadn't hurt anything. Not everyone's real careful with stuff in here." She looked at the floor and tears again rolled down her cheeks.

Officer Bishop waited until Lottie looked up, and then she said, "Then what, Miss Lottie?"

"I got to the ladder and saw him, saw Brother Six, just lying there, not moving." Lottie looked at the officer. "He was … dead."

Chief LaMond came through the door, looked at the three

of us huddled at the pew, and went over to Officer Spencer, standing a safe distance from the fallen ladder and the fallen Six. She talked to Spencer and conferred with the EMT beside the body. She then came over to us. She nodded, and Bishop told her what Lottie had said. Wisely, the chief told Bishop to continue and stood behind her and listened.

Officer Bishop turned to Lottie. "Was the front door locked when you got here?"

"Umm, yes." Lottie sniffled.

"Were lights on?"

Her trembling hand pointed toward the ladder. "Only the one back there … by Six."

"Was anyone else here?" Bishop asked.

"No," Lottie said, but she hesitated. "I don't think so."

"You said his name's Six," Bishop said. "Like the number?"

I remembered Six's answer when Charles had asked him that.

"Yes," Lottie said.

"First or last name?" Bishop asked.

"First."

"What's his last name?"

"Don't know. We don't talk about things like that."

I jumped in and told Officer Bishop that Lottie and Six were members of First Light and that they had been working on fixing up the storefront. She nodded and made a note.

I guardedly said to Lottie, "Lottie, I'm so sorry. I know you and Six were close." I paused to choose my words carefully. "Yesterday you said that he had been away for a few days but you didn't know where."

She slowly nodded.

"Do you know when he got back?" I asked.

"Didn't know he was. This was the first time I'd seen him." She gasped and struggled to catch her breath.

I waited a few seconds. "Know where he could have been?"

"No," she said.

"Did he have a car?"

"No, but he has a license." She gave a weak smile. "Sharp has an old Ford; Six borrowed it once. Sharp made him show a license before he would lend him his car." She put her head between her legs. "Now he's gone and I won't be able to ask where he was."

I heard the distinct sound of a siren as an ambulance pulled up in front. The EMT politely edged Officer Bishop aside, said he needed to get Lottie to the hospital, and asked her if she was able to walk to the emergency vehicle. She muttered yes and slowly stood.

"One more question," Bishop said. "Who else had keys?"

Lottie thought for a moment. "Don't know about all of them. Six and Sharp did, and so did two other guys who help occasionally, don't remember their names, and then there's Charles. Sorry, I'm not certain who else, but I remember when Preacher Burl handed them out; he had a handful. He might know who else, but he's not big on names."

After the EMT helped Lottie to the ambulance, Officer Spencer came over to Officer Bishop, Chief LaMond, and me.

"Looks like he was on the ladder, probably standing on the top where you're not supposed to stand. Nobody reads that warning." Spencer pointed to the ladder. "He grabbed the ceiling-tile grid, and it gave way. The ladder fell and he landed wrong. He must've fallen a dozen feet or more. I'd say the fall broke his neck."

Chief LaMond approached the body and glanced up at the

broken ceiling-tile grid. "Or the ladder started to fall, and he reached and grabbed the grid to catch himself."

I stood far enough away that I wouldn't contaminate the scene, looked at the ceiling, and said, "It wouldn't have stopped his fall."

"Either way," the chief said, "he hit the floor wrong. A tragic accident."

"I read that each year more than four hundred people are killed falling off ladders," Officer Bishop added.

"Seems strange," I said.

All three officers turned to me. "Why?" the chief asked.

"Doesn't it seem unusual that the only light in the room that was on was the one by the ladder? When I came in, I flipped the switch by the front door, and it turned the rest of the lights on." I pointed to the overhead fluorescents. "The lights near the ladder are on a switch by the back door."

"So?" Officer Bishop said.

I looked at her and back at the lights. "Lottie said that the keys Burl gave out were to the front door. Why would Six come in the front door, lock it, and not turn on the lights until he'd walked across the dark room to the switch in the back?"

The chief looked at the lights and then at me. "I'll get you-know-what ordered today," she said.

The two officers looked at her as though her cryptic reference had thrown them, but they didn't ask their boss what she had meant.

A badge was the last thing I wanted, but Six's death made me angry—enough to get involved, regardless how much the law enforcement community would try to discourage it.

"You have a theory?" Officer Spencer asked.

"What if Six, like Lottie, had come in early to work," I said. "He had a key to the front door, so he would have entered there.

It was dark, so he would have flicked the light switch by the door. Most likely, he wouldn't have locked the door since others could show up to help."

"Then someone else came in, and ..." Spencer paused. "Chris, are you saying that someone came in to kill him?" He pointed to the body beside the ladder.

"That's precisely what I'm saying," I said with certainty, probably more than I had. "The new arrival probably locked the door. Six may or may not have been on the ladder. If he was, the killer could have tipped it over. Six would have grabbed the drop-ceiling grid, pulling it loose but not stopping his fall. Grabbing it could have made the fall worse, even, twisted his body or disrupting his balance."

"It would have been risky to assume that the fall would kill him," Officer Bishop said.

"Yes," I said. "But the fall would have done some of the damage, and if it didn't kill him, it could have incapacitated him. The killer could have then hit Six in the head with something to make it look like the floor caused the blow."

"I don't know when it happened," Officer Spencer said, "but there aren't any curtains or blinds on the windows, so wouldn't there have been a chance that someone saw whatever was happening in here?"

The chief now spoke up. "Following Chris's logic, the killer could have turned on the back lights before killing Six and could have then walked to the front and locked the door, if it wasn't already locked, and turned off the main lights so a passerby would have much more difficulty seeing what was happening."

"Yes," I said. "The afternoon sun's strong on this side of the road. The front window has tinted film on it like I have next door. That makes it hard to see in. And Six would have known the killer well enough to feel comfortable with him or her being here."

"It could have been an accident," Bishop said. "The second person might have been afraid that he or she would get in trouble and turned off the lights, locked up, and hightailed it out of here."

"It wasn't anymore an accident than was JJ's assassination," I said to the chief. "Add the murder of Mendelson to the mix, and the only thing connecting the three deaths is this," I waved my hands around the room, "First Light."

As if to punctuate my displeasure, Charles stormed through the door, flailing his cane in the air. "I saw the commotion." He stopped to catch his breath before he continued, "Chris, I was afraid something had happened to you next door, you being old, you know."

I didn't comment; I wasn't the one out of breath.

"What in blue blazes happened?" He looked around the room and fixed his gaze on Six.

He plopped down beside me, threw his Tilley on the pew behind us, and took another deep breath. This was the first time that I'd seen Charles since I'd broken the news about the gallery, so I knew he was still angry, but I was touched that he was concerned about me. I knew what to say, and what not to say, to prevent a hundred questions, so I took the lead with the explanation. It took a few minutes but would have taken much longer if anyone else had tried to tell him.

He rose and slowly walked over to examine Six, and then he looked up. "It could have been an accident," he said to the broken ceiling grid.

"I would agree," I said, "if Lottie hadn't found the door locked and the front lights off."

Charles turned and faced me. "Any way to verify her story?"

All eyes but Six's turned to Charles.

"Not really," I said.

Charles scratched his head. "She could have done it and lied about finding him?"

Her scream had sounded real, but Charles could have been right. She and Six didn't appear to be that close, but her reaction to not being able to ask where he had been indicated more intimacy than I would have guessed. They had growled at each other a few times when I had seen them together, but more could have been going on. She also would have been able to get close enough to Mendelson without making him suspicious before she rammed a knife in his back.

Cindy said that she wasn't convinced that it was murder, but she called Detective Callahan to let him know what had happened and to ask for his help. Her overview had been briefer than the one I had shared with Charles. She rolled her eyes and waited when he put her on hold. A couple of minutes later, he returned to the phone. Cindy told him who was in the room, listened, and hung up. She'd said that he and Detective Burton would be over and that she needed to secure the crime scene. She smiled and added that Callahan had instructed Charles and me to wait in the gallery.

She also emphasized that he had called this a *crime* scene. I wasn't the only one who thought it was.

CHAPTER 20

Charles and I had been waiting for the detectives in the gallery for an hour, and during that time, my friend had said barely a dozen words. He was furious. He had stared at each of the images on the walls, shaken his head, and then looked out the front window. He poured more coffee and opened the back door and stared into the alley. I tried to talk about what had happened next door, and he only said "hmm" and continued to dart around like a Roomba. He asked how Karen was; I told him. He said, "Good."

Silence had never been Charles's strong suit, but he was carrying it off quite well. If I wasn't feeling so bad about the hurt that I'd caused, I would have told him how impressed I was. I soon gave up on conversation and did some paperwork, a task that expanded to fill the time, another reason to be thankful to shut this shop down.

I would never have thought how happy I'd be to see a detective walk through the door than I was when Detective Callahan entered.

"Have coffee back there?" he said, pointing toward the back room.

I fixed him a cup as he spoke to my angry friend. Charles hadn't gone mute, as I was beginning to suspect, and he interrogated the detective instead of the other way around.

Callahan took a sip, and I asked him where Detective Burton was. Far, far, away, I hoped, but I knew better.

"First, how's Karen?" he asked as he set the cup on an empty spot on the cluttered table.

I updated him.

"She'll be okay. Strong lady." He hesitated. "Back to Burton, I suggested that he stay over there and gather evidence before the crime techs arrive. I told him that with his vast experience, he could be much more valuable there than talking to you." He smiled. "Besides, I know what you think of him, and I doubt you're one of his Facebook friends. Figured both of you would be better off separated by a wall."

Callahan was perceptive, bright, and right.

The detective flipped open his notebook. "Okay, Chris, take it from the top."

I began with Lottie's scream and went through the arrival of the EMTs and the police. He took copious notes and asked clarifying questions. I limited my comments to what I had seen and heard this morning. Charles had leaned back in his chair and didn't say anything. Callahan was clueless about how odd that was. I almost missed his butting in and constant disruptions.

Callahan closed his book, verified that Charles hadn't arrived until after the police, and turned to me. "Chief LaMond says that you're certain it wasn't an accident and that it's tied to the hit-and-run death and the murder of the stockbroker."

"I am," I said and told him once again that JJ's death had been intentional. I then told him that I was just as certain that Six's "accident" had been anything but, then reminded him that no one had disputed that Mendelson's death was a homicide.

Callahan reached for his notebook, which he'd returned to his inside coat pocket, but he pulled his hand back, placed both elbows on the table, and leaned toward me. "And you think this has something to do with the new church?"

I leaned toward him. "Don't you?"

"What's the connection? Each person attended, but so did a lot of other people. The guy over there and the hit-and-run victim were homeless. The stockbroker had more money than I'll make the rest of my life. We have no evidence that he ever talked to the other two outside church and maybe a couple of times next door. So, what's the connection?"

I wanted to scream, "That's your job; figure it out!" Instead, I said that I couldn't see anything beyond the obvious and conceded that the murders may not have had anything to do with the church. What I didn't waiver from was that they weren't accidents.

Callahan turned to Charles and asked what he thought.

Charles stood, walked to the coffee pot, poured a refill, and moved behind my chair. "I didn't see JJ get hit. I didn't hear Lottie this morning or walk in on whatever happened. Chris saw the car smack JJ and heard Lottie." He put his hands on my shoulders. "If he says they were murdered, they were murdered."

Callahan tilted his head, took out his notebook, and said, "Have either of you attended First Light?"

I said that I'd been once and Charles added that he was a semiregular. The detective asked Charles if he saw any connections among the victims. Charles said that he didn't remember JJ, did know that Mendelson had donated a large amount of money to the church, and knew Six mostly from his volunteer work at the storefront. Charles had never seen Mendelson and Six together.

We had exhausted our knowledge of the victims.

"I suggest that you talk to Burl Costello, the preacher," I said. "If anyone knows of links, he would."

"That's my next stop," Callahan said.

Charles picked up his cane and pointed it at Callahan. "What do you think?"

Callahan smiled. "That thing's not loaded, is it?"

Charles lowered the cane.

Callahan looked at me and then said to Charles, "I don't know much about your friend here, but I know that the best detective in our office thinks the world of him. I know that your police chief says he can be a pain in the butt but that he's usually right." He chuckled. "And I definitely know that Detective Burton thinks that Chris is a royal ass and should be shackled. That's the clincher. If Chris thinks they were murdered, that's how I'll pursue the case."

"Thank you," I muttered.

"I'd better get back," Callahan said. "I suspect that Detective Burton has gathered all the evidence he can, if he's still awake."

He thanked me for the coffee and my description of what had happened, said that he had Karen in his prayers, and nodded to Charles as he left the gallery.

Charles turned to me. "You really think they were murdered?"

I nodded, and Charles abruptly said that he had to go and was out the door. He was still angry.

"Yes," I said to the empty gallery. "They were murdered, and I'm going to make sure that a killer doesn't get away with it."

I may not have been furious, but I was damned mad.

CHAPTER 21

When I left the gallery that evening, the body had been removed, crime scene tape was wrapped around the entry to the storefront, and a steady stream of lookie lous walked past and pressed their faces to the window to peek inside. I locked the gallery and walked home. The sun may have been out and the sky blue, but all I felt was a heavy weight on my shoulders, and my mind was cluttered with clouds of anger, frustration, and sadness.

I was unlocking the front door when my phone rang. The screen read Mayor Newman. The way things were going, I feared the worst and hesitated before I answered.

"Chris, it's Brian. I'm at the hospital and just talked to the doctor. He said that Karen's out of her coma and talking coherently. They've upgraded her condition. You there?" He had said all that in one breath.

"Fantastic," I said.

"The doc said that she's asking for you. Irritating that she hasn't asked for dear old dad, but anyway, thought you'd want to be here. We might be able to see her in an hour or so."

"I'm on my way," I said.

Thirty minutes later I walked into the waiting room, with a smile on my face for the first time. Three deputies in the far corner smiled and nodded at me, so I assumed that Brian had told them about Karen's improved condition. The mayor jumped to his feet with a spring in his step that I hadn't seen since before the shooting and greeted me with a handshake and an awkward hug.

"They said we could come in," he said. "I waited for you."

I thanked him as he punched the button beside the door to the ICU, electronically unlocking it. We entered the nearly all white, sterile, and frightening world of life-saving machines and antiseptic smells that was Karen's current home.

A young nurse greeted us and said that the doctor had an emergency but had asked her to take us to Ms. Lawson. She warned us not to be alarmed by the medical stuff attached to the patient; it was normal, and Ms. Lawson was doing remarkably well. I appreciated her sensitivity but wasn't worried since I had been here before when Brian had been hooked up to a surfeit of life-saving paraphernalia after his heart attack.

When we got to Karen, I appreciated the nurse's warning more than I had expected. To resort to a cliché, Karen looked like death warmed over. Her chestnut-brown hair flowed in all directions, her arms looked like pin cushions with all the tubes and wires attached, her eyes were sunken into their dark sockets, and she was as pale as the sheets. Her eyes were closed, but she was breathing on her own. My heart sank.

Brian stutter-stepped closer to the bed and reached out to touch her arm but hesitated. I walked to the other side and whispered her name.

Her eyes popped open. "What took you so long to get here? Find another gal?" She managed a weak smile. Her lips were dry and cracked, and she looked like she had lost ten pounds that she didn't have to lose.

Brian cleared his throat, and Karen slowly turned her head in his direction. "Hi, Dad. How're you doing?"

Brian laughed. "I might ask you the same." He leaned down and kissed her forehead.

"Mom always said hamburgers and fries were bad for my health," she said, her voice getting stronger with each word. "Won't be going to Shake Shack again."

I was glad she was looking at her dad. I had tears in my eyes, tears of joy. Brian glanced up as I wiped my cheek, so he distracted her with a couple of comments about the friendly nurses. She kept her eyes on him but moved her right arm toward me. I hesitantly took her hand but was careful not to touch the IV.

She turned back to me. "Well, girlfriends?"

I joked that I had accumulated a couple since she had been vacationing at Resort ICU, but now that she was back to the world of the living, I had ditched them.

"You'd better have," she said.

Karen's doctor stepped up to the bed and panted like he had been running a marathon. "I see you've become reacquainted," he said when he caught his breath. "She's on the road to recovery but far from her destination. Let's give her a break now so she can rest."

He had smiled when he said it, but it was clear he meant that visitation was over. We said our good-byes and followed the doctor out of the ICU. Brian asked how much longer she would be there, and the doctor said that if she continued progressing the way she had the last twenty-four hours, she may be able to move to a regular room in a couple of days and possibly could be released three or four days after that. He cautioned us not to get our hopes too high; she had almost died and had a way to go. He also said it would be best if we didn't visit again today.

We thanked him for taking such good care of her. He shrugged it off and said that he was only doing his job.

It may have been his job, but to me, it meant the world.

Brian asked me to give him a minute, and he updated the deputies who had been keeping a rotating vigil on Karen's condition, shook their hands, and said how much he and especially Karen appreciated their concern. He said that he would call the sheriff's office if there was any change and that they should get back to their families.

"Are you going to Al's with me or not?" Brian said after he escorted the deputies out of the waiting room. "I'm famished."

He pulled his shoulders back and relief filled his eyes. I told him that he couldn't stop me from going, and we took the elevator down. He had only been to Al's once, but Karen had often talked to him about it. Al had treated her like a queen, and she had been impressed.

We stepped from blinding sunlight into blinding darkness as we entered the restaurant. From the jukebox, the Supremes were asking "Where Did Our Love Go?" and the low roar of multiple conversations told us that it was a busy day in the local hangout.

"Look, look, look who it is," Al said as he gingerly stepped from behind the bar to greet us. "If it isn't the mayor of Folly Beach and the father of the loveliest detective in South Carolina."

Brian smiled and reached out his hand to shake Al's. Al pushed Brian's hand aside and gave him a bear hug. I thought I saw Brian blush. "How's my favorite detective?" Al asked.

Brian leaned close to Al so he could hear over the din of the restaurant and gave him the good news. Al hugged Brian again.

I moved close to the bonding males. "Yo, Al, I'm the boyfriend of the loveliest detective in South Carolina."

Al turned to me and frowned. "Will wonders never cease."

He hesitated but then broke into a smile and hugged me. He stepped back and told us that God had brought him a full restaurant and that we would have to wait for a table. We said that it would be worth it as we sidled up to the bar. I inhaled the comforting smell of frying burgers and listened as Marvin Gaye entertained the diners with "I Heard It Through The Grapevine."

As we waited for a table to be available, I was pleased that Al was busy. Most of the times that I had been here were during off hours, when the crowds were nonexistent and Al was barely getting by. Brian didn't appear in a hurry as he sipped a Budweiser, listened to the music, and watched the room full of happy customers.

Fifteen minutes later, a two-top by the front window emptied. It was small, and the large plate-glass window the table was pushed up against radiated enough heat to make it uncomfortable, but I wasn't about to complain. Brian was on his second beer and seemed content to have a seat anywhere. Al took our order, and Brian leaned back in the rickety wooden chair.

"I don't know what I would do if I lost her," he said, more to himself than to me.

It was the kind of statement for which any response would be inadequate, trite, and unnecessary, so I simply nodded.

He quickly switched to talking about fond memories of her childhood, how she had been so stubborn and hadn't wanted to listen to anyone who told her that she couldn't do something.

I smiled. "I know." I asked him what he thought would happen after she was released. Brian said that she would stay at his condo until she could be on her own. He had a spare bedroom and worked close enough to get home in five minutes if he was needed. We talked—hopefully not prematurely—about the logistics of her move to his condo and how I could check on her when Brian was running the city.

Our food arrived as our talk about Karen's arrangements had begun to wind down.

I took the opportunity to broach another delicate topic. "Let me bounce something off you about the recent murders on Folly."

"Here we go," Brian said.

The Miracles' "Shop Around" ended, and the late George Jones crooned "He Stopped Loving Her Today." A groan came from two other tables, and Al had a sly grin on his face. He had selected the country classic just for me, much to the chagrin of his Motown-leaning regulars.

Brian seemed oblivious to the music. "Chris," he said, clearly irritated, "is there some flaw in your DNA that makes you think that you have to get involved in every nefarious death you hear about?"

I took a bite of a fry, more to stall for a better answer than out of hunger. "You probably won't believe this," I said, "but until I moved here, I had never been close to a murder. My only involvement in crime was watching *Columbo*."

"Why the obsession now?"

"I'm not obsessed!" I said, clenching my fists. "I stood in the middle of Arctic Avenue and watched a man get intentionally run down. I was nearly killed, and he was murdered!" I was surprised at my anger and tried to pull myself back when I noticed a gentleman at a nearby table staring at me. I gritted my teeth and said, "Then, next door to my gallery, a Christian working for absolutely no pay was trying to help renovate a church when someone murdered him. Right next door!"

Brian leaned over the table and put his hand on my shaking arm. "Chris, I've been a cop longer than many of the folks in here have been alive. I know what you're feeling, I really do. Unnatural death is appalling. I've seen enough of it for many lifetimes; it makes me livid. But think about it. I have no doubt that you think JJ's death was murder, and I'm not in a position to argue with that. But if it was, you've got to leave it to the police to figure out who did it."

I held my palm up to his face. "The police still believe it was an accident. They're giving me lip service but won't be looking much beyond that. So tell me, how'll they figure it out?"

Brian took a bite of his cheeseburger, looked down at the drink-stained tabletop, and then up at me. "Karen says that Callahan's good. He may not tell you everything about the investigation, but that doesn't mean that he's not working it."

I was still angry, but not at Brian. God knows all that he had been through, but he was the only person I could vent to. "How can anyone say that Six's death could have been an accident? Could anyone be dumb enough to think it was a mere coincidence that JJ, Mendelson, and Six all died in a short period of time and all three were tied to First Light?"

"No cop is a fan of coincidences." Brian gave me his patented police stare that he apparently hadn't retired when he was elected mayor. "I know Chief LaMond will continue to investigate." He grinned. "I'll make sure of it. And I'm sure that Detective Callahan won't drop it. If you want, I'll talk to him."

I told him that I'd appreciate it.

"But dammit, Chris, it's police business. Butt out, you hear me? Butt out."

I didn't say that I would take his pointed advice. I didn't say anything.

Because I knew that I wouldn't.

CHAPTER 22

I spent the next two days dividing my time between being at the hospital and wandering around Folly to distract myself from thinking about Karen, the gallery, and the deaths. The doctor determined that Karen had made remarkable progress and moved her to a regular room, where visiting hours were more accommodating. She had little memory of what had occurred at the Shake Shack beyond walking in, hitting the floor, hearing the ambulance's siren, and waking up to see the smiling face of a nurse. She didn't know if this happened in hours or days. Her biggest concern was whether anyone else was hurt. I assured her no one had been and that the shooter had been quickly apprehended. I didn't tell her about Six's death.

Bob stopped by Karen's room each morning to spout tirades about blankety-blank drug-addled bums robbing stores to get money to feed their blankety-blank drug addictions while law-abiding citizens nearly got killed simply trying to buy a blankety-blank hamburger. She told me that the entire time he ranted, he held her hand and caressed her head with his other hand. Bob was a supersized carafe of contradictions.

Al had visited three times in two days and told Karen that he was there to visit his daughter Tanesa, an ER doctor, and he just happened to stop by Karen's room on his way back to the bar.

His story would have been more believable if he hadn't told me previously that he never dropped in on his daughter because he didn't want to disturb her life-saving work. I walked in on the two of them during his third visit. Karen was in the reclining chair next to her bed, had a towel draped over her lap, and was munching on one of Al's cheeseburgers. They were laughing, and I almost expected to see Al's jukebox in the corner playing Bob Marley's "I Shot the Sheriff."

And speaking of the sheriff, a steady stream of deputies visited. Nurses tried to limit the number of visitors, but they were fighting an uphill battle.

Of the law enforcement officials to visit, I was most pleased to see Detective Callahan, not because he was there to see Karen but because I wanted to ask what he had learned about the deaths. I waited for him to express his best wishes to the patient and then cornered him in the corridor and asked if I could walk him out.

He said he appreciated the offer but could find his own way. He laughed. "After all, I am a detective."

I acknowledged that he could find his car but said that there was something I wanted to talk to him about. He stopped laughing and smiled. "I know. You want to know what's going on with the investigations. I'm a detective, remember."

"Guilty," I said, and I asked if he had a few minutes. He said that a walk around the block would do him good.

We walked in silence for a couple of minutes, and then he stopped.

"Chris, I'm telling you this because I know Karen trusts you and her dad likes you. If any of this gets back to me, I'll deny saying it."

I waited.

"I wish I could say we've made an arrest in the Mendelson

murder; I wish I could say we have solid leads. We haven't and don't. I suppose it's a sign of the times, but the stockbroker had a passel of unhappy clients, a couple more vocal than the others in blaming him for ushering their money into losing stocks. The most outspoken client sent a dozen scathing e-mails and left rambling, nearly incoherent, voice mails threatening him."

"I take it that he had an alibi?" I said, although I already knew that he was talking about Renee Baker. I was also careful to not to say *she*, since I didn't want Callahan to suspect that I had a source.

Callahan frowned and shook his head. "Airtight." He started walking again.

"What next?" I asked as I followed him down the sidewalk.

"We've subpoenaed the suspect's bank records and are trying to trace money that may have been paid to have Mendelson killed. It's a slow process. The suspect's fairly wealthy and has more accounts that I have ties. Much of what the person spent was cash, so we may never be able to trace anything. Frustrating."

"What about JJ and Six?"

Callahan stopped and turned to me. "I told you after Six's death that I would look at them closely. I'm doing what I can, but to be honest, there's zero support in the office for your theory. Detective Burton says you're as wrong as the flat-earth proponents, and the sheriff says that we have enough real murders to keep us busy without inventing some."

"They're wrong," I said. "What did the ME say about Six?"

"Inconclusive, but the injuries were consistent with a fall from a ladder." He held up his hand. "I'm not saying that they weren't killed. I honestly don't know. But, I assure you that I will do whatever I can to keep the cases open. All I'm saying is I've got no official support."

"Not until there's another murder," I said.

"I'm doing what I can do," Callahan said sharply. "I need to get back to work."

I walked him to his car and thanked him for stopping to see Karen and for doing what he could. He apologized for not being able to do more. I told him that I understood, but I didn't.

I had been at the hospital most of the day and wanted to get back to more familiar territory and somewhere that wasn't a constant reminder of how precarious life could be. Folly had mysteriously drawn me in eight years before, and that draw continued today. Instead of going home, I grabbed my Tilley from the backseat and walked to River Park, at the edge of the Folly River. Out on the long pier on the edge of the river, I sat on a wooden bench. Two small sailboats were circling near the new bridge, and two men were unloading their small fishing boat into the stream.

I watched the late-afternoon sun reflect off the boats' white sails and thought about someone who hadn't visited Karen: Charles. I also wondered what else I could do about the murders. Who was killing the First Light flock?

Letting time pass was the best way to deal with Charles's anger. He was hurt and probably felt helpless about the gallery closing, and no amount of words could change that. He had come around before; I prayed that he would again. Time was not on my side with the murders, though. The longer a gap between the crime and the solution, the worse, much worse, chance there was to catch the killer. And that was when the police actually believed that a murder had been committed.

There was one thing that I could do. It had been a few days since I had asked Chief LaMond to do background checks on JJ, Timothy Mendelson, and Preacher Burl. I called but became more frustrated when I got her voice mail. I told her why I was calling and then leaned back and watched the two sailboats continue to go in circles. I knew the feeling.

***

Cindy returned my call at six thirty the next morning. She started by saying that she was sorry to wake me, so I told her that I was already awake.

"Liar, liar, pants on fire," she mumbled.

I repeated that I wasn't asleep, and after we traded a couple more insults, she got around to what she had learned.

"Sorry I didn't call last night, but my sweetie wanted to take me to supper. Who was I to refuse?" She paused and then chuckled. "And when we got home, he wanted dessert, if you know what I mean."

I suspected that I did, but I did what I do well: played innocent and asked what she meant. She said it was none of my business. I didn't disagree.

"First," she said, getting back on task, "I didn't learn anything about your boy JJ that you don't know. He didn't leave much of a footprint on the world, and I doubt kiddos in the next century will be reading about him in history books. I don't see anything that ties him to anything."

"Mendelson?" I asked.

"Decent reputation in the industry," she said. "Lot of clients, appeared to have done well for them—or that's how it looked to me, but I know as much about the stock market as I do about Bengali."

I didn't know what Bengali was, nor was I Charles, so I didn't care. "Detective Callahan said that he had some disgruntled clients. Anything about them?"

"Nothing besides a few complaints in the last two years,"

she said. I heard papers ruffling. "No one accused him of doing anything illegal, just hawking the wrong stocks."

"That's it?" I said.

"That's it about Mendelson." She hesitated. "Your preacher man's another story."

"Oh?" I said.

"It seems that he … never mind. Got a few minutes?"

"Yes."

"I'll be there in ten."

True to her word, ten minutes later, Chief LaMond pulled her navy-blue unmarked city vehicle in my drive. It was a pleasant morning with low humidity, so I'd waited for her on my front step.

"Coffee?" she asked, pointing to Bert's next door and then at my cottage.

I had a pot brewing, so I said that we wouldn't have to go to Bert's to bum one. She said that walking wasn't her favorite hobby and beat me inside.

"Now to the reverend, preacher, minister, or whatever he's called." She took a sip of coffee.

I waited for her to swallow and get comfortable in the chair.

"The boy's a church-birthin' machine," she said. "First Light is the fourth church that Mr. Costello has opened, founded, or whatever you call starting a church. The first reference I could find was about a congregation he begat—like my Bible lingo?—in some small town I've never heard of in southern Mississippi."

She didn't give me a chance to praise her Bible lingo.

"No arrests, no warrants, no problems with the Mississippi cops."

"How long was he there?" I asked.

"That's what's interesting," she said. "Only two years. That doesn't sound long to me."

I agreed.

"Then he popped up next in the part of Florida where you can't see an ocean in any direction; small burg outside Starke. Always wondered why anyone would want to live in the middle of Florida."

"You know where Starke is?" I said.

"Sure, looked it up," Cindy said. "It's a dot smack-dab in the center of the state."

"Any problems there?"

"Not that there's a record of. There was one brief report about some members of the Baptist church being upset that Pastor Burl, as he was called then, was starting a second Baptist church in their town. They didn't like the idea, but their concern seemed to fizzle out."

I was surprised that Burl's church had been Baptist. "It sounds like his church was more mainstream than First Light."

"The first two were. Apparently he started out trying to open name-brand churches. That was until he moved to Indianapolis to birth church number three." She looked around the kitchen. "Got anything to eat?"

"Stale bread and peanut butter," I said. She should have known not to ask.

"Chris, you make Larry look like that culinary guy on television who opens restaurants and fixes the best sauerkraut this side of Baden-Baden."

Thank goodness I had missed that show. I offered to go next door and get something to eat if she'd keep telling her story.

"Nah," she said, going over to the counter. "I woke up this morning hankering for a good slice of stale bread smothered in peanut butter. Don't suppose you have a knife?"

I got up and helped her prepare her culinary delight before we returned to the table and the story.

"The good preacher started a church in a lower-middle-class zip code in Indianapolis. Called it the Way, probably a play on the Indy 500 Speedway; that's my guess. Any*way*—get it, *way*?—the church was going gangbusters, had a hundred members in the first year according to a newspaper story."

"Why was there a story?"

"Hold your spatula," Cindy said. "I'm getting there."

There was no better chance of finding a spatula in my kitchen than there was of finding a grand piano, so I held my coffee mug up.

Cindy took a bite of "breakfast," unfolded a scrap of paper she had in her pocket, and said, "Richard Keen."

I took a bite of nothing and said, "Huh?"

"The late Richard Keen is the reason there were newspaper articles about the church. It seems that Mr. Keen was helping the preacher fix up an old gas station that Keen had donated for their church building. I suppose Indianapolis isn't as warm in January as it is here." She paused and took a sip of coffee.

"What happened?" I knew that the story was going somewhere and hoped she'd get there before getting food poisoning.

"You're getting as impatient as Charles." She grinned. "The concrete-block walls in the garage were nearly thirteen feet high, and the top two rows 'accidentally' fell and conked Mr. Keen on the noggin. Killed him."

"Concrete blocks don't just fall off walls," I said. "What happened?"

"Pastor Burl told the police that Richard accidentally hit the wall with a sledgehammer that he had been using and jarred the blocks off. Richard was the only other person in the garage and wasn't able to make a statement, being as that he was deader than a seven-year-old cricket. The report didn't say it, but if

I'd been investigating the death, I'd be mighty suspicious, but suspicions don't go far when the only account of the accident was from a man of the cloth."

"Sounds similar to Six's accidental death," I said.

Cindy nodded. "Burl closed down the Way, packed up his Bible and collection plate, and moved here two months after the walls came tumbling down."

I didn't tell her that I was impressed by her biblical reference; besides, I couldn't get the image of Six or the thought of how similar his body must have been to Richard Keen's out of my head.

CHAPTER 23

Still in my kitchen, Cindy explained that she had a meeting with the mayor to justify two new patrol cars. She was frustrated with the budgeting process and said that if the council had its way, her officers would be patrolling on skateboards. She asked me to remind her why she had accepted the chief's position, and after I had given her the "you're good for the city" rah-rah speech, she said, "Twaddle." I asked her to share what she had learned about Burl with Detective Callahan, and she said that she had a call in to him. She wiped a smattering of breakfast off her cheek and headed to city hall.

Had Preacher Burl killed the man in Indianapolis? If he had, wouldn't it make sense that he was responsible for the three local deaths? What was his motive?

Thinking about the various scenarios made me miss Charles more than ever. When faced with similar questions in the past, we had bounced ideas off each other. Some of them were terrible, some were plain stupid, and occasionally some were on target. He apparently wasn't going to break the ice, so it was up to me to take the first step.

He was seldom home at eight thirty, but I called anyway, and was pleasantly surprised when he answered. I was less pleased when he recognized my voice and said, "What?" There was nothing pleasant about his tone. I tried to not let his attitude affect me and said that I had learned some things about the deaths that I thought he'd want to know. "What?" he repeated. I suggested that it'd be better if I told him in person. I nearly slammed the phone down when he continued his one-word responses with, "Why?"

"Because I need your help," I said. "I thought we could meet and talk it out better than we can over the phone." For Charles, being needed overcame many evils, and he thawed a miniscule amount. I said that I'd buy him supper, and he reluctantly agreed to meet me at six at the Grill and Island Bar.

I arrived at the popular restaurant at five thirty, knowing that to Charles, that equaled six o'clock. He was already seated on the patio close to the sidewalk. I walked past him to get to the entry, and he didn't look up from his beer to greet me. *This is going to be fun,* I thought.

The owner, Jason, met me at the door and said that Charles told him to have the chef start preparing the most expensive item on the menu and to make sure that I got the check. He laughed and said that he thought that Charles was kidding. I said he probably wasn't and headed out to face the music.

Charles glanced up from his beer. "How's Karen?"

I told him.

"Great," he said. "So, what's so important?" No preamble, no smile, only hurt and anger.

Since it was Saturday, the tables quickly filled. A harried waitress stopped and asked if I wanted anything. I ordered a glass of chardonnay and turned to my borderline hostile friend and shared what Cindy had told me about Burl's church in Indianapolis.

When I finished, Charles stared at me. "So now you're accusing Preacher Burl of killing people all over the country?"

"I'm not saying that," I said. "But doesn't it seem odd that there are now four deaths—four that we know about—that are related to his churches? How would you look at it?"

My wine arrived, and Charles ordered another Budweiser. I asked if he was ready to order supper, and he said, "Later." We watched the waitress leave, and then Charles stared out at Center Street.

"I don't know what I'd say. I don't know what I'd say about anything." He put his fist to his forehead. I waited. Charles shut out the distractions around us as if he was praying. He finally said, "Preacher Burl is a fine man. He's doing lots of good things for many people. Chris, he's a man of God. John Adams said, 'We recognize no sovereign but God, and no king but Jesus.' Preacher Burl speaks the words of Jesus. How could he have anything to do with the deaths? How?"

I felt like a heel. Charles was hurting, and I didn't know how to help other than to say I was keeping the gallery open. I put my hand on his arm and was relieved that he didn't pull away. "Charles, I don't know what's going on, but I thought we could figure it out."

He looked at me and sniffled—perhaps allergies. "I'm not sure I can help. I don't want to change the subject, but I can't get some things off my mind. Here I am in my sixties, and what have I accomplished? If I die tomorrow, who would care? Heather, maybe. And I don't know what to do about her. So why was I put on earth? All I've done is fill space. Why? Why?" He put his head down.

I started to speak but thought it better to remain silent.

He looked up. "God, I miss Melinda."

I squeezed his arm. "I know."

"Then, you think you have to close the gallery, and I hate it."

"I don't want to close, but you know it's a money pit. I'd keep it open if I saw hope, but I don't."

Charles looked down at his second empty beer bottle and then up at me. "I've been thinking. Lord knows I'm not wealthy, never have been, never will be, that's one thing I'm certain of." He grinned. "I haven't touched—well, haven't touched much of—the money poor Margaret Klein left me. Didn't rightly feel like I deserved it." He looked back at the bottle.

Margaret Klein had been an elderly widow who owned the Edge, an oceanfront boardinghouse, and rented rooms at extraordinary discounts to people who couldn't normally afford the luxury of living at the beach. Charles and I had saved her from a brutal killer and a deadly hurricane four years before, and even though she barely knew us, she left each of us a substantial amount of money when she died a few months later. I had used most of mine keeping the gallery afloat.

"You saved her life," I said. "She didn't have any family and wanted you to have the money."

"Anyway," Charles said, "what if I bought the gallery? I think Ms. Klein would think it a good idea."

"Charles, I couldn't—"

He raised the empty bottle close to my face. "Let me finish, please. I'd let you keep your photos in it, and if you want, we can keep the same name. Your photos are better than mine anyway. Heck, I'd let you work there and wouldn't pay you anything. That way you wouldn't have to worry about taxes." He grinned again.

"It'd still lose thousands each month; rent alone eats up big chunks. I couldn't let you take on the expenses."

"What else do you think I have to spend money on?" He waved his cane in the direction of the ocean. "I've lived here decades and haven't spent as much the entire time as people who come over here each summer and rent a condo. Besides, I sort of like the idea of getting business cards that say that Charles Fowler is the owner of something. Why not a photo gallery?"

The waitress returned and asked if we wanted to order. Charles looked at me and up at her. "Believe so." He glanced at the menu and then at me. "You're buying, right?"

And he wants to buy a photo gallery.

His fingers walked down the price column, and he chose the most expensive item. I didn't think he even saw what it was. I stuck with the midpriced flounder. More beer and wine rounded out our order.

The waitress headed toward the kitchen, and Charles said hi to an elderly couple walking along the sidewalk in front of the restaurant, and then he turned back to me. "Will you consider it?"

I didn't have the nerve to shoot him down again and said that I would.

"Good," he said. "Now that that's out of the way, let's figure out what's going on with the dead bodies."

Charles and I finished our supper and each added another drink to the increasing tab and were having a civil conversation, our first in days. The patio was packed, and from my vantage point, I could see several groups waiting for a table. I felt guilty about hogging the valuable real estate but not guilty enough to give it up. Our waitress gave up on nudging us along and focused on other tables. The increased volume of laughter and conversation from the adjoining tables forced me to lean close to hear what Charles was saying.

We talked through everything we had learned about JJ, Six, and Mendelson, and I threw in what Cindy had found out about Burl's church in Indianapolis and the "accidental" death of one of his followers. We agreed on two things. First, if there had only been one death that appeared accidental, it could simply have been a terrible tragedy. Now there were three, regardless what the police or anyone else said, it couldn't be coincidence. Second, we knew that we didn't know much of anything about the victims or, for that matter, about Preacher Burl.

Dude and his look-alike canine companion got Charles's attention as they walked past the patio. If dogs were weapons of mass destruction, Charles could be America's secret defense. He could spot one a mile away with his eyes closed, and that was only a slight exaggeration.

"Dude, whoa!" Charles said as he jumped up and rushed to the wall separating the patio from the sidewalk. "Bring Pluto over so he can give me a kiss."

"Ew," Dude responded. "Bad germs. Make Pluto sick."

Charles waved toward the table. "Join us."

"No way, Chuckster," Dude said. "Pluto's chow time. Gotta be home." He pointed toward the beach. "Be at First Light *mañana?*"

"Probably," Charles said.

Dude squatted down and rubbed Pluto's belly. "Good. Preacherman Burl said be boss to have bunch there."

"Why?" I said, still sitting.

"Being dead lowers numbers," Dude said. "Preacherman wants to show flock still behind church."

"We'll be there for sure," Charles said.

I assumed that I was part of *we*.

"Whoa," Dude said. "There be more."

"What?" Charles asked.

"Sis. Lottie, bro. Sharp, bro. Victor be afearin' for life." Dude nodded like we knew what he was talking about.

"Be afearin'—I mean, afraid of what?" Charles asked. Dude-speak was contagious.

"Attend First Light, end up bye-bye. Who be next? That's what they be afearin'."

I was afraid that's what Dude had meant, and I reassured him that Charles and I would be at the service.

"Who's Victor?" Charles asked after we once again said we would be there.

"Bumster," Dude said. "Helped Sharp and Six with heavy liftin' at church store." Dude reminded us once again that he had to get home to feed Pluto and literally skipped down the sidewalk.

Charles returned to the table and took a sip of his warming beer. "I really like Preacher Burl." He shook his head. "I can't imagine him having anything to do with this."

Bob's strong feelings about Burl and what Cindy had learned about his experiences in Indianapolis were foremost in my mind. "I hope not, but things aren't looking good for him."

Charles looked at Dude, who was now a block away, and then down at his empty bottle. "Ronald Reagan often said, 'Trust, but verify.' It was good enough for him, so I suppose we need to give it a try."

I nodded and realized that it had been more than two hours since Charles had mentioned the gallery. I didn't want tonight's conversation to revert back to it and said that I was tired and had to go but that I'd meet him at the First Light service in the morning.

CHAPTER 24

Charles and I weren't on such good terms as we had been before I told him about closing the gallery, but we'd made progress. He waved good-bye over his shoulder as he headed in the direction of his apartment, and I turned toward home.

Unlike in the off-season when it was easy to cross four-lane Center Street, traffic was heavy, and anyone trying to jaywalk was tempting disaster. I walked two blocks to the nearest crosswalk and waited for a break in traffic. My mind wandered to "Trust, but verify." Excellent advice, but how could we do it?

The traffic coming from off the island eased, and only a couple of cars were moving in the other direction, so I crossed two lanes to the center of the street and paused as the car in the nearest lane to me slowed to stop. I smiled at the festive sounds and live music coming from Planet Follywood and the Crab Shack as I started across the next lane.

Just then a car that had been parked in front of the Crab Shack thirty yards away pulled into the street and accelerated. Its headlights blinded me, and all I knew was that it was loud and barreling toward me.

As I leaned in its path, my only hope of avoiding being hit was to lunge toward the sidewalk. The car was no more than fifteen feet away. I pushed off with my right foot and dove gracelessly toward the curb. The landing would hurt, but it beat the alternative.

My right foot glanced off the bumper of the speeding vehicle at the same time my arms struck the pavement. I hit hard and rolled to the sidewalk. The car continued to accelerate toward the off-island bridge.

Four people on the sidewalk rushed over and asked if I was okay. I was out of the road and immediate danger, so I stayed still as I caught my breath. I wiggled my legs, and both worked with no serious pain. My elbows were scraped, but my arms and hands appeared to function. One of the ladies leaned over and instructed me to remain still, as her husband had called 911.

Another car had stopped at the sidewalk, and now it inched past me and pulled to the curb. The driver, a man in his seventies, rushed over, pointed toward the bridge, and yelled to no one in particular, "The drunken maniac nearly killed that guy!" He pointed at me.

I slowly sat up. My arms burned from sliding along the asphalt, and my foot hurt from its encounter with the bumper. I took a deep breath and was relieved that nothing else hurt.

A Folly Beach police cruiser soon pulled behind me and blocked the lane so no one else could accidently hit me. I recognized Officer Bishop's voice before I saw her.

"Don't move," she said authoritatively. "EMTs are on the way."

I started to say, like most men would, that I was fine, but I realized that I may not have been, so I obeyed. The siren from the fire-and-rescue truck cut through the night air as it left the fire station fewer than two blocks away. I turned, and the lights from the cruiser blinded me, so I put my hand up to block them. Patrons from both Planet Follywood and the Crab Shack clustered on the sidewalk.

Officer Bishop crouched beside me. "You're Mr. Landrum, right?"

I said I was.

"Hold still until the EMTs can check you over," she said and looked toward the bridge. "What happened?"

Before I responded, the gentleman from the car that had stopped pushed his way between two onlookers. "I'll tell you," he shouted. "A damned fool didn't pay one bit of attention to the crosswalk and plowed through like a bat out of hell!"

"What kind of car?" Bishop asked as she stood and ushered the gentleman away from the crowd.

"No idea," he said. "All I saw was that poor guy nearly getting killed by the damned drunk."

The black fire-and-rescue truck pulled in behind Bishop's patrol car, and the same two EMTs who'd been at the scene of Six's death came over. One asked if anything was obviously wrong with me. I said no and started to stand.

"Hold on," the other medic said. "Let me take a look."

I closed my eyes while he professionally rubbed his hands over my legs and arms and asked if anything hurt. My foot felt better, so I said that only the scratches stung, and he said that was good. He felt around my neck and slowly twisted my head and asked if there was any pain. I said no, and he repeated, "Good."

Another patrol car then arrived, and an officer I didn't know asked if anyone in the gathering crowd could identify the car or the driver.

One women said that it had looked like a white Ford; her male companion said it was a Kia. Someone behind them said, "No way, it was a Mazda."

While there appeared to be little agreement on the make of the vehicle, several people said that it had been in front of the

Crab Shack, but no one could say for how long. Its windows were tinted and they couldn't see the driver, but everyone agreed that he had to be drunk. Another lady stepped forward and said it definitely was a Kia because she had one like it. The officer pulled her aside and out of my earshot.

The EMT continued to probe for injuries, and the crowd began to lose interest when it became apparent that I was going to live. Officer Bishop had finished interviewing the driver who had stopped at the crosswalk and a handful of others who had been close to the action. She came over and asked the EMT how I was.

"Lucky," he said as he wrapped bandages around my elbows. "Only some scratches." He offered to have an ambulance take me to Charleston for a more thorough physical. I refused, saying that all I needed was to sit down a few more minutes and then head home. He said it was my call and helped me to the bench in front of Planet Follywood.

Officer Bishop followed and asked for my version of what had happened. I said that the car's headlights were in my face and that I couldn't identify it other than that it was a light color. I couldn't see the driver.

I looked out at the sidewalk and at Officer Bishop.

"There's one more thing," I said, looking down at the sidewalk again. "It wasn't a drunk. It wasn't an accident. Whoever was driving had seen me at the Island Grill, figured that I would be walking home, and parked back there." I pointed to the Crab Shack. "Then he or she waited for a chance to run me down. Officer Bishop, it was intentional."

She protested and told me what the witnesses had said, but I put my hand up, palm toward her, and repeated, "It was intentional."

She stared at me a moment, jotted down a note, and sighed. "Hop in. I'll give you a ride home."

I slowly put weight on each leg and walked to the patrol car. Officer Bishop didn't say much as I gave her directions to the house, but she did say that she would tell Chief LaMond my version of events.

I thanked her, said my good-byes, and headed inside. I first headed toward the refrigerator and the ever-present bottle of chardonnay, but I took a detour to the bedroom, flopped down on the bed, and said a prayer that I was thankful to be saying a prayer. Sleep came mercifully quickly.

CHAPTER 25

The next morning I walked out the front door and gingerly moved down the front steps. So far, so good. My foot ached but not too badly, the scrapes on my elbows and knees stung, and I felt like I'd been hit by a truck. Fortunately, I hadn't even been hit by a light-colored Ford/Kia/Mazda. I was way too old to be taking swan dives on a city street.

I looked left and shaded my eyes from the sun glaring over the ocean. It reminded me of how the oncoming headlights had blinded me. I had no doubt that the driver had targeted me. I had countless doubts as to why. What had I done to anyone? What did I know that was such a threat to the driver? No answers immediately popped in my mind. I was a hundred yards from the beach and fifty more from the First Light church. I stopped, shook my head, looked back toward the center of town, and was thankful that I was walking to church—walking anywhere.

I thought about the reason Dude had wanted Charles and me to attend, but despite last night's near disaster and some recent bumps in the road of my life, I had much to be thankful for. Karen was making a remarkable recovery, and despite Charles's anger and hurt, I had fantastic friends. Yes, much to be thankful for.

When I arrived, the preservice lemonade social was breaking up, and Preacher Burl was herding his flock to temporary seats so he could begin the service. Charles, wearing the same long-sleeved University of Arkansas T-shirt that he had worn the last time we'd been at church, scampered up to me and asked where I had been all morning. He then noticed the bandages on my elbows.

"What happened? I left you in perfect condition."

"Later," I said.

He pointed his cane at my arm. "But—"

"Shall we begin?" Preacher Burl said.

Burl asked us to turn to page seven of the photocopied songbooks, stand, and sing the first three verses of "When Morning Lights the Eastern Skies."

I wasn't familiar with the hymn and didn't attempt to hum, much less sing, along. The First Light flock may have made a joyful noise to the Lord, but I doubted that even a tone-deaf Lord would have called it pretty. I looked around while the gathered worshipers butchered the hymn. Mad Mel and his significant other, Caldwell, were in the row behind me and next to the owner of a local CPA firm whom I recognized but hadn't met. The two elderly couples who had been at the previous service were huddled together trying to sing. They failed miserably. City council member Houston was standing behind the chairs with three people I didn't recognize, and two of the three surfers from the previous service were standing beside their boards with Dude, who was without a surfboard. Lottie and Sharp shared a songbook. And I wondered if one of the devoutly praying flock members had been behind the wheel of last night's potential murder weapon.

Proof that God did answer prayers came when we finished

the song. Preacher Burl said, "Amen," and I suspected it was for us finishing rather than for any liturgical purpose.

Burl held out his arms and lowered them for us to be seated. His robe hung loosely from his shoulders. "Brothers and sisters," he began, and then he paused a few seconds. "Once again we have come under the cloud of death. Brother Six passed away after a tragic accident. None of us know his inner thoughts, but I am as certain as I am that there're fishes in that sea that God had a greater purpose for taking Brothers Six, JJ, and Timothy from us."

He had finally acknowledged JJ's death. The comment also made me wonder what purpose God had for sparing me last night.

Burl gave a dramatic wave toward the Atlantic and returned to the notes on his portable lectern. "Attending church doesn't make you a Christian anymore than standing in a garage makes you a car. Christianity is in your actions. Brother Six gave his talents and time helping prepare the foul-weather sanctuary for you and me. He never asked for anything in return. He exemplified what First Light is. It's people helping people; people helping spread the word of our Lord and Savior; people walking hand in hand with those in need. It is your actions. God loved Six as he loves each of you. Please join me in a silent prayer for our departed brother." He bowed his head and gripped the lectern.

Were those the same words he had used to eulogize the member of the Way in Indianapolis after a similar "tragic accident"?

Burl emoted another amen and looked over the congregation. "Brother William is unable to be here today, and I know you will join me in regret that he will not be able to share with us his glorious voice." He chuckled. "I believe God will understand if we skip the singing that would now normally take place."

Another prayer answered, I thought.

"Brothers and sisters," he said without benefit of a musical interlude, "let me tell you a sad fact. Some people who proclaim to be Christians sneak around and whisper condemnations of First Light. They erroneously say that we are not a 'real' church"—he air quoted *real*. "They spew that we are nondenominational, like that is a word straight from the devil's venomous mouth." He flipped through his notes. "Truth be told, nondenominational churches are the third largest group of churches in this great country. We're only exceeded in followers by Roman Catholics and Southern Baptists. Yes, I know, our critics speak from ignorance. What they really mean is that First Light doesn't worship in the manner that they're accustomed to. We're not constrained by walls, or a rigid structure, or a bureaucracy that has been the downfall of many an organized church."

"Oh, so true," said someone seated behind me.

"Brothers and sisters," Burl continued, "I pray for their enlightenment. I pray that they gain insight into what we stand for. I pray not that they throw off their traditional religions but that they learn to accept us in their hearts for what we are. First Light is for you, the downtrodden, the oppressed, the stepped on, and," he paused and smiled, "even for those of you who have more blessings and fortune than many in our flock combined."

That covered all bases, but I understood what he was saying. And I agreed.

Burl tapped his hand on the lectern. "As the contemporary prophet Joe South said, 'Don't it make you want to go home? All God's children get weary when they roam. Don't it make you want to go home?' First Light is here for the weary, for they are among God's children."

Preacher Burl then made reference to Bible verses to bolster his message—verses that were a couple thousand years older than the words of Joe South. My mind drifted as I wondered how many of those listening knew that Joe South was a singer and songwriter from the 1960s. I doubted that Preacher Burl would quote another of South's ditties, "The Purple People Eater Meets the Witch Doctor."

Burl closed the service with a prayer that was more like the greatest hits from the last forty-five minutes and was nearly as long. Repetition was important to learning, but I was acutely conscious of how hot it was. There wasn't a cloud between us and heaven, and sweat poured out around Preacher Burl's collar. I couldn't see the elderly attendees but figured they were miserable. Even Charles, who had sat in rapt attention, scooted his foot in the sand and pulled the brim of his Tilley down in back to block the sun.

Brother Burl had apparently forgotten how terrible our singing was, and following his final amen, he asked us to join him in singing "The Battle Hymn of the Republic."

Everything bad that I had thought about the length of Burl's final prayer was forgotten with his choice of closing hymn. I loved the Civil War–era lyrics more each time I heard them, and tears came to my eyes when we reached,

> In the beauty of the lilies Christ was born across the sea,
> With a glory in His bosom that transfigures you and me.
> As He died to make men holy, let us live to make men free,
> While God is marching on.

I had spent less than a minute with JJ and had never met Timothy Mendelson or the dead parishioner in Indianapolis. I had only talked briefly to Six. But Burl was right, we were all brothers and sisters under the Lord, and someone was taking our brothers and sisters from us. And now, for some reason, I was in the crosshairs.

The flock quickly scattered. The surfers were back in the waves before I noticed that they had left. The elderly couples rushed slowly to their cars, others hurried to the nearby air-conditioned restaurants. Mad Mel and Caldwell, Dude, Houston, and Lottie and Sharp briefly stopped and asked about Karen and my condition.

"Clumsy me, just scrapes," seemed to satisfy their curiosity about my elbows since their primary interest was Karen.

Charles was in deep conversation with Preacher Burl, and I joined them. Charles said that he had invited the preacher to lunch at Loggerheads and asked if I wanted to go. Charles seldom invited anyone to lunch, so I knew his motives were not quite as pure as those behind the morning's sermon, and I quickly agreed. Lottie and Sharp busied themselves folding chairs and told Burl that they would get everything back to the storefront and wouldn't need him. He gave a halfhearted protest, but with perspiration running down his back, he said he saw the benefits of the air-conditioned restaurant.

Burl asked about my arms, and I gave him the stock answer. He nodded as we made the two-block walk to the elevated restaurant.

Charles glared at me, mouthed, "Later," and, turning back to the preacher, said, "I was terribly saddened to hear about the untimely death of Brother Six."

Charles could make a chameleon green-eyed by his ability to alter his speech and body language to match most anyone's. It was one of his secrets to getting more information out of unsuspecting people. Another one of his secrets was an overabundance of pure luck. At times, I couldn't tell the difference. Burl was his current focus.

The preacher wiped sweat from his forehead and agreed with Charles.

"Did you know him outside church?" I asked while keeping step with Burl and the cane-wielding chameleon.

He shook his head. "Brothers Six and Victor were the first two followers who volunteered to help after Brother Timothy made it possible for us to secure the storefront. I will be forever grateful to them."

We trudged up the restaurant's steps and were told that it would be a twenty-minute wait for an inside table. The hostess said that one was open on the patio, but Burl declined. He had had enough heat. We stood in the shade of the bar and waited.

I hadn't met Victor and didn't think I'd seen him at the storefront, so I asked Burl what his story was.

"Brother Victor was at the first service on Folly, just a year ago, come to think of it. He came a lot at first." Burl leaned closer and spoke in a lower tone. "He had anger issues, demons. I never pried into his past, but I got the impression that he has had more than casual contacts with the law. I pray for him daily. Now back to your question, after we acquired the storefront, he and Brother Six were always there, always working, cleaning, scraping, painting, doing whatever needed to be done."

I still couldn't picture him. "Was he here today?"

"No," Burl said. "He's in and out. Establishing roots is a foreign concept to many who find First Light. Brother Victor is a drifter and will always be."

"Were Six and Victor friends?" Charles asked.

Burl smiled. "Funny thing. They were at always each other's

throats. Both had short fuses, but despite their sniping, they seemed close."

"Six told us that he had a drinking problem and that you were responsible for his kicking the habit," I said.

"The Lord gets the credit," Burl said. "All I did was point out that there was another way for him to live. I think that may be why Six and Victor were close. I had the impression that Victor had gone down a similar path, but I don't know if he kicked the habit. Why the curiosity about Brother Six and Brother Victor?"

I looked at Charles. He looked at the bar. And Preacher Burl waited.

Finally, Charles said, "No reason, really. I didn't know Six well and was thinking about him during the service. Sorry he's gone."

It was a poor explanation, but luckily the hostess came for us before he had to elaborate.

The dining room was still packed, and the noise of happy customers and the multiple televisions made it difficult for two semielderly citizens and one middle-aged preacher to hear one another, but that didn't stop Charles from trying.

"Tell us more about you," he said, leaning into Burl's personal space. "I've never known anyone who started a church."

The waitress appeared, and Burl ordered two glasses of water and a Mediterranean wrap. The disruption had thrown Charles's interrogation off, and he quickly ordered a burger without looking at the menu. I stuck with a chicken-finger basket and waited for Charles to get back to learning more than anyone should know about the minister seated across the table.

Burl smoothed his mustache and smiled. "Brother Charles, you are inquisitive, aren't you?"

He had said the same thing about me.

"Only about things I'm interested in, Preacher," Charles said. "You're a fascinating person, so yes, I'm inquisitive." He tilted his head in my direction. "My friend here would say nosy."

I laughed. "Amen to that."

Burl chuckled. "Okay, but stop me when boredom arrives."

"Deal," Charles said.

Our drinks arrived, and Burl downed the first glass in two gulps.

"I was reared on a small cattle farm in southern Illinois," he said. "Nothing special. Dad did enough to get by. It's where I learned to work from dawn until dark. I didn't take much to the farming but enjoyed working with my hands, especially in carpentry. Mom and Dad didn't much cotton to churchgoing, so I didn't get exposed to the Lord and his work until I dated a minister's daughter from a town a stone's throw away." He took a smaller sip of water and chuckled. "Before you ask, not all preachers' kids are wild. I couldn't manage to get as much as a peck on the cheek out of Sadie until we had dated for six months."

He closed his eyes and slowly shook his head. I suspected that he was reliving that memorable peck.

"When did you decide to be a preacher?" I asked. I wanted to move the story along before Charles could ask a thousand questions about Sadie, her church, her friends, and about each of their dates.

"I was in my third year of college in California. Sadie was a distant memory, but I had held on to studying the Bible and doing the work of the Lord. Students could attend the Golden Gate Seminary while they were still taking undergraduate classes elsewhere. Killing two doves at the same time." He chuckled again.

Charles and I smiled to let him know that we caught the joke—weak as it was.

"That's impressive," Charles said. "Working on two degrees at the same time."

"Umm, yes," Burl said. "I was honored to get to know some people in school from Mississippi, and together we started a tiny church there. It was a wonderful opportunity; I could spread the word of the Lord and spread my wings at the same time. I was sad to have to leave."

"What happened?" Charles asked.

"The church ran out of steam when some of the members decided to attend a large church a few miles away, and, umm, we had to shut down."

"That's too bad," I said.

"It was God telling me to move on, and while I didn't believe it at the time, it was for the best."

Our food then arrived, and Burl vigorously attacked his wrap. Charles, to his credit, waited until Burl had taken three bites and wiped his mustache with his napkin before continuing his questions.

"Why for the best?"

"Moved to Florida," Burl said. "The hand of God sent me to another small town, this one near Starke, and prayer led me to open a church there. It was a gleeful experience, preaching the gospel, touching souls, watching God's miracles." He put his hand over his face. "And then lightning struck."

"What happened?" Charles asked again.

Burl pointed to the ceiling. "Honest to God, lightning struck. Saturday night, the seventeenth of October, the devil got his way." He held out his hands, palms up. "The church building, the building that I built with these callused hands, was gone in minutes. Then two days later, I had a heart attack and nearly left this flawed earth."

"We're glad you lived," Charles said.

Now I asked, "What happened?"

"I had nearly died, my church was gone, and I'm ashamed to say, so was my faith. I left organized religion, or should I say, it left me."

Yet here he was, Preacher Burl Ives Costello, founder of Folly Beach's First Light Church, starter of two churches that no longer existed, and he hadn't said anything so far about the Way in Indianapolis—in my mind, the only link between four murders. Interesting.

CHAPTER 26

Before long, the tables closest to us emptied, and we could talk without shouting. Burl had finished both glasses of water and asked for a refill. Charles had worked his magic, and the preacher seemed comfortable talking about his past. After he had shared that his second church had been destroyed by lightning, Charles had bemoaned how terrible that was. I'd heard stories of churches that had suffered both natural and manmade disasters and how their dedication to rebuilding had made them better than ever. Yet, Burl had moved on after the first church left him, and then he had left the second church when it burned.

"What did you do then?" Charles asked.

Burl shook his head. "Believe it or not, I did a little bartending to make ends meet. Not much different from preaching with all the listening and talk about spirits." He paused to smile. "Then I hooked up with a man from Orlando who called himself a good Christian. He said he needed other Christians to sell beauty products to ladies who couldn't afford the high-priced products sold in salons. He said that every woman deserved to look as good as the wealthy ladies."

"Did you have a store?" Charles asked.

"No, I sold them door-to-door and was asked to recruit other good Christians to help spread the word about the products."

"Like Amway?" I asked.

"That's what I first thought," Burl said. "And I learned a lesson that turned my life around, again."

"What was that?" Charles asked.

"When I was growing up, Dad would say, 'You are what you do, not what you think or say.' He was big into music and said he got the line from a song. In fact, that's where he got my name. Took it from his favorite singer, Burl Ives."

Charles straightened in his chair. "'A Little Bitty Tear,' 1962."

Burl smiled. "That's the one. Anyway, Dad said that people are always saying 'I'm going to do something' or 'I think I'm going to do something,' but all the talk and thinking won't put food in the cow's belly." He took a sip of water. "Dad's words flowed back to me when I realized that just because someone says, says, and says again that he's a Christian doesn't make it so."

"Going to church, not Christian; man in garage, not car," Charles interjected.

Burl smiled. "Ah, you did listen to the sermon."

"Of course."

Burl continued, "It took me five months to figure out that the man didn't care if his beauty products worked; all he wanted was to con folks into buying crates of it and con more folks into recruiting other unsuspecting good Christians into doing the same. He professed to be a Christian to get others to fall for his pitch."

"A pyramid scheme?" I said.

"Exactly," Burl said.

"What happened then?" Charles asked.

"One afternoon on the way to an appointment to sell a trusting lady a box of worthless face cream, I heard a voice in my head and pulled my Buick Roadmaster to the side of the road. I realized that the voice was really me reminding my sinning self what I already knew. I was born to minister, not to sell crap, excuse my language. I realized the reason my first two churches had irritated God was I was trying to fit into the traditional mold, trying to make them like all other churches rather than ministering to the sick, downtrodden, the lost souls, those who had been inoculated against traditional religion."

Charles nodded. "Thomas Jefferson said, 'I do not find in orthodox Christianity one redeeming feature.'"

Burl frowned at Charles. I was used to my friend pulling obscure presidential quotes out of the air. Charles had claimed to have read every book in his house except the cookbooks; I suspected there were hundreds of quotes by presidents among the millions of words surrounding him. They probably also contained quotes from Shakespeare, the Buddha, and Daffy Duck, but he hadn't started dropping those into conversation—yet.

"Brother Charles," Burl said, "I don't have the intellectual capacity to be challenging Brother Thomas, but I wouldn't go that far. I was trying to be part of a church where words like Baptist, Presbyterian, or Methodist said what they were. Those and all the other wonderful denominations provide life, support, and hope for millions of people. But they aren't me, and by trying to make my church like them, I wasn't *doing*, I was only *saying* and *thinking*."

Charles held out both hands, "I'm not agreeing with good ol' Tom J. I'm just sharing his thought."

I thought this had gone on long enough, so I repeated Charles's question: "Then what happened?"

Burl smiled. "I rolled down my window and threw my

last two boxes of face cream in the ditch. I prayed for God to forgive me for littering and turned the car north and headed to wherever God was to send me. For reasons I never questioned, I ended up in the fine city of Indianapolis, Indiana."

I knew some of what happened there—thank you, Cindy—but wanted to get Burl's take. "Did you start a church?"

Burl took a bite of wrap and leaned back in the chair. "In fact, Brother Chris, I did. With the help of God and some citizens I met at a homeless shelter, quite frankly, where I went to get a meal, I started holding services in a nearby park. It didn't take long to see that the weather wasn't going to be as accommodating as it had been in Florida, so with answered prayers and a few hundred dollars my new friends donated, we were able to acquire a sanctuary in an old filling station not far from the famed Motor Speedway."

"So," Charles said, "First Light was born?"

"No and yes," Burl said. "Unlike my first two churches, my—our church in Indiana was nondenominational. I didn't want the rules, regulations, constraints, and biases of the traditional churches to interfere with what I knew God wanted me to do. I would love to have taken credit for its name, the Way, but that goes to one of my flock, Richard Keen, God rest his soul. Brother Richard was mildly retarded and from a large extended family. He had tried every church in the area and finally found a home with us. He said that his parents and even his brother and sister were upset about his attending, but he was at every service. Notwithstanding his intellectual shortcomings, he came to me after one of the first services and said that since we were meeting near the famed Indy racetrack, perhaps we could drop *Speed* from Speedway and name the church the Way. I thought it was God inspired and told him so."

My right leg was cramping, so I stretched it out as far as I could without kicking Burl.

Charles being Charles, the collector of trivia and an outstanding listener said, "Did something happen to Keen? You said, 'God rest his soul'?"

"Yes, Brother Charles, Brother Richard passed." He opened his mouth to say something else, but he paused before adding, "The Way grew more rapidly than I could have imagined. We had more than a hundred regular worshipers after the first year."

I thought *passed* was a bit of an understatement since Richard Keen had been killed by concrete blocks to the head when Burl was with him. I didn't know how to bring his death back into the discussion, and Burl clearly wanted to move on.

I had shared with Charles what Cindy had said about Burl leaving Indianapolis under the cloud of suspicion, so I wasn't surprised when he said, "If the Way was going well, how come you're here?"

Burl's eyes darkened, and his mouth formed a tight line. At first I didn't think he was going to respond.

"The part of town where the Way was located was conservative. Within a mile of our sanctuary there was at least one church of every denomination. Our unorthodox approach rubbed some area residents raw. I suspected that one or more of the area ministers egged their congregations along, but I couldn't prove it. Even if I could have, I was in no position to affect change in their hearts." He shook his head. "I was a coward. I felt it best to move on rather than fight. And now I am here."

"We're a far piece from Indianapolis," Charles said. "Why Folly?"

"Don't laugh," he said and smiled. "God spoke to me through an Iranian clerk at a convenient store in Jeffersonville, Indiana."

I had grown up directly across the Ohio River from Jeffersonville and thought this was getting interesting. I leaned closer to Burl and asked, "How?"

"I was headed back to Florida, maybe to start another church, maybe to go back to construction, when I stopped for fuel for my car and myself. When I paid for the gas and two candy bars, I asked the clerk how long it would take me to get to Florida. It was loud in the store, and he thought I'd said Folly and got a big grin on his face. He said he loved Folly and hoped to move there someday. I told him that I'd never heard of it and asked where it was. He pulled a map of the southeastern United States off the shelf and pointed to it."

Burl chuckled, and I waited for him to say it was the will of God that he was here. Instead, he continued, "I figured, why not? Didn't have anywhere to go in Florida. So I paid for the gas and candy, bought the map, and headed toward South Carolina. I spent the night in Columbia and pulled onto this magical island before noon. I realized that I was hungry and stumbled upon Bert's Market and the door that changed my life."

"Door?" Charles said.

"God works in mysterious ways, Brother Charles," Burl said. He mimed pulling two doors open. "Bert's two glass doors. When I first saw them, as I walked into the tiny shopping emporium, I knew that if there were members of God's flock on Folly Beach who needed nontraditional worship opportunities, this was where they could be reached. And, on the same doors, there was a handwritten note seeking a renter for a charming dollhouse-like apartment slightly off the beach. I figured that meant a tiny dump with no view, but God had led me to Bert's and to the notice, so it was meant to be. Besides, I couldn't afford anything better. I pulled the note off the door, jotted down the phone number, and turned the paper over and printed in big letters: 'Come say hi to God, Sunday, eleven o'clock, on the beach near the pier. Come as you are. *All* are welcome.' I stuck the note back on the door and prayed."

"Did anyone show up?" Charles asked.

Burl raised his hand over his head. I glanced around the room; no one appeared to notice or care.

"Yes, praise the Lord!" he exclaimed. "First Light Church was born with five people plus a humble preacher. Victor and a young woman whose name I can't remember were there, more out of curiosity than a calling from the Lord, I would guess." Burl looked at me and turned to Charles and giggled. "Your friend Dude sat quietly through the service and told me later that the only reason he came was to say a few words to his sun god and sit in a chair while he did it. Of course, he didn't use that many words. I told him that was as it should be and that he could worship any god he wished as long as he kept peace in his heart and gained strength from the experience. He said, 'Cool,' and has been to most every service since."

"That be Dude," Charles said.

Burl laughed. "Two surfers sat off to the side on their surfboards. After I finished, they told me that they had been frustrated by the calm ocean and sat through the sermon as they waited for the waves to pick up. I told them that God often calmed the waves in life that people were struggling to overcome. They asked me to put in a good word to him to throw a few big ones their way."

"Did you part the sea for them?" Charles said. "Make boss waves, as Dude would say?"

Burl smiled. "I said that I'd try but not to get their hopes up. They said that I was nicer than most preachers, and they've become semiregulars."

"Sounds like a good start," I said.

"I was blessed," Burl said. "We haven't grown by leaps and bounds, but we've had steady growth and more acceptance on this little slice of heaven than I would have ever expected. By the next Sunday, Sister Lottie and Brother Six, God rest his soul, had shown up along with three couples who said that they had gone to one of the other churches for years but thought First Light sounded like more fun. I didn't wish to discourage them but made it clear that fun wasn't the main reason that we were worshiping. The next couple of months, several others became regulars. Brothers Mel and Caldwell, Sharp, a couple more surfers, and, well, so many others whose names I can't remember."

"What about JJ?" I asked.

"He was a strange one," Burl said. "I didn't remember his name until someone reminded me about him the other day. The thing I remember most was that he appeared more interested in the past than in the present." Burl spread his arms to emphasize that we were in the present, or else he was practicing his breast stroke. "In hindsight, I did have a couple of conversations with him. I think I told you about his interest in Leviticus."

I nodded.

"The other time he wanted to know about my church in Indianapolis. I don't know how he knew about it since I hadn't mentioned it in my services. Again, interest in the past."

"What kind of questions?" Charles asked.

"Nothing special," Burl said. "Thanks for coming to church today. I was afraid—"

"Some examples?" Charles interrupted.

I knew that he wouldn't have let the preacher get by with "nothing special."

"Umm ..." Burl stroked his chin. "Like how many members

I had." He smiled. "Oh yeah, here's a strange one. He wondered if I had any trouble when I was there. Strange, huh?"

"What kind of trouble?" I asked.

"He didn't say. I told him there wasn't any trouble, and he let it go. Again, thanks for coming today. As I started to say, I was afraid that with the tragic deaths our ministry has suffered, some in need of pastoral care would avoid attending. My fears were unfounded, thank God."

That was twice that he had steered away from talking about JJ, and this was new information about what he'd talked about with JJ. Otherwise, his story was consistent with what he had said earlier.

"When did Timothy Mendelson start attending?" I asked.

"A few months ago," Burl said. "Brother Timothy was a true gift from God. His legacy will carry us forward, praise the Lord."

I wondered what that meant. Charles not only wondered, he asked.

Burl looked down at the table and up at Charles. "Umm, he wanted us to be secure even if something happened to him."

"Did he leave First Light something in his will?" Charles asked.

"He perhaps found it in his heart to do so; I'm not certain." Burl abruptly turned to me. "Forgive me for not asking sooner. How is Sister Karen's recovery?"

I told him the same story that I had repeated to everyone who had asked in the last day or so, and he said that he was praying for her and that I should let him know if there was anything he could do.

He looked at his watch. "Oh my, where has time gone? Sorry, I must be going. I have to minister to one of my elderly followers. He's expecting me at his house."

Burl halfheartedly offered to get the check, and Charles generously told him that I would take care of it. We then watched the minister squeeze between the other tables on his way out.

"The good reverend sure got in a hurry to talk about Karen and leave when the topic of Mendelson's legacy came up," Charles said.

I watched Burl go down the stairs. "About as quickly as he brushed over what happened in Indianapolis and the suspicious death."

"Is he for real?"

"Don't know," I said.

"Later is now," Charles said.

"Huh?" Charles's transitions were as smooth as Mt. Everest.

He pointed at my elbow. "Let's hear about 'clumsy me, just scrapes.' And remember, you just came from church."

He deserved the truth, and even if he didn't, he'd find out somehow. It'd be much worse if he didn't hear it from me. I walked through everything that had happened after we went our separate ways the night before. He interrupted only three thousand times before I finished; approximately half the interruptions were variations on the question, "Are you certain it was intentional?"

The common thread in each of my answers was *absolutely*.

CHAPTER 27

I spent the next morning photographing Charleston's narrow and stunningly beautiful avenues south of Broad Street. The seawall and promenade called the Battery, White Point Garden adjacent to it, and the stately antebellum homes that overlooked both comprised one of the country's most historic areas, and it probably offered more photo opportunities than any other spot of equal size anywhere.

Some people escaped the trials and tribulations of the real world with golf. Others escaped with strenuous activities like skiing, skydiving, or an ungodly obsession with running. Photography was my escape, and while it usually worked, this morning was the exception. Every time I saw a tourist crossing a street, my mind flashed back to JJ and his last moments and my narrow escape from the same fate two nights before. Each time I passed one of the majestic churches, I thought of Preacher Burl's humble gatherings and my misgivings about his motives. And each time I saw one of the many painters on extension ladders refreshing the façade of one of the stunning homes, I thought of Six's lifeless body in the storefront.

By ten o'clock, I surrendered. I was mad, and walking around with the camera viewfinder to my eye wasn't helping, so I drove two miles to the hospital. My heart stopped when

I entered Karen's room and found it empty. I rushed to the nurses' station and was told that she had been taken for X-rays and had tried to convince the aide that she could walk rather than being transported by wheelchair. I realized that I didn't know if I could take more bad news. My anger was now heavily seasoned with fear.

A frown on Karen's face turned to a smile when she came back and saw me waiting. She gently pushed herself out of the wheelchair and turned to the middle-aged aide holding the device. "Next time, I'm walking," she said.

The aide rolled her eyes. "Just following orders, Miss Karen." She backed the wheelchair out the door.

"They treat me like a danged invalid," Karen said.

I walked over and kissed her on the cheek. "Such a lovely invalid."

She rammed her fist into my arm. "I'm not helpless. You've got to spring me from this joint!"

Instead of getting back in bed, she lowered herself into the chair and smoothed her hospital gown over her legs.

I didn't think springing a police detective from the hospital was a good idea and instead asked how much longer she'd be there. She said that she'd gotten more information out of her most reluctant doctor but shared that he had mentioned that she might be able to go home in two or three days. I said that was great, she said it was an eternity and that I wouldn't think it so great if I were stuck in this god-awful hospital room.

After she vented about the extended hospital stay, she asked how I was doing. I told her that I thought the three deaths on Folly and the death in Indianapolis were connected. I didn't mention what had happened to me or explain why I was wearing a long-sleeved shirt. This was a tactical error on my part. She gave me a look that made the glare she had flung at the aide pushing her wheelchair seem downright pleasant.

Karen slammed her right hand on the chair's arm. "Chris, dammit, leave it alone. Detective Callahan is working the Mendelson case, the one that's actually a homicide."

"Karen, he's good, but even he agreed that there's a chance that the two other deaths might not be as they appear. Add the one in Indianapolis and there's a better chance of winning the lottery than of them being unrelated."

She glared at me. "And you shared all that with Callahan and Chief LaMond."

Her dad must have already told her my concerns. "Yes."

"And they're taking it seriously?"

"Said they were."

"And they're the trained professionals with resources at their disposal?"

She'd backed me into a corner, but I wasn't ready to give up.

"Yes, they'll do whatever possible. But they're busy. Callahan's working other cases; Cindy has a department to run. There's no harm in my asking questions, looking for a possible connection among the victims. I'm not stupid enough to try to catch the killer."

Karen shook her head and smiled. "History says otherwise."

"Ancient history," I said, but I realized how feeble it had sounded.

"Will you promise not to put yourself in danger?" she asked.

"I promise that if I learn anything, I'll call Detective Callahan or the chief."

We both knew that didn't answer her question.

Two deputies from Karen's office stuck their heads in and asked if she was entertaining visitors. She waved them in, and I got up to leave to give her time to visit. She said that we'd talk about it further.

I had no doubt that we would, but I still wasn't going to back off.

***

An hour later I was home, had changed into a more comfortable short-sleeved shirt, and was stretching my aching legs. The scrapes on my elbows and knees were healing nicely, so I had trashed the bandages. I realized that I'd been on the go since my fateful walk with JJ. It felt good to rest, and then the phone rang.

"Are you still alive? Getting into trouble? On Folly?" Bob asked before I could say hello.

I said, "Yes, no, yes," to Mr. Congeniality.

There was silence; I guessed that he was figuring out which answer went to which question. "Meet me at Rita's and I'll let you buy me an early supper. Got to meet a client in an hour, so hurry." The phone went dead.

It was in the upper eighties, so Bob was seated inside at one of the window booths. His wrinkled camp shirt was sweat stained, and he was breathing heavily. A half-eaten plate of fries was in front of him with an empty Budweiser bottle to its side.

"About time," he said. "What'd you do, stop for ice cream?"

I smiled, set my Tilley on the bench beside me, and took one of his fries. "Going to sell an overpriced house?" I asked.

"Of course, but that's not why I called. All I wanted to know was how the lovely, she-of-bad-taste-in-men detective was doing."

"You could have asked over the phone," I said.

"Yeah, but I wouldn't have gotten a free meal."

Despite his bluster, Bob was a good friend. He just enjoyed

pestering me. At least I hoped so, because he spent a lot of time doing it. He was concerned about Karen, and I suspected about the deaths and my involvement too. He would never have admitted it, but I knew he worried about my friends and me. I gave him the update about Karen, including how much she wanted to get out of the hospital and what a hard a time she was giving the staff.

"Smuggle her in a bazooka," he said. "She could blast her way out."

I told him that he had been watching too much television.

He pointed at my right arm leaning on the table. "What happened?"

I looked down at it like I hadn't noticed anything wrong and gave my clumsy-me answer.

"And I'm supposed to believe that drivel," he said. "What—" He waved his hand in my face. "Never mind. Has that damn preacher been harassing her?"

The waitress brought Bob a second beer. He ordered two barnyard burgers and pointed to me as he told the waitress that I might want something and to make sure that I got the check. I ordered fish and chips and a chardonnay, and the waitress left before Bob could buy everyone in the restaurant a drink, on me.

Bob had strong opinions about most everything, but I had never heard him as vociferous about anything as he was about Burl.

"What's your problem with Burl?" I asked. "He's been to the hospital several times, he's got a loyal following, and he doesn't seem to be harming anyone." I didn't want to share that I suspected he was a murderer.

Bob stuffed three more fries into his mouth, glanced out the window, and turned back to me. He exhaled almost like the air was being let out of him as he slumped.

"Dad died when I was in the tenth grade," he said in a quiet voice—for him, anyway. "Massive heart attack. Was only forty-two. He was a successful insurance broker. We lived in a small rural farming community, and Dad was at the top of the economic food chain."

"That's terrible," I said, wondering what it had to do with Burl.

Bob stared out the window. "Yeah. We were devastated, especially Mom. She was in a fog. At the time, I thought she was just sad. She was probably suffering from acute depression and was maybe even suicidal, but as a sixteen-year-old, I couldn't see beyond my own nearsighted world." He turned to me. "Anyway, three months later our little village was *honored* with a visit from a dynamic, charismatic, and I guess to women, handsome preacher. All I remember about him was he had a mouth full of pearly white teeth. Isn't it terrible that that's all I can remember?"

I shrugged.

Bob picked up two more fries and then put them back on the plate. "The pearly-white-toothed preacher pitched a tent on the edge of town, a big ol' damn circus tent, and a huge sign inviting everyone to his nightly revival services. Mom was at her lowest and thought that a revival of her spirit and rededication to the Lord would be the answer to her loss." Bob's hand balled into a fist. "The damned weasel pounced on her like a raptor on a three-legged chipmunk. And she wasn't alone. The fraud convinced two other widows that God had told him to build a glorious temple unto the Lord right there in our little town. I didn't know a hell of a lot, but I sure as shit knew that the Lord wouldn't have picked a field full of chiggers and prickly weeds in the middle of Nowhere, USA, for some smooth-talking scoundrel to build a temple."

The waitress interrupted Bob to see if we needed anything. Bob ordered a third beer, and I asked for more water.

When she left, Bob continued, "The faker slathered on the praise; told the ladies how God had sent him to them and how great an honor it would be if they helped him find a way to honor God's wishes." Spit spewed from his mouth. "Mom was told that her donations to the building fund would be repaid many times over, and while I doubted he used these words, he told her that God was personally paying attention like he had an adding machine in the sky."

He turned back toward the window and stared out. I didn't know what to say and was relieved when the waitress returned with our drinks. His attention finally drifted back to me.

"You're a bright fellow, Chris. Venture to guess what happened next?"

"Your mother gave him most, hopefully not all, of her money, and the preacher skipped town."

Bob slowly nodded. "All of it."

"I'm sorry," I said.

"The devil was not only in the damned rogue, he was also in the details," Bob said barely above a whisper. I leaned closer to hear. "Two days, forty-eight hours, before Dad's heart attack, he took out a second mortgage on our house so he could buy some stock that couldn't lose. He stashed the money in a savings account until he could get with his broker. That never happened and the money was still in the account when he died. So, not only did the damned charlatan convince Mom to give him Dad's large nest egg, as he called it, he convinced her to give him everything in savings, although she didn't know that a big chunk was from the second mortgage that would have to be repaid. The man cleaned my dear, sweet, gullible mother out of everything, and I mean everything. Fortunately, Dad had a life insurance policy that covered his first mortgage, but it covered none of the second mortgage or his nest egg."

"That's terrible, Bob."

He lowered his head and mumbled, "That's why I decided to get a degree in economics. Never wanted to be caught ignorant about money." He took a long swig of beer.

"I see why you'd be dubious of Burl," I said, stating the obvious, but I felt I needed to say something. "Did anyone try to catch the preacher?"

"Chris," Bob said as he set his bottle back on the table, "we're talking nearly sixty years ago. Our three-man police force wouldn't have known which way to turn. There wasn't any instant communication or easy way to track him. He was gone—poof! And Mom was broke and broken; her spirit, faith, and will to live left with the damned faker."

I shook my head.

"The town was tiny," Bob continued, "about the size of Folly without vacationers. There were four churches there when I was born; the same four are there today. Lord no, they're not perfect, and I seriously doubt any of them have a monopoly on God's master plan, but by God, they're still there ministering to the people." Bob looked at the beer bottle and picked at the label. Then he looked up at me. "The Baptist church was there for my mother's funeral six months after the bastard stole everything." He stared at the passing traffic for a moment before turning back to me. "Do I know if First Light and your Preacher Burl are different? Hell no, but I will say the same thing if you ask if I'll trust him farther than I can throw my car." Bob looked at his watch. "Crap, I'm late for my appointment." He pushed the table away and inched his way out of the booth. He patted me on the shoulder. "It was nice listening to you jabber on about nothing."

He turned and was gone.

CHAPTER 28

I felt a pang of guilt as I walked by the gallery on my way to peek in First Light's window. Should I have reconsidered closing? Sure, I could have scraped by, but why should I? Were Charles's feelings the only reason to keep the door open? I pushed those thoughts out of my mind when I saw Lottie and Sharp rearranging the large pews to make more room for chairs behind them.

Since they had been active in the church nearly from the beginning, I figured they were my best chance of learning something, anything, that might help me figure out who had a motive for killing JJ, Timothy, and Six and trying to add me to the list.

"Ah, help has arrived," Sharp said with a smile as he lowered his end of the heavy pew.

"Praise the Lord," Lottie said, plopping down on the pew. Her long hair appeared to have received about as much attention as I had given to thinking about why God created mosquitoes.

The air conditioner roared, but the temperature was still in the eighties, and the room smelled musty. I said that I only had a few minutes so that I wouldn't get sucked into a day of physical labor, heaven forbid. Lottie smiled and said that I didn't look like I could be much help anyway and that they needed a break, and she asked me to join them on the pew. I think I was insulted, but let it go—it beat work.

I bragged about how much they'd achieved.

"We don't have anything else to do," Sharp said. "No jobs here."

"Don't let him fool you," Lottie said as she brushed her hair out of her eyes. "He'd be here anyway. He loves Preacher Burl and his ministry."

Sharp gave her a cross look. "It's something to do. And I sure don't feel the same way you do about Preacher Burl."

Her head jerked toward Sharp. "What's that mean? The preacher saved me from myself and a life I hated. I owe him."

Sharp smiled. "You're sweet on him and you know it."

Lottie's face turned red, possibly from the heat, but I'd have put money on her blushing.

"That's … not true," she said, unconvincingly. "He's a father figure. He—"

"He's only seven years older than you," Sharp said, leaning forward. "Father figure?"

Lottie ignored Sharp and turned to me. "Okay, maybe he's more like my big brother. My home life sucked, that's why I got out as soon as I could. Dad was a drunk and Mom was, don't know, just always seemed out of it. I didn't have a big brother to take care of me. Preacher Burl is not only there for spiritual guidance," she pointed to Sharp and then around the room like the other followers were seated in the pews, "but I feel that he'd be there if I needed protecting. Know what I mean?"

I said yes.

She again pointed at Sharp while looking at me. "He wouldn't understand. His childhood was different." She turned to him as if it was his turn to speak.

He took the hint. "Sister Lottie thinks I'm a freak because I had a normal childhood, whatever that means."

"Not a freak," she said, "just not like any I know of. His parents weren't divorced, not on drugs, had a nice brother and sister, dad worked, mom stayed home with the kids. They probably had a white picket fence in front of their pretty white house with green shutters and yellow flowers by the front porch. That ain't the normal I know. You know anybody with a childhood like that?"

My childhood wasn't far from that except I didn't have siblings, but I understood what she was saying.

"Sister Lottie has a potent imagination," Sharp said. "All I've ever said to her was that we lived in a quiet neighborhood and that my dad worked. We didn't have much money, and yes, I had a brother and sister and a bunch of aunts, uncles, and cousins, something Lottie seems to have been deprived of, but all wasn't normal with them either."

Lottie stood and shook a finger in Sharp's face. "All I'm saying is I look at Brother Burl as the father, or brother, that I never had. I'm not sweet on him; he's my preacher, for God's sake!"

"You talk about him all the time," Sharp said.

"I'm worried about him," she said.

"Why?" I asked.

Lottie returned to her seat and looked toward the front door. "Rumor I heard at Bert's is that some do-gooder townies are saying that the deaths of Brother JJ, Brother Timothy, and," she glanced in the corner where the ladder had fallen, "Brother Six were hooked together."

"That's absurd," Sharp said. "How could that be?"

"It isn't," Lottie said. "But all it takes is a few devil-planted rumors for him to slip into people's minds and convince them of the impossible. Everyone knows that Brother JJ was hit by someone consumed with alcohol, and Brother Six," Lottie pointed to the corner and put her hands on her face.

I sat back, glanced at the corner, looked back at Sharp and Lottie, and realized that I was probably the townie who had started the rumor. What could I say?

"That's why we, I, appreciate you and Brother Charles attending church the other day." Lottie saved me from commenting, but this made me feel guiltier. "I'm afraid that if the numbers start going down because of stupid rumors, you know, people being afraid that something might happen to them, Preacher Burl might have to leave. If he did, the devil would do a victory dance right there on the beach."

"I don't know about that," I said. "And I don't know about Six's death, but JJ's wasn't an accident."

"We figured that was why you asked us the other day if we knew a connection between Brother Mendelson and Brother JJ," Lottie said.

She and Sharp leaned in my direction.

"How do you know it wasn't?" Sharp asked.

"I was there," I said.

"Thought someone said that was you," Lottie said. "Did you see who did it?"

I told them that I had been beside JJ but didn't get a look at the driver.

I realized as I was saying it that Lottie and Sharp had already known about my suspicions. Could that have been enough reason to want me out of the way? Did one of them think that I may have been able to identify him or her?

"Did either of you tell anyone what I was hinting at?" I asked as casually as possible.

Sharp turned to Lottie and back at me. "After you said what

you did, I started thinking who might have known more about them, so I asked Preacher Burl, and then Victor. I told Saylor. May have told some of the others."

"Who's Saylor?" I asked.

"One of the surfers," Sharp said.

"Okay, how about you, Lottie?" I asked.

"I mentioned it to Dude." She tilted her head. "It wasn't a secret was it?"

"No," I said, still trying to keep my intentions low-key since one of them could have been behind the wheel of both cars.

"I can't believe it," Lottie said. "Who would want to hurt Brother JJ?"

Sharp shook his head. "Probably because of all his nosiness. Maybe he got some answers he didn't need to know."

"He did ask a heap of questions," Lottie said.

"I still can't see a connection between JJ and Mendelson," Sharp said. "Didn't know either of them much, but Brother Mendelson was as rich as a king, and Brother JJ was as broke as, well, just broke. They could've run into each other here since Brother Mendelson was paying for it, but Brother JJ wasn't around enough to leave an impression."

I turned to Lottie.

"Can't think of anything," she said. "I still can't get my arms around what you said about Brother JJ. Not that I don't believe you, and I hope you don't take offense, but what do the cops think?"

"No offense taken," I said. "The police don't have any evidence that I know of that JJ and Six's deaths were anything but accidents, but they're suspicious about their both being followers of the church."

"See," Lottie said, "that's exactly what I was afraid of. It's just what the devil wants, people casting aspersions on Preacher Burl."

I mentioned during the conversation that there were two pieces of the puzzle that they weren't aware of, pieces that strengthened my conviction: the "accidental" death of Richard Keen, a member of the Way, and that someone tried to run me down.

Was the answer to the puzzle in Indiana?

***

I arrived at the hospital early hoping to be Karen's first nonmedical-related visitor. I was too late. When I entered the room, I saw the back of someone whose long curly hair covered the top of a tie-dyed T-shirt. With shorts falling just below his knees and day-glow green Adidas tennis shoes at the ends of his bird legs, it couldn't have been anyone other than Dude.

Karen gave him a hug and saw me standing in the doorway. "Look who came calling," she said with a wide grin.

Dude turned to see who it was, smiled, and said, "Whoops! Me caught wooing your Barbie."

"You can borrow her until she's well," I said.

She stuck her tongue out at me, a good sign that she was on her way to well.

"Me be stoked," Dude said. "Never been this close to copster without being attached by handcuffs."

Karen winked at me. She didn't ask Dude what he had meant, and I certainly wasn't going to open that door.

"Have a seat," Karen said as she lowered herself onto the bed and raised the back to a forty-five-degree angle. There was only one chair in the room, and before I could arm wrestle Dude for it, he moved to the wall and slid his back down until his rear end was on the floor. I considered being polite and joining him but was afraid that I wouldn't be able to get back up. I took the chair.

"K-cop say doc say she can boogie out next full moon," Dude said.

I looked questioningly at Karen.

"Three days in earthling speak," she said.

"That's great," I said. "Your dad'll be happy to get you to his place."

She rolled her eyes. "I'll give it a week before he's kicking me out or I'm throwing myself out."

"Crash with Pluto and the Dudester," the hippie surfer said.

"I'll remember that," she said.

Dude turned to me. "Chrisster, me hear you be trying to find murderer of JJ and Six even if they not murdered."

Besides seeing how Karen was doing, I had planned to tell her that I thought the key to the deaths was in Indianapolis and that I was going there to see if I could learn anything to make sense of them. I only told Dude that I was asking questions and that I was certain that JJ's death wasn't an accident and had reasons to think that Six hadn't fallen off the ladder without help. I didn't mention my brush with a car. He asked if I thought that Preacher Burl was in danger. I responded that I thought he was safe, but I didn't mention that it was because I had him pegged as the killer.

"Detective Callahan stopped by last night," Karen said. "He said that he understands your suspicions but can't find anything to substantiate them."

"Have they caught the alleged drunken driver?" I asked.

"No," Karen said.

"So there's no proof that it was an accident."

She sighed. "No. Just because you think it was intentional doesn't make it so."

"Dudester be having idea," said the voice from near the floor.

Karen and I said "What?" at the same time.

"Me not be detective like K-cop or crime-fighter Chrisster, so idea not perfect."

I motioned for him to continue.

"Stockbrokerman flattened JJ by accident; JJ's amigo Six found out, killed stockbrokerman. Karma got pissed and knocked Six off ladder." Dude leaned his head against the wall. "Voilà, there it be."

I figured that Karen was well enough to respond and waited.

She looked over at me and turned to Dude. "That's certainly something to think about."

"Okeydokey." Dude pushed against the wall to stand. "I'll leave you love-doves. High-five me later for solving crimes."

He was out the door before either of us could think of an appropriate noncommittal response.

I got up, kissed Karen on the forehead, and asked how she was feeling. She said she was fine except her strength had a ways to go. I asked if the doctor had said that was normal. He'd told her that he would've been shocked if she wasn't weak.

I explained my theory about Indianapolis and my plan to head there in the morning to see what I could learn. She sighed, frowned, and shook her head before asking if she could talk me out of going. I said no. That's what she had figured, she said, and that if I went, I should take someone to keep me from getting killed.

"How about Dude?" I asked.

"Be better off with Pluto."

I smiled and told her that I'd try to abduct Charles.

"Only if Pluto's not available." She smiled.

I called Charles on the way home and was surprised that he was home. I was afraid that I would have to wait until that night to catch him since he spent most of his days out and about. I told him my plans and asked if he wanted to go.

"I don't know," he said hesitantly. "I wouldn't have guessed that you would want to spend that much time with me with you closing the gallery so you—"

"Charles, I'm closing the gallery because of money. It has nothing to do with you."

When I had wanted him to go somewhere, even on multiple-day trips, before, Charles was in the car with his suitcase before I finished asking. He was still pouting.

"I'm not sure that I can get away. How long will you be gone?" he asked.

"What else do you have to do?"

"Well," he said, "there's the, umm, and I have to … oh, crap, what time are you leaving?"

CHAPTER 29

The sun peeked over the marsh as we crossed the bridge leaving Folly to begin our 750-mile trek through five states into the center of Indiana. Two hours later, we pulled into a Waffle House in Columbia. Charles had spoken no more than ten words. He was sulking, and a calorie-packed breakfast didn't improve his mood. I talked about rumors on Folly and what I thought about the recently completed beach renourishment, topics that Charles would normally have talked endlessly about, but all I got were grunts, nods, and whatevers. Pluto would have been a better traveling companion.

Charles became more talkative on a full stomach as I drove from Columbia to Asheville. He asked if I had read Carl Sandburg's poetry as we passed a highway sign about thirty miles before Asheville telling us that the poet's house could be reached from the next exit. If he had been in a better mood, I would have told him that I would rather stick pencils in my eyes than read poetry, but instead I took the safer route and said that I probably had in high school. To no surprise, he told me how much he enjoyed a biography of Abraham Lincoln. I faked interest.

Cindy called as we skirted around Asheville. "Found the car that nearly made you ground meat."

Instead of reminding her that it would be much more pleasant to start a conversation with something like, "Hi, Chris," I said, "Where?"

Charles tapped me on the shoulder, looked at the phone, and shrugged. I put it on speaker so I wouldn't have to repeat everything.

"White Kia Rio," she said. "It was reported stolen from the Harbor View Shopping Center on James Island about five hours before your incident. It was found less than a mile from where it was taken early the next morning."

"How do you know it was the same car?" I asked.

"One of the women we talked to at the Crab Shack remembered it. She said it was there when she and her beau got to the restaurant. Its windows were tinted, so she didn't think anyone was in it until it pulled away from the curb and took aim at you."

"How did you know it was the one that was stolen?"

"The woman must have been bored with her date; easy to do when eating with men, you know. She noticed the last two numbers on the license plate, 89, because that was the year she was born. That's 1989, not 89; she wasn't that old."

"Don't suppose you know who took it?" I said.

"How?" Cindy asked. "A picture of you on the seat with a note saying 'I'm going to run down the nosy, irritating, buttinski,' and signed by the bad guy?"

"That'd be nice," I said.

"Sorry," she said. "The car was clean."

I thanked her and she asked where I was.

"Out for a ride," I said and tapped End Call.

Charles said that the call was interesting but didn't tell us much, and he regressed to silence as I navigated the winding interstate between Asheville and Knoxville. As we got to the

Gatlinburg exits, he started talking. I wished he hadn't. He reminded me of the trip we had made to the Smoky Mountains a couple of years earlier and how close I had come to getting killed by my ex-wife's murderer. I felt tightness in my chest as he reminisced, in excruciating detail, about what had happened. I had hoped that I was over the hurt of losing my ex for the second time, but it wasn't gone.

We shared the wheel so we wouldn't have to spend a night on the road. I wanted to get to Indy as quickly as possible, talk to as many people who might know something about Burl, and rush back to my comfort zone on Folly Beach. Charles's tongue loosened more as we headed north from Knoxville to Lexington, the destination of another road trip that Charles and I had taken a few years back. Again, we had been meddling in police business, and Charles took the opportunity to relive those experiences, and I took the opportunity to think, once again, that I would have had a less stressful trip with Pluto.

After road trips down memory lane, somewhere between Lexington and Louisville, Charles got around to asking the question that I had contemplated for the last ten hours. "So, what do *you* expect to learn?"

"Don't have a clue," I said and looked over at him behind the wheel.

He glanced at me. "Once upon a time in a land"—he looked at the odometer—"six hundred miles away, I knew a man, a strange fellow from somewhere around these parts, in fact, who would tell me every time I went off on a tangent, or as he called it, a half-baked wild-goose chase, that I needed to stop and analyze what I was searching for and come up with a plan."

"Hmm," I said.

He kept his eyes on the interstate, smiled, and continued, "I thought it was a rather boring way to live, but over time I gained a smattering of respect for the stranger's approach. It was still boring, but it did help all the passengers in this car solve a few murders, and it saved their lives more than once."

"Your point?" I said.

"My point is that when I got up this morning, I had miraculously become a ventriloquist, because my voice is now coming out of your mouth." He tapped the steering wheel. "No, wait, I'm not a ventriloquist. You've finally seen the light. You're now officially a half-baked wild-goose chaser."

I wasn't certain if Charles thought it was a good thing, but he had a point. I would have preferred a better plan before hitting the road, but I was confident that the answers to questions about the deaths were in Indy. I told him that I was sure that we'd get to the bottom of it; I simply didn't know how.

By the time we reached my hometown, we were fewer than two hours from our destination, hungry, and needing to get out of the car. It was rush hour and would be slow going out of Louisville, so we stopped shy of downtown for a decent supper. Charles, the consummate trivia collector, asked me approximately three hundred questions about my childhood and early adult years: where I lived, where I went to school, where I worked, who my friends were, and, no surprise, what pets I had. His questions were tedious, and it went against my grain to talk about myself, but I answered them because it deflected conversation about the gallery. It was good hearing Charles be Charles again. I hoped it would last.

Supper dragged on longer than I would have preferred, but it felt good to be out of the car, and it gave the interstate time to unclog from rush-hour traffic. We crossed the Ohio River into Indiana on the last leg of our trip. We passed through Jeffersonville, and I smiled when I thought about what Burl had said about God speaking to him through an Iranian convenient store clerk, but I caught my breath when I realized that we were driving by the town that had a connection to the deaths of three people on Folly Beach. I reminded Charles of what Burl had shared, and we drove for fifteen minutes with the only sound in the car coming from talk radio and the hum of the tires.

I broke the silence. "I'm not certain what we'll find, but I had to make the trip. The police are only going through the motions when it comes to JJ and Six. They're following every lead on Mendelson's murder, but until someone looks at all three deaths together, plus the one up here and my possible hit, the odds of solving them seem small. That someone is me. Charles, it's personal."

Charles turned the radio's volume down. "You mean *we*, don't you?"

I smiled.

"We have to be careful," he continued. "The last time *we* played detective, things got hairy."

Now I was the ventriloquist; that's something that I would have said. "We're only asking questions."

Charles tapped his finger on the center console and looked at me. "President Taft said, 'Enthusiasm for a cause sometimes warps judgment.'"

I knew little to nothing about William Howard Taft, but I hoped and prayed that he would have been wrong about our current jaunt.

Exhausted, stiff, and sick of looking at interstates, we pulled into a Super 8 Hotel south of Indianapolis. Charles asked the bored clerk if he had an old-man discount for his friend and pointed at me. The clerk looked up at Charles and said yes, that both of us would qualify for the AARP rate. Charles frowned, I smiled, and we were on our way to the room.

"So now what?" Charles asked after he hopped on his bed like it was a trampoline.

Good question, I thought and looked in the bedside table for a phone book. "I know the name of the reporter who wrote the story about the death in the church, so we can start by going to the newspaper."

"Got a better idea," Charles said as he went through the table beside his bed to find something to read. "First thing we do is get a beer."

"How about get a good night's sleep?" I said. It was only nine thirty, but the long drive had worn me out.

"How about catch a killer?" Charles said.

"How about a good night's sleep?"

"How about that beer?"

I was defeated. Besides, it was too early to sleep, and I thought some wine may help me unwind. The hotel didn't have a bar, but there were several restaurants in walking distance, so I suggested we find one with a bar.

"Great idea," Charles said. "Knew you'd know what to do."

The closest restaurant with a bar was a Japanese steak house three blocks away. It was near closing time, and the bartender looked at his watch before getting our drinks. It reminded me of sitting in Cal's bar when he was sweeping the floor around me and trying to close. Well, it would have if Cal had been Asian and his jukebox had been playing Tatsuro Yamashita. Charles drank his beer and said little. He would never admit it, but the ride had taken a toll on him too.

***

The *Indianapolis Star* was about five miles from the hotel. At each red light along the way, Charles asked why we didn't just call the paper and ask for the reporter. I ignored the question every other light since each time I did answer, I said that we'd have a better chance of the reporter talking to us in person.

He finally stopped nagging as we entered the paper's new headquarters in downtown Indy, where a smiling receptionist greeted us. I asked for Stephen Vest. She glanced at Charles and turned back to me and asked our names. Then she said she'd see if he was in. She wrote our names down and called someone, mumbled a few words into the mouthpiece, and said that Mr. Vest wasn't there but that she'd give him my number. I did, and she asked if she could tell him the nature of our visit. I explained that it was about a story he'd written about a death and that I had some information he might be interested in. *That should pique his interest enough to call.*

As we walked back to the car, Charles said, "Now wasn't that helpful?"

I ignored him, and in a few more paces he added, "Hmm, didn't I mention calling instead of driving all over Indianapolis?"

I simply said that we'd wait for the reporter's call.

"Then, while we're here, wouldn't it be nice if we could see where they have that race?"

I went out on a limb and assumed that he meant the Indianapolis 500, entered the Indianapolis Motor Speedway into the navigation system, and followed its directions.

We were in the Speedway gift shop's parking lot when the phone rang. I was relieved when the person on the other end identified himself as Stephen Vest. He asked what death I had information about, so I told him Richard Keen's. The reporter exhaled, and I heard a noise that sounded like a squeaky chair. He asked where we were. I told him. He gave directions to a nearby Grindstone Charlie's restaurant and said he'd be there in a half hour.

After two wrong turns, I found the restaurant. We'd beaten

the lunch crowd and had our choice of tables. We settled for one near the window, settled for coffee, and settled down to wait for the reporter. Vest arrived fifteen minutes late. He was in his late fifties, had slicked-back, jet-black dyed hair, a matching mustache, and a slight limp. He looked more like he was arriving for a drug deal than a meeting with two upstanding citizens from South Carolina—okay, one upstanding citizen and Charles.

"You're Chris," Vest said, not making eye contact with either of us.

"Yes," I said, and I introduced Charles.

Vest dropped a thick, wrinkled manila file folder on the table. It had drink stains on the top and looked like it had led a hard life, not unlike the alcoholic-red-nosed reporter. Vest settled in a chair and waved for a nearby waitress, who took his order for coffee and said that she'd bring refills for Charles and me.

Vest squinted. "What information do you have about Keen?"

So much for small talk. I told him where we were from and a little about the deaths. "So what?" he asked, and I told him how each of the victims had attended First Light Church. "So what?" he said again. I said that First Light Church had been founded by Burl Ives Costello.

That got his attention.

CHAPTER 30

The reporter stared at me, rubbed his fingers through his mustache, and said, "I've wondered what happened to him." He leaned over the table. "Tell me everything."

I told him about seeing JJ killed. I let Charles tell him about Timothy Mendelson. And I followed with Six's "accidental" fall. "The accident that wasn't an accident," Charles added. And I told him about the attempt on my life.

Vest tapped his fingers on the table, said that he'd be back, and pulled a pack of Marlboros from his coat pocket as he scurried to the door.

Charles looked at the file folder that Vest had left on the table. "Want to get a head start on what's in there?"

I told him no; we'd learn soon enough.

"Soon enough," Charles grumbled. "He was already fifteen minutes late."

Charles wouldn't have forgotten Vest's indiscretion. At least he hadn't verbally accosted the man about it.

When Vest returned, he said, "Keen's death's always bothered me."

"Why?" Charles asked.

"I've been a reporter thirty years. Covered everything: tornados, fires, fatal wrecks, and murders. Could say I've seen it all. When something bad happens, people always think they're the first that horrible things happen to, but when you've seen what I have, you learn that they almost always react the same way. Keen's death didn't feel right. Don't ask me why; I can't put my finger on it."

"Tell us about it," I said.

He opened the folder, pulled out a typed sheet, and stared at it. "Richard Keen was in his early forties—chronologically. He was mentally challenged, probably autism, but never had a diagnosis. His parents and his siblings said that he was loving and way too trusting; said he would do anything for anyone. He wasn't stupid, but according to members of his church, he seemed a notch or two off with his reactions. The family, especially his big brother and his sister," Vest looked at the paper again, "Patrick and Sarah, tried to protect him from, quote, 'the world taking advantage of Richie,' that's what they called him." He stopped, sipped his coffee, and gnawed on a fingernail.

Charles had all the silence he could handle and started to speak, but Vest beat him to it. "The family was poor, barely squeaking by. They were Methodist but not regular churchgoers. Then Richard found out about the Way, the church where Burl Ives Costello preached. Apparently Richard heard about it at the job he had stocking shelves at Kroger. One of the parishioners I talked to said that Richard liked the church because the preacher paid attention to him." He paused again.

This time Charles couldn't wait. "What happened?"

Vest chewed his nail and glanced at Charles. "Richard's immediate family was poor, but he had a wealthy uncle, a well-known industrialist over in Bloomington. He'd taken Richard under his wing. He knew of his nephew's limitations and slipped him money without his parents knowing. The uncle passed away a couple of years ago, and he left Richard almost a million bucks. Could've been enough to take care of him for the rest of his life. He also left him an old gas station building, one of those that actually worked on cars. It had three bays and a large room that sold food and crap. It was on the other side of the Speedway. Good-sized building; valuable land." He nodded in the direction of the Speedway.

The waitress interrupted and asked if we wanted to order. We all ordered cheeseburgers and fries, and then Vest reached inside his sport-coat pocket, started to pull out his cigarettes, but then returned the pack to the pocket. "That's when it started getting strange. Richard flat out gave the building to the preacher for the Way to make it their church." He raised his eyebrows. "You can guess how pissed that made the kid's family."

I wasn't thinking about Richard's family but about how similar this situation was to Mendelson's donating to First Light.

"Anyway," Vest continued, "as if giving the building wasn't enough, Richard talked to a lawyer he met at the Way about writing up a will so he could leave his newly acquired estate to the church. The lawyer couldn't tell anyone about the will, but that didn't stop Richard. A week didn't go by before everyone in the congregation knew." Vest pushed away from the table. "Be back," he said and once again rushed to the door, Marlboros in hand.

Charles watched him leave and turned to me. "Timothy Mendelson déjà vu. I'm thinking Richard's death is connected to what's happening on Folly."

I resisted the temptation to remind him that that was why we were here and said instead, "Wow, you are a detective. What else have you detected?"

He pointed to the front door. "That boy's going to single-handedly keep the tobacco industry in business, and Preacher Burl is up to his wooly-worm mustache in the killings."

Vest returned with the pungent smell of cigarette smoke.

"A few weeks later," the reporter continued, without preamble, "the preacher and Richard were in the building repairing leaks. According to the police report, Richard was standing close to the wall and swinging a sledgehammer to break old hydraulic equipment loose from the floor to get to the leak. He somehow hit the wall, and the top two rows of concrete blocks fell on him. Killed him instantly. The preacher said he was on the other side of the building and didn't see it happen but heard the ruckus and saw Richard on the floor with blocks all over the place."

"The cops bought it?" Charles said.

"No reason not to. The preacher was the only other person there, and it looked like it happened the way he described it. Richard wasn't in any position to give his version, and who would suspect a preacher?"

"Was there an autopsy?" I asked.

"Yeah," Vest said. "Death from blunt-force trauma to the head. Duh!"

"From the blocks?" Charles asked.

"Concrete shards were found in the head wound."

The waitress arrived with our food, and Vest attacked his cheeseburger like he hadn't eaten in a week.

"What made you suspicious?" I asked between bites.

Vest held up his forefinger and continued to stuff burger in his mouth. Charles leaned back in his chair and stared at the reporter. My friend's patience was running thin, and I was afraid he was going to yank Vest's plate away.

The reporter took a sip of Pepsi. "I did the initial story about the death. A week or so later, I thought that since the Way was a new church, a follow-up story may be of interest. I'd been reading research that showed that traditional church memberships had been declining, so I asked my editor if I could pursue it. It was a slow news day, and I didn't have anything else to do except write a story about three cows that got loose on the I-65. How much could I say about that? I interviewed members of the Way, but all they wanted to talk about was Richard's family being angry about how the church had sucked Richard in. I went to talk to the family. That's when I learned about the will, and that got this old reporter's antenna vibrating."

Charles bobbed his head from side to side as Vest took another bite. "What happened?"

Vest glanced at me and then looked at Charles. "Here's the kicker. The gas station was never deeded to the church, and the will was never filed. The attorney told his family that Richard had taken the transfer documents and the will to study them and never brought them back. They weren't surprised because he was slow about doing things like that."

"Did the preacher know that Richard hadn't signed it?" I asked.

"Now you're catching on," Vest said. "No, *your* preacher was all prepared to accept the God-sent windfalls when the attorney broke the news: no signature, no building, no will, no big bucks. But the damage had been done. The Keens thought the preacher's story didn't follow some of the Ten Commandments, and they blamed him for trying to steal Richard's inheritance, hinting that Costello killed him. They spread their suspicions to the police, who talked to others in the church who had begun wondering."

"The police didn't find anything?" I said.

"Not really. One of the detectives I know told me off the record that he wasn't buying the preacher's story but had no way to disprove it. Other members of the Way began to lose faith in their minister and stopped attending."

"So then what?" I asked.

"Costello folded his tent, tucked his ministry between his hind legs, and hightailed it out of town faster than an Indy car."

Instead of elaborating on Burl's departure, Vest asked if we wanted dessert. He waved the waitress over and ordered a slice of apple pie. Charles and I said we were full. Vest attacked dessert with as much vigor as had his cheeseburger.

"Why'd he close the church?" Charles asked.

Vest wiped crust crumbs out of his mustache and held up his hand. "Hold that question." He rushed out the door before his lungs suffered clean-air poisoning.

Charles looked back at the drink-stained folder. "Think there's anything else in there for us?"

"If there wasn't, he'd be gone."

Vest returned and asked what the question was again. I said we wondered why Burl had closed the Way.

"He didn't return my calls, and then his phone was disconnected, so I never got his version, but from what I pieced together, it was a combination of things. First, Richard's family was pissed. They blamed the preacher and didn't hesitate to tell everyone that he was taking advantage of their son's lack of social skills, as they put it. They said Costello was trying to steal their son's inheritance, and they pulled the plug on the Way's using the building to hold its services. I also heard most of the members stopped attending. No one said it, but I suspected that Richard's siblings called each one and spouted off about the evils that their preacher was involved in."

"Why his siblings instead of his parents?" I asked.

"The parents were so traumatized that they couldn't do anything. They holed up in their house and wouldn't talk to anyone except their preacher. The kids had been close to Richard and helped him with many of the chores that normal people handled routinely—taxes, shopping, budgeting."

"You've been a reporter a long time," I said. "What's your gut tell you?"

Vest looked down at pie crumbs, glanced at Charles, and turned to me. "Your damned preacher man thrashed the Sixth Commandment."

"Thou shalt not kill," said Charles, probably the closest thing to a Bible scholar at the table.

"Can't prove it," Vest said, "and never will, but I know it as well as I'm on the road to lung cancer."

I nodded.

Vest glanced at his watch. "Don't have much time." He pushed the plate away, pulled the mysterious folder in front of him, and shuffled through a few papers. Finally he pulled out a folded sheet with a photocopied list of handwritten names on it. "This is everybody I talked to. Maybe you can figure something out. The preacher man's now your problem." He slid the paper toward me, but Charles grabbed it.

"Can we keep this?" Charles asked.

"Yeah, I have the original."

I saw that some of the dozen or so names had phone numbers next to them, some had addresses, and about half had brief notes beside them. "Any problem with us contacting them?"

"No," Vest said. "There won't be any confidences broken since all of them were mentioned in the article. Tell them that you got their names from the paper's archives."

I thanked him, and he closed the folder, popped out of his seat, and headed to the door without saying anything. He stopped before opening the door, turned, and returned to the table.

He looked to see if anyone was nearby, rested both hands on the table, and said, "I'm a reporter and report only facts, so you didn't hear this from me." He waited for both of us to nod.

"I hope you get that freakin' faker and they fry his ass." He saluted, asked us to call if there was a story about what we find, and was gone.

Charles tilted his head up and sniffed as the door slammed behind Vest. "Notice how much cleaner the air smells?"

"Uh-huh," I said. "The clean, healthy aroma of hamburgers, fries, and onion rings."

"Now I'm ready for dessert." Charles picked up the photocopy and read the names out loud.

It was now well past the lunch hour, and the waitress didn't seem bothered that we were hogging the table, so we ordered bread pudding, and I asked Charles to see the list. The first four names were Richard's immediate family members—parents Reginald and Sandra Keen and siblings Patrick and Sarah. A phone number was printed beside Reginald's name. I wished that I'd looked at the list before Vest had left; he had put a star beside Sarah's name and names of three other people. What'd it mean? He'd written "hostile" beside Patrick and Sandra. It was understandably a distraught and angry family.

The next starred name was Calvin Song, accompanied by a phone number and the note, "Minister, 2nd Methodist Church, Keen's family pastor." Other names on the list were Chance Arnold, Vivian Clem, one that I couldn't make out, and Detective Powers, with "Only the facts, Jack, Powers," beside it. I didn't know if that was meant as an insult, an inside joke, or a compliment, but I figured that if he had been the detective on the case, it would be a good place to begin.

Our desserts then arrived, and Charles had his mouth full when I punched in the number listed beside Powers. I got a recorded message that said that he was no longer with the department and referred me to the Metropolitan Indianapolis Police Department's nonemergency number. I hit End Call, told Charles what the message had said, and suggested that it would be a waste of time to weave my way through the maze of people I'd have to talk to at the police department to find out anything. Besides, we already had Vest's version of what the police thought, and it wasn't helpful.

Charles glanced down at the list and started singing "Son of a Preacher Man."

His voice wasn't nearly as bad as his girlfriend Heather's, but I wasn't certain why he had chosen to break into tune. I held out my hands in a what-are-you-doing gesture. He pointed to the list of names.

"Calvin Song," I read.

He stopped singing, nodded, and handed me my phone.

Our luck changed when a deep voice answered the phone with, "Reverend Song, how may I be of service?"

I told him who I was and briefly explained how he may be of service. He hesitated and said that he would be at the church for another hour. He gave me the location and said that he would talk to me if I could get there soon. He church was across town, but I said I'd hurry. Hearing this, Charles hurried his last bite.

Would talking to the reverend be as unproductive as our conversation with Stephen Vest? I hoped not since I would have to hear about it for a dozen hours on the ride home.

CHAPTER 31

Fifteen minutes later, with the aid of the navigation system and Charles's "help" repeating each command that the device's stilted female voice gave me, we pulled into Second Methodist Church's parking lot. The small, white, brick church was located in what appeared to be a working-class neighborhood. Its lawn and parking lot islands were well maintained, but age had taken its toll on the building, and the "Office" sign was faded and nearly illegible.

The door was locked, but there was a Ford Focus in the lot, so I knocked, and a six-foot-three gentleman who was roughly my age opened the door. He wore a coat and tie and looked like he should be presiding at a funeral. We shook hands, and I introduced Charles and me. The pastor's expression was guarded.

Reverend Song escorted us to his small office and offered us the chairs in front of his cluttered desk, apologized for the papers and reference books strewn across its surface, and said that he had been working on his sermon. The closest thing to high tech that I saw was a hand-cranked pencil sharpener attached to the wall behind him.

"You mentioned that you were interested in the death of

Richard Keen," he said as he settled into his chair. "Please explain your interest in the tragic loss."

I was beginning to think that this would be less helpful than our conversation with the reporter. I told him where we were from, that there had been a death of a member of a small congregation there that was surprisingly similar to Mr. Keen's demise. I didn't want to confuse the conversation by mentioning JJ and Mendelson.

"How, pray tell, could a death in your beach community have any connection to Mr. Keen? In fact, how would you have even heard of Mr. Keen's death in North Carolina?"

"South Carolina," Charles corrected.

"Good questions," I said quickly, since I didn't think Charles correcting the minister in his church would be a fruitful beginning. "The congregation on Folly Beach is headed by a man named Burl Ives Costello. He—"

Reverend Song exhaled so loudly that it interrupted my thought. "Now I see," Song snarled. *Quite unminister-like*, I thought. "I assume that is the same man who claimed to be Mr. Keen's preacher."

I said that it was, although I couldn't imagine how there could have been more than one, and I added that we had learned about Song's church from newspaper accounts about Richard Keene.

"How was the death similar to Mr. Keen's?" Song asked. He gritted his teeth but now appeared less antagonistic.

I explained the falling ladder and the fatal head injury. Reverend Song nodded and didn't interrupt.

He leaned back when I finished and gazed at the ceiling like he was searching for the correct words. "Did the victim of your accident by chance leave a large amount of money to the Way?"

"Preacher Burl named his new church First Light," Charles said.

Correction number two. *Please let the minister talk.* "It is similar to the one he started here. And no, the man who died was homeless and had nothing to leave to the church."

"Hmm," Song said, "that would be a big difference from the gold-digger Costello's ministry here."

"You're not a fan of Burl Costello," Charles said.

Song turned to Charles. "Let me tell you a few things, Mr. Fowler." Song waved his hand around the room. "Second Methodist is not a wealthy church. We've been in this building since 1953. By the grace of God, our members, through sacrifices far beyond what should have been expected, paid off the mortgage in 1978. We run a small soup kitchen in one of the poorest parts of town that's staffed by members of the congregation who do so for no earthly remuneration. If one of our members suffers a tragic loss of home or property, we step in to help. We have been here sixty plus years, and God willing, we will be here for the next sixty."

"You do great work," I said.

"It is our mission." Song balled his left hand into a fist. "And then someone I will munificently call a minister comes in, feeds upon the inaccurate perceptions of an unenlightened few, and starts a church, one with no history to judge it against and no ability to do good for our community. He gives it a culturally cute name and waylays some of our existing members, especially those who might be slower in intellect or who appear to be able to donate to the new endeavor." He paused and took a sighed. "Such a lad, Richard Keen, fell for Costello's psalm and dance." A glimmer of a sly grin broached the corner of his mouth at his own humor. But it didn't last. "Richard was the perfect foil. He was slow of thought, enamored with the attention the preacher showered upon him, and believed that the Way was his salvation. Richard followed the man around wherever he went; he was under the preacher's spell. It was no wonder that Richard promised to give the building to the Way and almost made that man the beneficiary of his ample estate."

"Did Richard's family try to talk him out of attending?" I asked.

"Oh, did they ever," the reverend said. "His God-fearing parents made personal pleas to Costello to loosen his grip on Richard, to no avail. His sister told me that she would never step a foot in the Way and never wanted to see Costello. Said she would rather confront the devil. Richard's death did more damage to his lovely family than any bomb could. His mother blamed her husband for Richard's straying and left him for her hometown in Arizona, taking her remaining son with her. Richard's sister had a mental breakdown and was institutionalized for months. I pray for the family every week." He stared at his desk for a while and then looked up at me. "I don't see how any of this can help you. What did you expect to gain from the lengthy trip?"

I told him that we didn't know but that I was convinced that whatever happened began with Mr. Keen's death. "Did you ever meet Burl Costello?" I asked.

"Never," he said sharply.

I asked if he happened to know Jeremy Junius Chiles, or someone who went by Six.

He wrinkled up his nose. "Six, like the number?"

Please, Charles, don't say, "Do you know any other kind of six?" I quickly said, "Yes, maybe at church or from the soup kitchen."

He slowly shook his head. "Don't believe so."

I had one more question but wanted to save it for last, so I asked Charles if he had anything to ask.

Charles took the handoff. "Is there anyone in your congregation who'd been ripped off by Costello? Anyone we should talk to?"

"I doubt many others had contact with him," Song said. "Most of our families have been with us for years, generations even. I know that Chance Arnold and Vivian Clem each attended one of the Way's services to see what it was about. They returned the next Sunday and said they'd never stray from Second Methodist again."

I said I remembered their names from the newspaper, and he responded that he wished that nosy reporter had spent more time investigating the Way than pestering his members.

"I know you have to leave," I said, "but let me ask one more question. Other than trying to take advantage of Richard Keen, do you believe that Burl Costello had anything to do with his death?"

Song glared at me. "I sincerely believe that he killed Richard Keen, but I do not suspect that anyone of this world will ever know for sure. Let me tell you gentlemen something." He looked toward the ceiling. "The Maker knows, and if that man is responsible, he will receive his just rewards upon his departure from our world of sin."

If Burl killed Richard and the three men on Folly, I didn't want to wait for him to leave this world to receive his punishment. The question was, how could I prove he was the killer.

CHAPTER 32

Charles and I sat in the church lot. The Reverend Calvin Song had said a lot, but had we learned anything new? He resented the Way, but he would have had hard feelings about any church that reduced his ability to meet the spiritual needs of the community. We already knew that Richard's family was opposed to Preacher Burl and the Way. It was sad that their son's death had affected the entire family, and I felt sorry for them, but that didn't get us closer to answers.

It wasn't as hot in Indianapolis as it was at home—in the low eighties—and the air conditioner cranked out cold air.

"Don't know about JJ's connection," Charles said as he turned the vents toward his face and ran his hand through his long, thinning hair, "but there are a spooky number of similarities between what happened here and the demise of our stockbroker and Six."

"True," I said.

"Anyone else we need to talk to?" Charles asked.

"The other people the minister mentioned who had visited the Way only went once, so I doubt they'd know anything. I wouldn't impose on Richard's father and sister, even if we could find them, and his mother and brother are no longer here. Vest's list didn't have other promising names on it, so I suppose we've done all we can."

"Then why are we still here?" Charles said. "Let's head 'em up and move 'em out."

I didn't know when my friend decided that we were herding cattle, but I often didn't know what he was thinking. I told the navigation system to lead us home and followed its directions to the interstate and turned south. After four hours on the road, I said I needed to stop for the night. Charles called me a wimp but yawned as he said it, and we pulled off the road at a string of interstate hotels near Richmond, Kentucky. We checked into a room at the first one with a vacancy, and I called Detective Callahan to share what we had learned.

The person who answered told me that Detective Callahan was unavailable, so I reluctantly asked for Detective Burton. When I told him who I was, he reacted just as he had several other times over the years—with bored irritation. I told him where I had spent the day and why. He was still irritated but slightly less bored. Progress.

I shared that Burl Costello was the only other person in the building at the time of Richard Keen's death. I mentioned that Richard had told the preacher that he was leaving his substantial estate to the Way and explained the similarities to Six's death.

To his credit, Burton didn't interrupt or hang up on me. When I had finished, he cleared his throat. "The guy there was leaving a bunch of money to the church, and your guy was broke. How's that the same?"

"The circumstances of the two deaths were similar, but not the motive. My guess is that Mendelson had planned to leave money to First Light and was killed not by some angry client but by Costello to speed up the inheritance. Somehow, JJ and Six found out. JJ was always asking questions, and Six often worked at the storefront and could have overheard something either the preacher or Mendelson said. If Burl found out that they knew something, that would give him a strong motive."

"You think he was driving the car that almost hit you?" Burton asked.

I was surprised that he knew about it. "Yes," I said.

"Other than that he found you irritating, why would he want to kill you?"

I wanted to scream that it was because he knew that the police weren't smart enough to see that the deaths were related, but instead I said, "He had heard that I was trying to connect the deaths, and my search would lead to him."

"That's quite an ego and imagination, Mr. Landrum," the grumpy detective said. "Let me ask you something. You've been in Indianapolis since when?"

"Yesterday."

"And you've talked to a reporter and a preacher who didn't have anything good to say about the church up there."

I agreed. Charles bounced on his bed and pointed to his ears and the phone. I rolled my eyes and hit the speaker icon so Charles could hear Burton's end of the call. Charles gave a thumbs up.

"Did your road trip and two conversations provide you with one speck of evidence that the death of the guy there was anything but an accident?"

"No," I whispered.

"What I thought," Burton said.

Burton had a knack for getting under my skin. He had been helpful over the years, but most of the time he had been condescending and only marginally competent.

"Look, Detective," I said, "it doesn't take Sherlock Holmes to see that something connects the deaths. Richard, JJ, and Six are all dead, all were connected to Burl Costello's churches, and all are allegedly victims of accidents. Then throw in the murder of Mendelson—you do agree his was a murder, don't you? It's all connected, and I believe Burl Costello killed all of them."

There was silence on the line. Had Burton walked away from the phone?

And then he said, "I agree."

I nearly fell out of the chair. "Huh?"

"I agree with you, Mr. Landrum. You think I'm incompetent, but I've been doing this for nearly forty years. I know in my gizzard if someone's guilty; I can usually separate bullshit from fact. But let me tell you what I can't do. I can't arrest someone because of my gut. I'm restrained by this silly thing called the rules of law and evidence. Judges and juries aren't as bright as I am—heck, maybe not as brilliant as you. With the guidance of *helpful* defense attorneys, juries are forced to look for evidence. Silly, I know, but that's the system I'm stuck in."

He was right, and I told him so.

"Thank goodness," he said. "We finally agree."

I smiled. "So, what are *we* going to do about it?"

"We!" he shouted. "*We* are not going to do anything. *I* am going to share this with Detective Callahan, and *I* am going to interview your preacher again to get his version of what happened in Indiana. Detective Callahan and I will be going under the assumption that the deaths may not have been accidental, and he and I will be doing whatever necessary to uncover evidence—yes, there's that word again—that will lead us to the killer."

I thanked him for taking it seriously, and he thanked me for the call. He almost seemed sincere. He said that he knew he was wasting words but that I should stay out of trouble. I said I would try.

"Sure you will," he said. The line went dead.

***

Charles didn't say much on the drive from Richmond to Knoxville, but at the first billboard announcing one of the many attractions in Gatlinburg, he said, "Let's hop over there and get some fudge for Karen."

Charles was a thoughtful person, but his idea seemed fishy, especially since a side trip to Gatlinburg would add a couple of hours to our already long ride home. I cocked my head. "Fudge?"

He kept his eyes on the first Gatlinburg exit, which I passed without slowing, and said, "Sure, she'd love some. Umm, and while we're there, we could drive up in the mountains and you could take photos for the gallery. You don't have many mountain pictures."

Now it was becoming clearer. Why would I need photos for a closed gallery? He had gone almost two days without mentioning the sore topic, and I didn't want to get into an argument with him when we had six more hours together in the car.

"That's a good idea," I said, "but we have a long way to go, and I wanted to stop at the hospital before it gets too late."

How could he argue against my seeing Karen? *Please, Charles, don't go down the gallery-closing road.*

He turned from the window and smiled. "Okay, but I'm going to tell her that I wanted you to get her fudge."

Whew! I had avoided a verbal disaster. Ten miles farther, I learned that I was wrong.

"What's the biggest expense at the gallery?"

"Rent," I said without hesitation. "Eighteen hundred a month is more than I bring in most months, then add utilities and insurance, on and on."

"And that doesn't include the huge nonsalary you pay your executive sales manager," he said and smiled.

I was happy to see a smile. "Nor the absurd salary, dividends, and retirement benefits for the owner." I hoped we could keep the conversation light.

Charles's smile faded slightly. "Now, let's get back to the big cost. Before Bob conned you into renting the run-down building, it had been vacant for a while, and before that it had been a souvenir and T-shirt shop for what, thirty years?"

"Twenty-seven." I felt good correcting Charles for a change.

"Close enough," he said. "My point is that Folly now has twice as many T-shirt shops as it did when the gallery was one. The building's in no better shape. And I bet it'll take years to rent."

"Probably."

He looked down at my phone. "So why don't you call Bob and see if he can get you a much better deal if you renew for a few more years."

Bob had already talked to the landlord and had surely gotten the best possible deal, but I didn't want to spend the rest of the day trapped in the car with a hostile executive sales manager, so I figured there was nothing to lose by calling. Charles volunteered to call and put the phone on speaker in case he had any brilliant suggestions to add. I cringed and smiled at the same time.

"Are you dead yet?" a blustery voice said over the speaker.

I hated caller ID. "Yes, Bob," I said. "I'm calling to haunt you."

"I think you're pulling my shapely leg," the Realtor said. "This better be important. I'm at Al's getting ready to chow down."

I heard Randy Travis singing in the background. "Say hi to Al for me," I said.

"Tell him yourself."

Bob yelled something away from the phone, and then Al came on. "Hi, Chris. How's Karen?"

"She's getting out of the hospital tomorrow," I said.

"Wonderful. Be sure and—"

"Give me the damn phone, old man," Bob said in the background. "He called me, not you."

There was a clink, and then Bob boomed, "So what's so damned important that you interrupted my lunch and pleasant conversation with Al?"

I told him that I was closing the gallery unless I could significantly cut expenses. He said something to the effect that maybe I should take prettier pictures so that I'd sell more. I didn't take the bait and said that the problem was on the expense side of the ledger. He said that I was sounding mighty accountanty and may need to dumb it down for him. I reminded him that I knew that despite the impression he gave, he was a Duke graduate and could probably grasp my ledger talk.

"What-the-hell-ever," Bob said. "What do you want me to do?"

I suggested that he contact the landlord and use his Realtor charm to lower the rent by half or he would lose his long-term tenant. Considering the economy and the increasing number of shops, the space would sit empty for years if Landrum Gallery closed.

Charles smiled and gave me the okay sign with his thumb and forefinger.

Bob wasn't as positive. "Crap, Chris, want me to walk on water too? How about me figuring out how Al's fries can cure cancer and the common cold?"

"Not necessary," I said. "All you need to do is get the landlord to cut the rent in half."

The line went dead.

"Good job," Charles said. "Bob will take care of it."

Bob was many contradictory things, but I doubted miracle

worker was among them, and such a big cut in the rent would definitely qualify as a miracle. I didn't share my pessimism with Charles. We were still miles from home.

Fifty miles down the road, Charles mumbled something that I couldn't understand. I asked him to repeat it.

"I've decided. I can't marry Heather," he said.

"Why not?"

He looked out his window. "It's not me. That may not be a good reason, but I can't see myself married, to Heather or anyone else, when I look down the road. It was stupid, but I proposed because it was what Aunt M. wanted." He turned his gaze from the passing landscape and toward me. "Am I making a mistake?"

"The only mistake you could make would be if you did something you knew was not the right thing to do."

He tapped the console slowly. "Then it's the right thing to do."

"Does she know?" I asked.

"I told her the night before we left."

"How'd she take it?"

"Said she understood, but I know she didn't. She cried, got angry, then cried some more. Said she didn't want us to break up. I said we weren't, that I just couldn't get married."

"How'd you leave it?"

"Told her I still wanted to, umm, date and that she was the greatest gal I've ever known. She said she'd have to try to sort through all of it. Then I left."

I told him that I was sorry and that I'd be with him regardless what happened. He thanked me and resumed staring at the South Carolina pines as they slipped by.

We arrived in Charleston at rush hour. Luckily we were going in the opposite direction from most of the traffic and made it to the hospital before six. Karen's room was empty, and we started toward the nurses' station to check on her when I saw her walking, unaided, down the corridor and laughing at something that a long-haired man wearing a tie-dyed T-shirt walking beside her had said. It was a great sight.

Dude saw us first and snapped his fingers. "Be caught courtin' your chick." He leaned on Karen's arm. "Again."

"Hmm," I said and faked a frown.

Karen stepped away from Dude, held her arms out, and pirouetted. "Escape tomorrow."

Charles clapped, I smiled, and Dude said, "K-cop be movin' in with the Dudester." He smiled. "Be joshin'."

I cautiously hugged Karen, but she said that she wouldn't break and squeezed me tighter. "We're heading outside. Come with us," she said and waved for Charles and me to follow. Although Karen was thrilled about being released, she still walked at about half speed, and it took us awhile to reach the benches. It was hot and breezy, but she said that after being in her hospital room, it was heavenly.

When we settled on the bench, Dude asked where we had been. I told them about our trip, and while Dude expressed interest in whether we got to drive around the Speedway, Karen's mood darkened.

I told them about our visit with the reporter and the minister and gave a capsule version of what we had learned about Richard Keen.

Dude interrupted, "Keen like smart or like knife blade?"

"Like a name," Charles said.

"Just clarifying," Dude said.

Karen asked, "So what did you learn?"

Charles and I exchanged a glance. "Umm," he said, "we learned that big-city reporters smoke like a forest fire."

Karen smiled. "Sorry, I mean what did you learn that was important?"

Charles shrugged and looked at me again.

"I suppose nothing other than Keen's minister's feelings about Burl's church. We didn't know what we would learn unless we went," I said defensively.

Dude waved his hand like he wanted to be recognized. I looked at him, and he said, "Epimetheus."

"Huh?" Karen took the word right out of my mouth.

Dude turned to Karen. "Be Prometheus's brother."

Great, I thought. *That explains everything.*

"Skip the family tree," Charles said. "Why did you say Epimetheus?"

"He be Greek god of hindsight," Dude said.

"Got it," Charles said. "Hindsight be twenty-twenty."

Dude smiled and nodded.

And I thought of how great it was to be home—among friends.

CHAPTER 33

The next morning I woke in my own bed, but I ached from balding head to arthritic toe. The older I got, the more uncomfortable it was to sleep away from home. Add a strange bed to riding fifteen hundred miles in three days, plus the aftereffects of my dive on the street, and my back felt like I had been riding a bucking steer. My legs throbbed, and my elbows still reminded me of their close encounter with the pavement. I thought about walking next door to Bert's for coffee, but my back muscles requested that I keep my movements to a minimum, so I performed about the only task I knew how to do in the kitchen: I fired up Mr. Coffee. I twisted and turned in the kitchen chair to get comfortable and replayed my conversation with Detective Burton. His gut—gizzard—had told him that the deaths were related and hardly accidents, but I knew with his workload and lack of enthusiasm for the alleged accidents that he would have little time for and minimal interest in aggressively pursuing them.

Vest had said that everyone believed that Burl had killed Richard to inherit nearly one million dollars, a plan that had backfired because the will hadn't been finalized. If that were the motive, I had to know if Timothy Mendelson had left anything to First Light. It hadn't been enough time for the information to meander its way through the legal channels and be made public, but if anyone could find out, it would be Sean Aker, one of Folly's four practicing attorneys.

Marlene, Sean's office manager, answered my call and said that he wasn't in. She laughed and said that I should know better than to call him before nine o'clock. "It's not like he has a real job and has to be at work like normal people," she added.

I'd met Marlene and her boss the first year I had been on Folly. Sean had done some legal work for me to get Landrum Gallery open, and we had become friends after Charles and I had proven his innocence when he was accused of killing his law partner. He had said that he owed me favors big-time, and I had already taken him up on a few. He was a source of legal information and of the stories behind the never-ending controversies that swirled around the small island.

I told Marlene that I must not have been thinking. She agreed and said she would have him call as soon as he elected to grace the door. A cup of coffee later, the phone rang.

"My slave-driving office manager told me I had to call you," Sean said without any semblance of a greeting. "Said I couldn't sip my coffee, take a bite of my scone, or start my midmorning nap. Enough about me. What's up?"

I laughed. "Good morning, Sean. Beautiful day, isn't it?" This was part of my effort to return civility to my corner of the Low Country.

"Yeah, yeah," he mumbled. "May your life be filled with blessings. You didn't call to give me a Hallmark greeting."

"You know about Timothy Mendelson's murder?" I said.

"Did Marlene say that I'd just flown in from Mongolia? Of course I know. I even know how to read; taught myself after I finished law school. You may not know this since you didn't go to law school or journalism school, but the newspaper thought the murder of a prominent Charleston stockbroker would sell papers. Stuck it right on the front page."

"Right," I said and chuckled. "Know anything about his will?"

"Not a period, comma, or clause," he said.

"Can you find out?" I asked.

"Why? No, don't tell me. You're mixed up in solving his murder and want to see who inherits because you read in *Catching Killers for Dummies* that most murders are committed for money or love."

If there was such a book, I hadn't read it, but I'd bet that Charles had. "Close, but I believe Mendelson's murder is connected to other deaths."

I had to jerk the phone away from my ear when Sean yelled for Marlene to bring him coffee and told her he was listening to a tale that couldn't be interrupted.

"Let's hear it," he said to me.

I gave him the short version, including the two "accidental" deaths here, the one in Indiana, and my close encounter with the car on Center Street. Once Sean put his mind to it, he was a good listener and had a lawyer's analytical mind.

"Quite a collection of coincidences," he said. "What do the guys who get paid to solve crimes say?"

I told him my take on how much time and energy the detectives were devoting to the cases.

"You think that whomever inherits did it?" he said.

"Only if it's Burl Costello or First Light," I said.

"No promises. Let me make some calls."

I thanked him and asked if he'd been on any scuba diving trips or gone skydiving recently, two of his hobbies.

"No, but did you know you don't need a parachute to skydive?" He paused. "You only need a parachute to skydive twice."

He cackled, and I pretended to laugh.

I told him to be sure to thank Marlene for looking out for me. He said, "No way," and hung up. I had more work to do with my civility lessons.

I had done all I could do until I heard back from my skydiving buddy. Karen was to be released in a couple of hours and had asked me to pick her up. The mayor had a day-long meeting about the city's budget and had confessed that it was the last place he wanted to be but knew that unless he was there to look out for his priorities, his fiscal policies could take a tumble. I was at the hospital an hour early, which would have made Charles proud, but as I should have predicted knowing what I did about bureaucracy, my promptness was rewarded with a two-hour wait before the paperwork was complete and Karen was wheeled to the exit in the requisite wheelchair.

Karen hopped out of the chair, looked at the beautifully sunny day, and said, "Take me to Al's. I'm famished!"

She pooh-poohed my concern that she may not be well enough but conceded to ride instead of walking the short distance.

"Praise the Lord," Al said as the door closed behind us. "There's the person I prayed I'd see again."

My burgeoning detective brain told me that the bar's owner wasn't referring to yours truly as he delicately stepped out from behind the bar and came our way. My instincts were reinforced when he spread his arms and gently hugged Karen.

"You can do better than that," she said as she put her arms around him again. "I'm not made of china."

"You, my lovely friend," Al said, "are fine porcelain, and I'm elated that you're walking, talking, and, alive. Praise the Lord."

I reached over and tapped Al's arm. "I'm alive too."

He rolled his eyes. "Of course you are." He turned his attention back to Karen. "Let me help you to a seat."

There were days when Al's arthritis was so bad that he could barely make it out of bed, so I took Karen's elbow and escorted her to the nearest table. We ordered, and Karen sighed. Al headed to the grill and Karen said, "I didn't think I'd ever be here again."

I nodded and told her how good it was that she was here and mentioned my conversation with Sean. She didn't look happy, but once again said that she knew that I would do what I had to do and wouldn't try to dissuade me. Al then returned and said that he had heard me talking about Preacher Burl and wondered if the good minister had converted Bob yet. I said that it was more likely that Burl would surrender to the skepticism of Bob Howard.

Al laughed. "You're probably right." He turned serious. "Anything new on the killings?"

I told him that Charles and I had spent the last two days in Indianapolis and what we had found out.

"Got a thought," Al said. "Let me grab your food and I'll bounce it off you."

Five minutes later Al returned with two cheeseburgers, two orders of fries, a beer for Karen, a glass of chardonnay for me, and something that I hadn't considered.

I moved over so Al could have the seat closest to the aisle. He looked at Karen and then turned to me. "Now y'all have a lot more police experience than me, so I'm just talking from the little I know."

Karen nodded, and I had to reluctantly agree.

"Preacher Burl seems like a fine Christian gentleman." He paused and grinned. "He'd have to be to keep him from smacking Bob upside his fat head with a Bible after the way Bob talked to him in here."

So true, I thought.

"Anyway," Al continued, "is it possible that you have the situation ass backward?"

"Meaning?" I asked.

"You think that the preacher is killing those folks to get money out of them or to keep them from telling something that they've found out. Is that correct?"

"Yes," I said. "The man in Indiana was leaving nearly a million dollars and a building to Burl, and I think Mendelson may have been leaving him something, and—"

"Now," Al interrupted, "what I'm thinking is maybe someone has a powerful heap of something against the preacher and is killing people so he'll shut down his church. Didn't you say that's what happened in Indiana? Someone died, and it ran him out of town. The same something could be going on here."

I thought about it and looked over at Karen. "But Al, Burl was with the person when he was killed in Indianapolis. No one else was there."

"Oh," Al said. "I didn't know that. I don't have it all figured out. That's what the police should be doing."

I told him that it was an interesting theory and that I'd give it thought and share it with the detectives.

Karen waved her right hand in the air. "Enough murder talk. Let this recuperating gal eat in peace. You didn't have to eat the stuff they called food at the hospital."

Al said what she needed was another beer. "Bless you," she said, and she went back to her fries. Al left to wait on another table, and James Brown and then Johnny Cash filled the air while we ate in peace, with no further mention of the murders or her near-death experience.

Karen was exhausted when we finished lunch and dozed on the way to Brian's condo. She struggled up the stairs to his second-floor unit and collapsed in his lounge chair. She said that she didn't need anything, so I said I'd check on her in the morning. On my way to the door, she said that she'd be really, really pissed if I got myself killed.

I got in the car, turned the air on high, looked up at Brian's condo, and wondered why she'd said that. Did she know something that I didn't know?

CHAPTER 34

If Folly Beach had a chamber of commerce, Wednesday morning's weather would have headlined its website. A broken line of Charmin-white clouds passed overhead, the sun made its presence known, and the temperature was in the low seventies with unusually low humidity. I had woken before sunrise and was thinking about taking a leisurely stroll on the beach when Charles appeared at the door.

"How about a photo walk?" he asked. He had his cane in hand, his digital camera over his shoulder, his canvas Tilley cocked at a thirty-degree angle on his head, and a long-sleeved white T-shirt with "UAM Men's Golf" and a cartoon image of something I couldn't begin to describe on the front.

I violated one of my rules, but I couldn't help asking what it was as I pointed at his shirt.

"A boll weevil, of course. University of Arkansas-Monticello."

"Bring your clubs?"

"Funny! Are we photo walkin' or not?"

Only someone who knew Charles well would know that this was as close as he would get to an apology for being upset about the gallery.

One of my most favorite activities was to take leisurely walks around the island with Charles. I would take photos of seascapes, beach scenes, and anything else that caught my eye. Charles specialized in images that could kindly be called avant-garde or simply weird. Crumpled candy and gum wrappers appeared to be his specialty, but he would occasionally see the beauty in a squashed Pepsi can or a rock that he would swear looked like Aunt Jemima. Regardless, our excursions were fun filled and definitely entertaining. I suggested that we venture west of Center Street to avoid the spot where JJ had taken his last breath, yet I still caught myself staying far to the side of the road and glancing over my shoulder every few steps. We had walked five blocks when my phone rang and the screen read "Sean."

"Is this my favorite attorney?" I said, abandoning my crusade to be more conventional with phone introductions.

"You don't have to suck up," my favorite attorney said. "I have your information."

I was impressed that he could have found anything that quickly and told him so. He told me how intelligent and resourceful he was, and I asked where he had gotten the information. He said that if he told me that, I wouldn't need him anymore. With the foolishness out of the way, I asked what he had learned.

"Timothy Mendelson's will was revised nine days before his death. Would you like to guess who was added as primary beneficiary of an estate that's estimated to be worth approximately five million, including his paid-for mansion on the beach?"

"The Most Reverend Preacher Burl Ives Costello," I said. Charles stared at me.

"That would be an astute, and accurate, observation, Mr. Landrum."

I had hoped that I'd be wrong. "Anything else?" I asked.

"Crap, Chris, you can't afford what I've already told you. Quit while you're ahead."

"One more thing," I said. "I'm going to tell the police about the will. Can I let them know where you got the information?"

"No, no, no," he said. "Tell them that they should contact Mendelson's attorney, Dawn Smith, with Breathitt, Jackson, and Eslinger on Broad Street. Have the cops tell her that they were touching all bases and see if she'll tell them about the will. I went to law school and not police school, but it sounds like the will's what they call a big-ass clue." He was gone.

We had reached Wave Watch, a small community playground at the end of East Cooper, and Charles commandeered two swings. I took off my Tilley and wiped sweat from my forehead.

"What about Preacher Burl?" Charles asked, motioning with his arms for me to hurry.

"It seems that Mr. Mendelson changed his will and left his estate, roughly five million dollars, to First Light."

Charles took off his hat and waved it in front of his face. "I wish you hadn't said that."

"I like Burl, but it would take one whopper of an explanation to pin the murders on someone else."

We were the only two in the playground, so I figured there wouldn't be a better time to tell Detective Burton about the will. He answered on the second ring and said that he was busy and for me to be quick. I told him about the "rumor" I had heard about Mendelson's will. I either got a flicker of interest or he burped. I shared the attorney's name, and Burton said he would check it out.

I summarized the conversation for Charles, who watched an old Ford Explorer pull up to the park only to turn around and leave. "Remember what you said about Burl needing a whopper of an explanation?"

That had been only ten minutes before, and I told him that I did recall.

"Why don't we give him a chance to lay that whopper on us?"

I could think of several reasons off the top of my sweating head, such as interfering with police business, clueing the preacher in on our suspicions, and, oh yeah, putting us in the crosshairs of someone who had already killed four people and had made one attempt on my life. I knew these would be wasted on Charles. Besides, I wanted to know if there was a reasonable reason not to think he was a cold-blooded killer.

"Now?" I said.

Charles had already picked up his cane off the mulch and flung his camera strap over his shoulder. "Good idea."

I reminded Charles twice before we left that it wasn't the brightest idea, and he suggested the compromise of talking to the minister-murderer in a public location, preferably one without ladders and concrete blocks. Charles had Burl's number, and he grabbed my phone to call after we decided to ask him to meet us at the closest restaurant to wherever he was. We figured that an offer of a free lunch should be enough to entice his presence.

Burl was at the storefront and could meet us at the Folly Beach Crab Shack. He was at a rustic wooden table on the patio when we arrived. On the table were three glasses of water, two containers of complimentary unshelled peanuts, and a basket of hush puppies. Preacher Burl had come about his football-shaped physique the old-fashioned way, by overindulging.

"How's Sister Karen?" he asked before we sat.

I told him that she was out of the hospital and resting at her dad's condo.

"Praise the Lord," he said, and he crammed another hush puppy in his mouth.

Charles commented on the wonderful weather, and then the waitress arrived. I looked out at the spot along the street in front of the restaurant where Burl, the person now sitting across from me, had waited in the stolen Kia for me to cross Center Street. I bit my tongue in reverence to the reverend.

We ordered, and Burl said, "Don't get me wrong, I'm always appreciative of a meal." He chuckled and patted his stomach.

Charles and I smiled.

"But," Burl continued, "I have a feeling that there's more to the invitation than to break bread together." He looked from me to Charles.

Charles smiled. "You found us out, Preacher Burl. Chris here," he nodded in my direction, "has a friend who works at one of those hoity-toity Charleston law firms. Snooty bunch; don't know what they see in him. Anyway, his friend told him that he was sorry about the death of one of Chris's fellow islanders, Timothy Mendelson. The lawyer thinks everyone on Folly knew everyone else—go figure."

The yarn that Charles was spinning was getting interesting, and I leaned closer so I wouldn't miss anything.

"The lawyer said his firm was handling Mendelson's business affairs and had heard from another firm involved with his will that the stockbroker had left most of his estate to a start-up church on Folly."

Burl gave a slight nod, cracked open a peanut, and slipped it in his mouth.

"So," Charles said when Burl remained silent, "First Light is the only new church I know of. The lawyer said it was all hush-hush since it wasn't finalized but that the church was aware of its good fortune. If that's true, it has to be the most exciting news your ministry could get. We didn't know who else might know, so we wanted to congratulate you secret-like."

I didn't expect Burl to throw up his hands and confess to killing Mendelson, but I was interested in his response to Charles's tale.

Our food arrived along with drink refills. Burl wiped a crumb from his mustache and asked us to pray with him over the bounty with which to fill our stomachs and the friendships to fill our hearts that the Lord had bestowed upon us. I bowed my head but couldn't quite manage to pray with a devious killer. Charles faked it better than I.

Burl took a bite and looked at me. "Gentlemen, it is true. Brother Timothy, God rest his soul, felt it in his heart to leave a substantial sum of money to First Light. I only learned about it two days ago when his attorney contacted me. I would be less than honest if I said I wasn't overjoyed. I am only human."

I'll bet he's overjoyed, I thought. *After all, he stabbed Mendelson to get the money.*

Burl slowly nodded. "The night the attorney called me, I took a long walk on the beach. I stopped and prayed for guidance at the spot where First Light meets. I walked to the storefront to which Brother Timothy donated so freely. And then I walked by the lovely Catholic Church and admired its presence and thought about how fine it met the spiritual needs of its congregation. On my walk back to my humble apartment, I reflected on the church I pastored before coming to your island and felt pangs of guilt for leaving my followers. I must confess." He closed his eyes.

Maybe he was going to confess to murder after all.

"Confess to what?" Charles asked.

Burl opened his eyes and looked down at his plate before turning to Charles. "Brother Charles, I was a coward. Instead of following the teachings and example set by Jesus, I ran from adversity instead of confronting it. I will not make that mistake again."

"What happened?" I asked.

"I told you before that I started a church in Indiana and that a tragic accident took the life of a member of my flock, an accident that I witnessed."

"I remember, but you didn't say much about it," Charles said.

"That's true," Burl said. "The young man had sought out the Way because he felt that his traditional house of worship wasn't meeting his needs. His former church and several of its less tolerant members blamed the Way for his death. Some of them, including his family, blamed me directly; they said that I killed him."

"Why'd they say that?" I asked.

"Brother Richard, the young man, had a learning disability, and his family said that I had coerced him into attending. He inherited some money and told his parents that he was leaving it to the Way when he went to meet his maker."

"And they thought you killed him for the money?" Charles said.

"Yes!" Burl hammered his fist on the table. "And they polluted the minds of other members of their church, inundated the police with their accusations, and pestered a newspaper reporter until he wrote stories about the unfortunate event. And I received threatening calls saying they would get even, saying that my followers would learn what hell was really like."

"Who were *they*?" I asked.

"Don't know, but in my heart, I suspected Brother Richard's family."

"Do you think someone would actually harm you and your followers?" I asked.

"If you'd heard the calls, you'd know the answer. Instead of doing the right thing, I took the cowardly path and ran. I will not do that here, despite … never mind." He looked down at his fork but didn't touch it.

"Despite what?" I asked.

"Nothing," he said. "I'm just being paranoid."

That answer simply wouldn't fly with Charles. "Paranoid about what?"

"I feel like a dark cloud is hanging over me. The accidental deaths of Brother JJ and Brother Six brought back memories of the tragedy in Indianapolis."

Would he have mentioned them if he was the killer? "Do you think they're related?" I asked.

"Don't see how," he said. "They just bother me. Are my churches doomed? I don't know. I simply don't know."

"Did the Way get the inheritance?" Charles asked.

I had wanted to ask but didn't know a kind way to put it. Thank goodness for fearless Charles.

Burl shook his head. "No. It seemed that Brother Richard never followed through on his desires. We never closed on the building nor was there a valid will."

"It sounds like your church's luck has changed," I said.

"Brother Chris, as I've said before, money is necessary to a church, but I have refrained from asking for anything from my flock."

Burl's phone rang. He listened and said a few words that I couldn't decipher, waved the waitress over, asked for a to-go box, and told us that a member of his flock had fallen while getting off his fishing boat and had broken his leg. An ambulance was taking the man to the hospital, and his wife had asked Burl to meet them there. He apologized for leaving, and Charles generously offered to have me get his check.

He then started to rise but hesitated, looking at the

nearby diners and at Charles and me. "Yesterday I called Brother Mendelson's attorney and told him that First Light is extraordinarily appreciative of his client's generosity, but I refused to accept it. I asked him to prepare whatever legal documents were necessary to donate the vast bulk of the inheritance to the Golden Gate Baptist Theological Seminary."

"All of it?" Charles exclaimed.

Burl shrugged. "I requested that First Light receive enough to finish renovating the storefront. I thought that three thousand dollars should be plenty." He smiled. "The attorney sounded perplexed but said that he would honor my wishes."

He then took his to-go box and left.

CHAPTER 35

"Does that mean what I think it means?" Charles asked after Burl had gotten in his car.

"It means that we were wrong about Burl," I said. I had a nagging feeling that I knew something else, but I couldn't put my finger on it.

"Not to overstate the obvious, but who in the navy-blue blazes killed those folks?" Charles went back to his lunch.

"Good question," I said, "but first, let me call Burton and tell him about the will."

"And eat crow."

The detective answered. "Holy hell," he said after I told him about Burl's refusing the inheritance. "What are you going to tell me next, little green men from Mars are killing everyone over there?"

I told him I thought he would want to know that Burl didn't have a motive. He impolitely told me that while he suspected the deaths were murder, he never thought that Burl had killed anyone, that I was the conspiracy theorist, and that I should get my freakin' nose out of things that were none of my business. I slipped one more rung down the courtesy ladder when I hung up on him.

I was angry at Burton, I was angry with myself for trying

to pin the murders on Burl, and I was irate with whoever was killing residents of my small island. I also had a headache, so I excused myself to go home, take a shower and a nap, and spend a few hours with Karen. I didn't want to give another thought to First Light, Preacher Burl, or murder.

The evening with Karen did the trick. We took a leisurely walk around the condo complex and sat for an hour on a bench overlooking a wooded area. Her memory of the shooting was returning, and she talked about being shot, blood gushing out of her body, and then blackness. She said she hadn't been in nearly as much pain as she had been exasperated that her life might end not in a shootout while saving civilians from a crazed killer or while saving a child from a burning building but while standing in line to buy a hamburger. She talked about how glad she was to reconnect with her dad and to spend time with him, time she hadn't gotten when she was growing up when he was stationed all over the world.

She put her head on my shoulder and said, "I wasn't keen on leaving you either."

I smiled.

We comfortably drifted into an inconsequential conversation about a blue heron that called a small pond near the condo home and the pesky flying insects that made our peaceful evening difficult. We avoided exactly the topic that I had hoped we would.

It was nearly midnight when I got home, but I still had trouble falling asleep. It had been quite a day, and my mind kept replaying the various conversations. I still had the feeling that I had missed something critical. Sleep came before the answer.

I was up before sunrise. I still had the nagging feeling that I knew the key to the mystery but couldn't summon it to my consciousness. I dressed quickly, grabbed coffee at Bert's, and headed to the pier. I passed a couple of early-morning fishermen as I made my way to the end of the landmark. The sun had yet to appear over the horizon, and I settled on one of the wooden benches. Some of my best thinking had been done while seated here, and I stared at the soothing waves as they rolled onto the beach. I hoped for my safety and sanity that history would repeat itself.

Instead of answers, all the tide ushered in were more questions. Was Al's theory right that someone was out to get Burl and to sabotage First Light? Who would have benefitted from the deaths? Why had I been targeted? JJ and Six didn't have any money, and although Mendelson was loaded, his fortune was going to a seminary in California. Love didn't appear to be a viable motive. What was going on?

All I had accomplished after an hour was seeing a beautiful sunrise and a fisherman's young son whooping and hollering as his dad hauled in a two-foot-long bull shark. When I saw the dad using a boning knife to cut the fish off the line, it struck me. When I had told Dude about what happened in Indianapolis, he had asked if Keen was "like smart or like knife blade." *Sharp* and *keen* were synonyms. Hadn't the minister in Indiana said that the family had been torn apart by Burl and his church? Was it possible that Sharp was actually Richard Keen's brother, Patrick, and that he went by Sharp so Burl wouldn't recognize the name?

But if Sharp was Patrick, wouldn't Burl have recognized him at First Light? Not necessarily, I realized. Pastor Song had said Richard's parents had confronted Burl, but he hadn't mentioned Richard's siblings talking to the preacher. Sharp would probably be about Patrick's age. Could he be hiding in plain sight?

If I was right, and I realized that it was a stretch, answers to some questions became clearer. Hate, revenge, and discrediting the preacher and his new church could have been powerful motives. Sharp would know that Timothy Mendelson's money was helping First Light expand its influence. He would have wanted to stop it. But why kill JJ and Six? Could they have found out about Keen and had to be silenced? Or would he have killed them just to throw a shadow over Burl's ministry in hopes of annihilating the preacher's dream? Could he have killed Six to send a message to Burl, the person he was convinced had killed his brother? Both deaths had taken place in Burl's church buildings, both had been freak accidents. Burl might not admit it, but he had recognized the similarities and would have been terribly wounded by them, possibly enough to give up on his dreams, his church, and his spirit.

If Sharp had murdered three innocent people simply to send a message to Burl, what length would he go to before stopping? He had already attempted to kill me, probably because I had asked questions. Were Burl's other followers in danger? Was Burl's life at stake?

I had no proof, and as far as I knew, Sharp may have never set foot in Indiana. The circumstances surrounding Mendelson's murder weren't anything like the deaths of JJ and Six. But if the police were going to solve the murders, they had to have all the information.

Once again, I swallowed my pride and punched in Detective Burton's cell number. Instead of his cranky voice, I listened to an electronic voice telling me that the detective was unavailable and to leave a message. I crammed my thoughts into a one-minute message and then told him to call if he had questions. I took a chance that Detective Callahan was in and called the sheriff's office but was told to leave a message there too. I didn't.

The more I thought about how unstable Keen—Sharp—had to be, the more I worried about Burl. The police were skeptical about the deaths being related, but they were talking to everyone who might have had information. Sharp could be worried that his window of opportunity for revenge was coming to an end. I didn't see him letting it go, and the logical final act of revenge would be to kill Burl Ives Costello.

Chief Cindy LaMond was the one law enforcement official I could trust. Granted, she had occasionally made fun of my theories, rolled her eyes, and treated me like a puppy that peed on the carpet when I'd shared off-the-cuff ideas, but in the end, she would take me seriously. I called her.

She sounded out of breath when she said, "What now, Chris?"

I skipped my lecture on civility and asked if she had a few minutes. She said that she was at the Tides Hotel helping one of her officers escort an alcohol-saturated interloper into a cruiser. I thanked her for the police report and asked if she would have a few minutes after she finished her Folly Beach version of *Cops*. She said for me, anything; I told her I was close and could meet her in the lobby in five minutes.

The cruiser carrying the alcohol-saturated interloper was pulling out of the lot when I arrived and found Cindy slumped down in a comfortable chair in the seating area off the lobby.

She looked up as I approached. "I'm getting too old for drunk rustling."

I told her that since I had many years on her, she was complaining to the wrong person about being too old. She laughed and said that she had forgotten that I was a fossil. I smiled, but only to be polite.

"What did I do to deserve this visit?" she asked.

I told her about the trip to Indianapolis and what Charles and I had learned, how we had concluded that Burl was the killer, and what he had told us to make us change our minds.

She interrupted with a couple of questions. And then I told her about what I had decided this morning. She said that one of these days I was going to find myself dead at the hands of one of the many killers that I stumbled over but that she was glad that I had brought my harebrained theory to her because if I had shared it with anyone else, she would be visiting me in a padded cell. I meekly told her that I had shared my theory in a voice mail to Detective Burton.

She lowered her head and covered her face with her hand. "Oh Lord, please forgive Chris, for he knoweth not what he doeth." She looked out at the ocean and then back at me. "Okay, what do you want me to do?"

I asked if she could have her officers keep an eye on Burl. She didn't have the staff to keep a close watch on him, but a few extra patrols by his apartment and the storefront would be appreciated. And if she or one of her guys could find a reason to stop Sharp and check his ID, it might help. She asked if he had a car; I remembered that Lottie had mentioned that Six had borrowed one from Sharp. It dawned on me that Six could have learned Sharp's identity if he found the car's registration when he borrowed it. I told her this but that I didn't know what kind of car he had. She said there wouldn't be much reason to stop and question him, but was creative, and I knew she'd find something. She said she'd try.

The more I thought about it, the more I worried about Burl. Would Cindy's trying be enough?

When I got home, I called Charles to give him my latest wisdom and to see if he thought I could be right. No answer. I walked around the house, stared at the phone, and wondered what, if anything, I could do next.

I got another idea and called Cindy. Apparently, the memo not to answer my calls had finally made it to her, so I suggested to her voice mail that she could contact the Indianapolis cops and have them e-mail a copy of Patrick's drivers license photo to see if he was Sharp. Then, not thinking of anything else I could do, I walked off several blocks of nervous energy and ended up behind the Sandbar Seafood and Steak Restaurant and watched the cloudless sunset from the restaurant's lawn. Charles's small apartment shared a gravel parking lot with the restaurant, but his lights were off, so I didn't stop by. I did stop in at the gallery to pick up an inventory list I wanted to update and was surprised when the bell over the door announced someone's arrival.

"What in the hell are you doing here in the middle of the night?" Bob Howard boomed.

He walked through the gallery to the door to the back room, where I stood and waited his arrival. He had on a T-shirt that may have fit when he was thirty pounds lighter; it said "Wipe Out Rodents: Kill Mickey Mouse." It was a one of his favorites; I'd seen him in it several times.

It was only a little after nine, but I didn't waste words telling him that. Instead, I said, "What are you doing here this late?"

"Plying my trade," he said. "Showing a house at the Washout to a couple from some freakin' small town in New Hampshire. It's a two-million-buck starter home at the beach, so I couldn't say no."

"You're all heart," I said.

"Damned right I am," he said, apparently not appreciating my sarcasm. "Anyway, I saw the light and remembered that your landlord called, and I figured I might as well tell you what he said."

"Well," I said, "what—"

The lights flickered.

Bob looked up at them. "You should pay your electric bill," he said.

They blinked again. “That’s funny,” I said. “The only time they’ve done that was when a power tool was running next door.”

“So what’s funny?” Bob looked at the wall separating the gallery from the storefront chapel next door. “Someone’s using a power tool.”

“Their lights were off when I came in, and that was a few minutes before you brought cheer, gaiety, and your charm to the gallery.”

Bob harrumphed. “So, Dick Tracy, I suppose you want to check it out?”

Normally I would have said no, but after my day of thinking about Burl and Sharp, I nodded and started next door.

I glanced in the window of the dark storefront. “See, no lights,” I said to my anti-Mickey friend, and I then in leaned closer. The main lights were off, but I saw a faint light coming from the back of the building. I couldn’t see anyone.

I tried the door and was surprised when it opened. I reached around the corner and hit the switch.

The room filled with light, and I filled with fear.

CHAPTER 36

The pews blocked some of the view, but I saw someone dressed in black standing over what appeared to be a large man splayed on the floor. Wires from the 220-volt outlet by the neon cross were twisted and snaked under the body.

Bob had followed me, and when I stopped, he rammed my back like a moose butting a tree.

"Shit!" he said and stumbled sideways.

The person in black now looked up, turned, and dropped a mop handle that he'd been using to move the wires under the person on the floor. His face was partially hidden by a black cap but visible enough for me to tell it was Sharp. His expression morphed from surprise to anger in a millisecond. He adroitly moved around the body and dashed toward the rear exit.

I rushed to the motionless figure, saw it was Burl, and took a step back. I'd had a close call with electrocution a few years back and knew I had to shut the power off before I could help the preacher—if it wasn't too late. The storefront had the same electrical arrangement as the gallery, with the panel on the side wall near the rear exit. I yanked a circuit-breaker switch that controlled the wall outlet.

The main overhead lights remained on. Bob bent over the preacher. "He's alive."

The skin on the back of Burl's left hand was ripped open, curled, and burned. The smell of burning flesh was in the air. His eyes fluttered, his breathing was erratic. He pulled his legs up and tried to sit, grabbed his chest, and fell back. His head smacked the floor with a frightening thud.

The electrical shock must have triggered a heart attack.

"Chest," he mumbled.

Bob put his hand under Burl's head. "Hang on, preacher," he said in the most calming tone that I'd ever heard from him. "Help's on the way. Everything'll be okay."

I grabbed my phone, punched in 911, and quickly gave our location and problem. I told the dispatcher to also send police.

Burl coughed. His breathing stopped.

Bob moved to the preacher's side and looked up at me. "I know CPR. I've got him. Don't let the bastard get away."

Easier said than done. Sharp had a head start, and it would be minutes before the police arrived, enough time for Sharp to get off the island. The alley behind the storefront paralleled Center Street. Turning right led to public areas behind some of the bars, so I figured he would have turned left where there was a lesser chance of being seen. The alley intersected a dark residential street with even fewer people. I gambled and ran in that direction.

Another reason that he would have decided to go left made it difficult for me to find him: it was dark, the only illumination from one streetlight a block ahead and one porch light on a house set back in a wooded area. Sharp could be anywhere.

Then, a hundred yards away, I heard angry barking, and I ran toward the noise, which came from one of the island's many elevated houses. There were no cars in the parking space underneath, but a large dog leapt against the ten-by-ten-foot chain-link pen behind it.

Sharp had chosen the wrong yard to cut through. I saw him crossing the adjacent lot and head behind an industrial-waste Dumpster in front of a house being renovated.

I didn't think that he'd seen me, but I wasn't sure. I also didn't know if he was behind the Dumpster or had continued to run. I pulled up ten yards short of the steel receptacle and caught my breath. Now what?

There was a temporary electric pole at the corner of the yard with a security light halfway to the top. The light threw ominous shadows from the Dumpster and a foot-high stack of plywood.

I cautiously walked toward them. If Sharp was still here, I was afraid he'd hear my heart pounding. What was my plan if he was still here? I had no weapon and twenty years on him. I had last been in a fistfight in the seventh grade, and I'd lost.

I heard rustling in the underbrush to the right of the Dumpster and turned, fully expecting Sharp to attack. I hadn't realized that I had been holding my breath until I exhaled when I saw the pointy snout and two beady eyes of an opossum about the size of a Fiat staring at me. The critter gave a deep growl. It must have figured that its posturing wasn't working, and it turned and scampered back into the bushes.

I took another deep breath and caught a glimmer of movement off my left shoulder. I turned in time to see a two-by-four flying at my face. I instinctively raised my left arm to protect my head. The weapon slammed into my already scarred elbow. Excruciating pain radiated up my arm.

I ducked before Sharp could swing the scrap wood again. I grabbed at him. He took a step back and tripped over the pile of lumber beside the drive. My momentum carried me with him, and we hit the gravel. The two-by-four flew one way, Sharp went the other.

I landed on my injured arm; it felt like I'd landed in a pile of burning coals. Sharp pushed me aside and was on his feet before I forced myself to ignore the pain and move. He looked around for the two-by-four, but it was under my good arm. I grabbed it. He looked at me and then toward town, where I heard the wailing of two Folly Beach patrol cars. I rocked up on my knees and stood. He then started toward me but stopped, turned, and jogged away from the patrol cars.

The smart thing for me was to remain in the safety of security light, wait for the police to come, tell them which way Sharp had gone, and get medical help. I caught my breath, smelled the freshly cut sawdust and Sharp's sweat on my shirt, and then rejected the wise course of action.

Sharp was not going to get away if I had anything to do with it. I held my left arm close to my side, squeezed the two-by-four tight in my right hand, and charged after him.

He didn't have as much of a head start this time, and I could see his silhouette. He stopped on the side of the road, bent over, and put his hands on his thighs. I was exhausted and wanted to do the same but didn't. My only chance to catch him was to keep going. Sharp then headed toward the off-island bridge a couple of blocks away.

I saw the red lights of an ambulance reflecting off the bridge and prayed that they could get to Burl in time and that Bob had convinced the police that I desperately needed help. I knew that would take time—valuable time.

Sharp was jogging through the small park and I finally realized where he was headed: not for the bridge but for an old Chevrolet parked on Center Street. He was so focused on the vehicle that I knew it had to be his escape vehicle.

I caught up with him in the middle of the park when my luck ran out. He sensed movement, stopped abruptly, and turned.

He saw me getting ready to swing the board, quickly moved to the right, and grabbed a three-foot-long branch from below a nearby oak. We looked like two bent, folded, and mutilated Jedi knights squaring off to do battle with light sabers.

He stepped toward me and swung the branch at my head. I leaned back and he missed. I swung the two-by-four, but Sharp reached up to protect his head. I squatted and swung at his legs instead, connecting with his knee. He shrieked and dropped to the sidewalk, grabbing his leg.

I stepped out of his reach and leaned the board on my shoulder like a batter stepping up to home plate. My elbow throbbed, but I wasn't about to let Sharp know. He tried to stand but collapsed as soon as he put weight on his injured leg. He was defeated and knew it.

I held the two-by-four in front of me to remind him what he would face if he tried to resume the fight. The police sirens wailed again as two, maybe three cars crisscrossed nearby streets. *It shouldn't be long before they get here.*

"Why, Patrick?" I said.

He looked startled. "How do you know who I am?"

"I know about your brother and why you'd want to kill Preacher Burl. But why the others, why me?"

He clutched his knee and mumbled a profanity. Then he said, "He killed my brother, ruined my family, tried to steal my brother's money. He wasn't going to get away with it."

"But the others?" I asked again.

He slammed his fist on the sandy soil. "The con artist preacher had to suffer before I killed him. Had to stop the stockbroker from paying for the church. Burl deserved misery, not money from do-gooders. I went to Mendelson's house and tried to politely tell him about Burl. He wouldn't listen. He laughed at me and then made the mistake of turning his back on me. What else could I do? Had to stop him. You can see that, can't you?"

A patrol car skidded to a stop in front of the park. "Chris, are you okay?" Officer Spencer shouted. He held his Maglite in one hand and firearm in the other. I lied and told him that I was fine. He looked down at Sharp. "Killer?" He holstered his flashlight and removed handcuffs from his duty belt.

"Patrick Keen, alias Sharp," I said.

Officer Spencer yanked Sharp into a sitting position and pulled his hands behind his back, slapped on the cuffs, and recited him his rights. Sharp gave out another loud groan as Spencer pulled him up and radioed for an ambulance.

"Why kill JJ and Six? Why go after me?" I asked.

Sharp looked at me. "You were the only one asking questions. I've heard about how you wouldn't let go once you started. And those nosy bums. JJ's damned questions and then Six's snooping. He found out who I really was from my car's registration papers and connected me to Burl in Indiana." He looked at Spencer, who was now about four feet away, and then turned back to me. "He fooled the cops into thinking my brother's murder was an accident. I wanted JJ, Six, and your deaths to look that way too. Wanted accidents to bring his church down." He looked at the ground and then back at me. "Time to ask for that lawyer." He closed his eyes and his mouth.

I asked Spencer about Burl, and he said that he was alive thanks to Bob Howard but that was all he knew. He smiled and added, "The cranky Realtor started yelling as soon as we arrived that idiot Chris with a death wish was out there somewhere and that we'd damn well better find him alive or Bob would have all our tin badges."

That's my Bob, I thought. I then told Spencer that I wasn't doing as well as I had led him to believe, and I slowly walked to one of the picnic tables to wait for an ambulance. My elbow throbbed, and I forced back tears. Adrenaline could only carry me so far.

The next half hour was a blur. Two more patrol cars arrived, one of the city's fire engines ambled to a stop at the park, and a firefighter who doubled as a paramedic spoke to Officer Spencer, glanced at the prisoner, and then came over to check my arm. Chief LaMond arrived with Bob, who rushed over and asked the paramedic, "Is the idiot who's always trying to get himself killed going to make it?"

The paramedic said I'd survive.

"That's what I was afraid of," Bob said. "He's going to be the death of me yet."

When the ambulance arrived, the EMTs loaded Sharp onto a gurney, and Officer Spencer handcuffed the killer to it. Chief LaMond asked if I'd mind hitching a ride in the ambulance with the prisoner if she went with us to prevent any fisticuffs along the way.

I smiled at the chief and said it'd be fine with me.

CHAPTER 37

The pain from my elbow shot up my arm with every bump the ambulance hit. I hadn't realized how rough Folly Road was. My consolation was that Sharp moaned with each jolt and that I wasn't wearing handcuffs. Chief LaMond said that she'd whisper sweet nothings in my ear if I thought it would distract me from the pain. I told her that I didn't want her hubby to break my other elbow. She said he would understand it was strictly medicinal.

"Oh, shucks," I said. We laughed.

Sharp and I went our separate ways in the emergency room. It must have been a slow night. I was whisked off for X-rays and talking to a fresh-eyed doctor in less time than it usually took to get registered. It entered my mind that Cindy may have used her East Tennessee charm to move me ahead of other patients.

The doctor nearly jogged into my cubicle and said that I had a fractured elbow caused by an acute traumatic event; the last part I knew without spending a minute in medical school. He said that I was going to live but would be stuck with a plaster splint for what would seem like forever. And then he was gone.

Bob somehow managed to sneak, or, more likely, bully, his way through the various hospital gatekeepers and showed up where I was waiting to be splinted.

"Want to arm wrestle?" He chuckled.

I was hurting, tired, and still traumatized by everything. I frowned. "How's Burl?"

"Damn," he said. "The doc remove your sense of humor?" He nodded. "Your favorite preacher's going to be fine. His weak heart nearly bit the dust, but according to the medic, I, yes, *I* saved his life." He reached over his shoulder and patted himself on the back. "I hear you didn't do so bad yourself even if your swing was barely inside the strike zone."

I was spared more comments when a nurse pushed the curtain aside and told the Realtor that he'd have to scat. He looked at her and turned back to me, "Oh yeah, as I was saying before the shocking—get it? *shocking*—event, your incredible Realtor got the landlord to reduce your rent by a third since you'll only be open two days a week."

I'd never said two days a week, but he then left mumbling something about my having to buy the two-million-dollar beach house if he couldn't find the couple that he'd been on Folly to meet.

It was the middle of the night before the doctor and nurses were done pushing, probing, sticking, and splinting me. Somehow I'd managed a few hours of sleep by the time Detective Callahan stopped by to get my statement. He also told me that I shouldn't have taken on Sharp by myself, but he thanked me for doing it. He was confident now that he knew who Sharp was, and he and Detective Burton would be able to put all the parts of the puzzle together. I figured one of them would.

Brian Newman and Karen were waiting to take me home once I was discharged. Cindy had filled the mayor in on what had happened after she left the hospital. Karen took way too much delight in pushing me to the exit in a wheelchair, something I had done to her not that many days ago.

As she helped me into Brian's Jeep, she said, "How's this for irony? You, a danged out-of-shape gallery store owner, get injured apprehending someone who killed three people, and I, a highly trained police detective, get shot buying a burger."

"Love you anyway," I said, patting her on the shoulder with my good arm.

***

Twenty-four hours of phone-turned-off rest later, Charles pounded on the door. He wore a long-sleeved green-and-white Wilmington College Quakers T-shirt and carried his cane in one hand and a six-pack of Budweiser in the other. I let him in, turned the phone on, and with one seriously sore wing, was ready to rejoin the world. He said that he was here so we could take a walk. I told him to dream on, grabbed a pillow off the bed, and put it on the arm of my living room chair to keep my arm elevated.

"Then let's party," he said. He put the beer in the refrigerator, pulled one out of the pack, and poured a glass of chardonnay. I didn't stop him, but I planned to leave the wine because of the pain meds I was on. The phone rang while he was asking if I had chips.

"If you're still alive, some preacher wants to talk to you," Bob bellowed.

The phone bumped something, and I heard a weak voice. "Brother Chris, this is Preacher Burl. How is your arm?"

A question Bob had forgotten to ask. I told him how I was doing and asked about his condition.

"They say that I'll recover. If it wasn't for you and Brother Bob—"

"It ain't Brother Bob," Bob yelled in the background. "I'm Bob, or Mr. Howard to my wife."

I was surprised to hear Burl laugh. "Your friend Bob's funny. He's already been here twice checking on me."

I was now convinced that God did work in mysterious ways. I said I was glad that he was recuperating.

His hand had come out worse for wear with the electrical burns, he explained, but he should get out of the hospital in a couple of days. "Bro—Bob and I will be praying that your arm makes a speedy recovery."

Bob again said something I couldn't catch. Preacher Burl said to him, "Now Bob, I'm not about to say that to Brother Chris." He chuckled. "Chris, Bob meant to say get well soon."

We said our good-byes, and I wondered if one of God's mysterious ways was the effect of meds on Preacher Burl. Bob on his best day could never have garnered two laughs—especially from a minister.

I told Charles about the other end of the conversation, and he scolded me for not having him there to cover my back during the chase. I pointed out that he was nowhere to be found, but he asked what that had to do with anything. He then asked for every detail of my adventure; I gave him the short version that included Keen's confession of killing Timothy Mendelson and Six.

"So why did he kill JJ?" Charles asked.

"His fatal habit of asking questions," I said. "He did ask about anything and everything. Sharp could have told him that he was from Indianapolis, and he could have pestered Burl into telling him that his last church had been there. Putting two and two together would have been JJ's downfall. But the cops may never know, and it probably won't matter. He killed Six and Mendelson and tried to run me down. And, if it hadn't been for Bob, he would have killed Burl. That'll be enough to put him away forever."

Charles grabbed a handful of breakfast Doritos, stuffed them in his mouth, and finished his second beer. "Speaking of Brother Bob," he said with a smile, "have you heard anything about the lease?"

I told him about what Bob had told me.

"Wow, great!" Charles said. "Signed the new lease yet?"

"Not yet," I said. I was about to tell him that I wasn't sure that I would but was saved by the bell—more accurately, the phone.

"Hey, lame one," Cindy LaMond said. "The mayor tells me that you're going to make it, but whoa, that's not why I'm calling. I have great news."

"What might that be?" I asked.

"Two things. First, I got a call this morning while I was working and you were goofing off playing patient. A friend in the sheriff's office told me that your favorite detective Brad Burton officially retired."

Cindy was right, that was great news.

"You haven't heard the best part," she said. "The now former detective has bought a house on Folly and will be moving here next month."

I couldn't grasp what was so good about that. "Where?" I asked.

She giggled. "Open your front door and look left. Yep, that's it. He's your new neighbor." Her giggle became a full-blown laugh. "You two can start a Neighborhood Watch program."

The phone went dead.

Yes, God did work in mysterious ways.

CPSIA information can be obtained
at www.ICGtesting.com
Printed in the USA
FFHW020118130219
50530896-55798FF